"Red Hawk, just give me a little time,"
said Kincaid. "Two weeks..."

"Three days."

Matt shrugged helplessly. "I would like more time,
but if that's all you can give, I'll have to accept it.
If, within three days, I have not given you satisfaction, I'll not ask you to trust me anymore. At that
time, if you choose to leave the reservation and seek
revenge, I will not ask any different of you. But if
that happens, we will be enemies once again."

Red Hawk looked down at the fallen boy, but refused
to allow the impassive expression on his face to
change. Then he looked again at Kincaid. "It is
agreed. You have three days. Nothing will bring this
young man to life again, but I do not wish to see
others die. If, after that time, your justice has not
worked..." his eyes swept the plains and his voice
became distant... "we will be at war..."

Easy Company

EASY COMPANY

AND THE LONGHORNS

JOHN WESLEY HOWARD

A JOVE BOOK

First Jove edition published June 1981

First printing

Printed in the United States of America

Jove books are published by Jove Publications, Inc., 200 Madison Avenue, New York, NY 10016

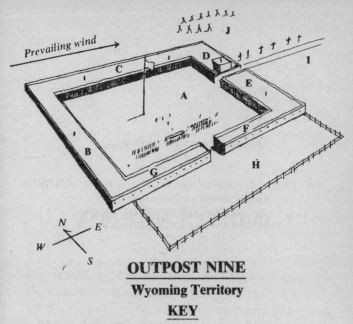

Prevailing wind →

N · E
W · S

OUTPOST NINE
Wyoming Territory
KEY

A. Parade and flagstaff

B. Officers' quarters ("officers' country")

C. Enlisted men's quarters: barracks, day room, and mess

D. Kitchen, quartermaster supplies, ordnance shop, guardhouse

E. Suttler's store and other shops, tack room, and smithy

F. Stables

G. Quarters for dependents and guests; communal kitchen

H. Paddock

I. Road and telegraph line to regimental headquarters

J. Indian camp occupied by transient "friendlies"

INTERIOR   OUTSIDE

OUTPOST NUMBER NINE
(DETAIL)

Outpost Number Nine is a typical High Plains military outpost of the days following the Battle of the Little Big Horn, and is the home of Easy Company. It is not a "fort"; an official fort is the headquarters of a regiment. However, it resembles a fort in its construction.

The birdseye view shows the general layout and orientation of Outpost Number Nine; features are explained in the Key.

The detail shows a cross-section through the outpost's double walls, which ingeniously combine the functions of fortification and shelter.

The walls are constructed of sod, dug from the prairie on which Outpost Number Nine stands, and are sturdy enough to withstand an assault by anything less than artillery. The roof is of log beams covered by planking, tarpaper, and a top layer of sod. It also provides a parapet from which the outpost's defenders can fire down on an attacking force.

one _____

There was a certain ungainliness about them, those almost pathetic creatures with the pointed beards, hairy fore-bodies, and bare rumps, whose rounded, short horns curled ineffectually from the sides of their heads and to a point before their eyes. Long, stringy, matted hair hung from their chests behind stubby front legs, and it nearly touched the tall grass as they grazed warily across the prairies in the semiprotected swale provided by two rolling ridges joined at an oblique angle. The buffalo, their yellow eyes constantly searching above the feast as tufts of grass were munched in their powerful jaws, moved unsuspectingly forward with the wind to their backs. The field of green shifted before them like undulating waves on an endless sea. Calves frolicked at their mother's sides, oblivious to time and danger, while the bulls raised their heads with every mouthful and searched the wind for some alien sight or scent that might indicate danger and send them scampering away with speed apparently uncharacteristic of their massive, humped torsos.

But the sun, angling toward the horizon on those northern

plains, revealed a signal of which the buffalo were unaware. Five blued rifle barrels glinted dully as they were aimed downward, motionless now and waiting silently for the herd of seventy-five animals to graze within range.

Lying flat on his stomach, with a chew of tobacco working noiselessly beneath his unshaven, bristly cheek, Samuel "Hoss" Boggs squinted down his rifle barrel while traces of brown saliva glistened at the corners of his mouth. His wide-brimmed hat, pulled low to his eyes and soiled with sweat stains, covered a wild shock of red hair that bulged out beneath the black leather hat and covered his ears in an unruly tangle. To his left were two of his sons, leering-eyed men who also squinted along warm steel, their fingers fairly itching for the pull of the trigger and the slamming jolt of a bullet being sent with a thudding smack into the bodies of the animals below. Daniel and Martin Boggs, twenty-three and twenty-four respectively, thought much like their father in that they believed the buffalo were nothing more than vermin to be exterminated from valuable rangeland better used to sustain the Double G cattle herds.

But off to his left, sweat trickling down his forehead, lay Timothy Boggs, eighteen and uncomfortable in the thought of the carnage that awaited. Clean-shaven and lacking the thick, massive body of his father and brothers, Timmy was tall and lean, with blond hair, and his upper lip was graced by the faintest wisp of a mustache. His eyes drifted to the rock-still figure of his father, who continued to stare downward and silently work the bulge in his cheek. There was an uncomfortableness in Timmy's eyes as they went back to the sights again, and he sighed as he shifted the rifle to a more comfortable position.

"Whatsamatter, boy?" Jake Barnes whispered thickly. "Got no stomach for this kind of work?"

Timmy's hat tilted with the slight shake of his head as he glanced over at the ranch foreman. Barnes was a man of medium height, barrel-chested, with thick, sloping shoulders supporting a bull-like neck and an ugly head. He had a wide gap between his front teeth. His beady, darting eyes matched the twisted sneer of his mouth. Barnes had a well-earned reputation for being one of the meanest, cruelest, and most unforgiving of all the barroom brawlers and gutter fighters ever produced in West Texas. And, as Timmy watched him, he again noticed the ragged scar where the lower portion of Barnes' left ear had been bitten off in one such fight. And he remembered the story of the conclusion of that brawl, in which Barnes had killed his opponent with a knife slash across the throat and then severed the dead man's ear and stuffed it into his mouth. "If you've got such a hunger for ears," Barnes had been reported as saying, "then here's a little somethin' for you to nibble on in hell, you miserable son of a bitch!"

Timmy felt a cold chill tickle up his spine, despite the heat. "No, Jake," he replied, "I'm not much for—"

An angry "Ssshhhh!"—coming from the elder Boggs—silenced the two men. "I'll drop that lead bull," Boggs said in a coarse whisper, without taking his eyes from the sights, "and the rest of you pick off the other bulls, especially the ones that look to run. Then we'll shoot the calves and cows. Should be able to get the whole damned bunch. Easy now, about ten more steps and we've got 'em."

There was silence on the plains, save for the whisper of shifting grass in the increasing wind and the occasional bleat of a calf that had strayed too far from its mother's side. Then a booming shot split the calm, and the lead bull went to its knees and flopped over on one side as though suddenly desirous of sleep induced by a .44-caliber bullet smacking into its head just behind the right ear.

Instantly, three other rifles spat their deadly poison and three more bulls crumpled in silent, almost obedient death. The remaining buffalo raised their heads with grass yet munching in their jaws, and watched their leaders with more curiosity than concern. Again, four rifles fired from above, and other animals on the periphery of the herd went down, the victims of well-aimed shots intended to kill instantly. Strangely, it was only the calves who showed alarm in their tail-high scampering to seek out their mother's protection. The slain animals had crumpled in the grass with nothing more than the occasional twitch of a stiffening leg, and since mature buffalo reacted only to alarm demonstrated by their leaders, which was not forthcoming in this case, they lowered their heads and again began to graze.

The shots from the high ground were well spaced now, and as quickly as one animal went down, another from the opposite

3

side of the herd followed suit, until all the bulls were dead and the weapons were turned on cows and calves with less concern for deadly accuracy. But still, one rifle had not fired.

Hoss Boggs rolled onto one side to jam fresh cartridges into his Henry, and his hands worked with mechanical precision while his grayish-blue eyes glared at his youngest son. "Damn you, Timothy," he said with a menacing growl, "let's put some heat down that barrel!"

Timmy continued to stare down his sights, but his trigger finger was motionless and his only movement was another slight shake of his head. "Don't cotton to killing healthy animals for nothing, Pa," he said cautiously, knowing the outburst that would follow.

"I don't give a goddamn what you cotton to, boy!" Boggs snapped in an enraged whisper. "And don't you never talk back to me, hear? Now I'm gonna watch you from right here, and the next buff that goes down is gonna fall to your gun." Boggs' eyes snapped to what was left of the herd, then back to Timmy. "Take that little feller there, the one trying to snatch a pull from his mama's tit."

Timmy looked toward the calf, but did not aim his rifle in that direction.

"I said take him, boy," Boggs warned, his voice ominous and threatening.

Slowly, Tommy's rifle barrel swung toward the calf while spaced shots continued on either side of him, and he saw more buffalo falling from the corners of his eyes. His sights lined up on the little animal, whose neck was arched beneath his mother's flank. His finger tightened on the trigger, but he hesitated.

"I said take him, Timothy. And don't miss. I know what kind of shot you are when you want to be. Take him, boy, and take him now!"

Timmy hesitated a moment longer, then the rifle belched flame and the tiny calf slammed into its mother's hind legs as the slug smashed through its heart. Boggs twisted, raised his rifle, and instantly the mother was dead as well.

"Nice shot," Boggs grunted, his eyes searching the herd for another target. "Had to get her quick, she mighta spooked the rest of the herd. Now keep shootin', boy. I didn't buy that rifle for you to use as a crutch."

In a space of ten minutes the entire herd lay strewn across

the prairie floor in motionless lumps, with the sighing wind twisting the hair across their backs in restless surges. The ridge was silent and the men lay their hot rifles in the grass to cool while they collected the brass cartridges scattered about them. Timmy could feel his father's searing eyes on his face as he picked up a mere four spent rounds, which he stuffed quietly into his vest pocket.

"Four shots, boy? Is that all you fired? Four lousy, chickenshit shots?"

Timmy nodded without looking at his father. "Guess so, Pa."

"Guess so? You damned well *know* so! Why?"

Barnes grinned as he massaged the gap between his teeth with a blade of grass. "Looks like the young feller ain't got much of a stomach for killin', Hoss."

Timmy glanced once at Barnes, then across at his father. "Jake's right, Pa. I ain't got much stomach for killin'. Especially when it's senseless, like that was."

The men were standing now, and Boggs' massive chest bulged beneath his cotton shirt and strained against the two buttons holding it closed over his distended but rock-hard stomach. "Senseless?" He spat viciously and took a menacing step toward his son. "You callin' what I order to be done senseless?"

Timmy watched his father's clublike hands forming into fists by his sides. His eyes went to the elder man's face, and the muscles worked along his jaw as he clenched his teeth. "Yeah, Pa, I am," he said softly. "Those buffalo weren't hurtin'—"

With flashing speed beyond what one would expect of a man so huge, Samuel Boggs' fist cracked across his son's chin in a glancing blow, and Timmy staggered backward but did not go down. Hurt filled his eyes and a tiny trickle of blood dripped from the corner of his mouth, but he seemed not to notice as he continued to stare at his father, whose rage had now grown to nearly uncontrollable fury.

"Those buffalo was eatin' Double G grass, that's what they was doin' wrong! They're nothin' but vermin and deserve to be shot like a damned coyote or prairie dog. We've got to protect our rangeland for our cattle, and 'sides that, a buff will mount a cow in heat quicker'n a fly'll come to shit. Don't want no buff blood in my herd, just like I don't want no backtalk from my sons!"

5

Off to one side, Daniel and Martin Boggs had been watching their father in apprehensive silence, and now their eyes drifted down to stare at the grass between their boots. But Timmy did not look away.

"This is our land, is it, Pa?" he asked softly. "Seems to me like the Arapaho were here first."

"Arapaho? Buffalo? Who gives a shit? One ain't no better'n the other."

Boggs' eyes closed to narrow, squinting slits. "This is government land, boy, and that makes it our land, what we can take of it, that is. When the buffalo are gone, the Indians will be, as well, and the government's given us permission to do that little trick. Even asked us to. What we're doin' is patriotic, somethin' for our country." His lips curled into a sudden, yellow-toothed smile, and he spoke to Barnes while continuing to stare at his son. "Ain't that right, Jake?"

"Right as rain, Hoss. When it came time to wave the flag, ain't neither of us had a slow hand."

Boggs' guffaw rolled across the silent land. "True for a fact." Then his lips went straight and his voice lowered to a sad tone. "You're different from the rest of us, Timothy. Yer ma done that by sendin' ya off to school. God rest her ignorant soul. Yer brothers is like me, but yer like yer ma. Too soft, too kind for Plains life. But I'll whip some toughness into ya, mind me I will."

"Maybe you will, Pa, but you'll be the loser if you do."

"You talkin' back to me again, boy?"

"No, Pa. Just telling you the truth."

"Truth, huh? Only truth is you got blood running out of yer mouth fer sass and you let me down today more'n any man could. Now wipe yer face clean and go get the horses. We got work to do back at the ranch."

Timmy continued to stare at his father for several seconds before stooping, snatching his hat from the ground, and moving toward the distant grove with long, proud strides.

Boggs watched him go and shook his head sadly. "Damn her fool hide," he muttered through gritted teeth. "I ain't got no time nor need for weaklings. She done that to him."

Barnes had begun slowly to jam fresh shells into his rifle, and he looked up from his work. "Maybe she did, Hoss. Maybe she did. Then again, maybe he's just made that way."

"Made that way my ass, Jake. He's my blood. His sister's got more spunk that he has."

Jake Barnes continued to watch Boggs' face, and there was no fear in his eyes. "You're wrong, Hoss. He's got half his ma's blood too. And as for Jennie, she's got more spunk than she's a right to, to my way a' thinkin'."

A glower came over Boggs' face again. "You talkin' down about my daughter, Jake?"

Again, Barnes' face was an expressionless mask of unconcern as he stared at the larger man. "No, Samuel, I'm not. Facts is facts. If they weren't, she wouldn't be bedded down with a gambler in Texas right now."

"You ain't nobody to be short-shootin' gamblers, Jake," Boggs said. "You've lost more money at poker than any man I know."

"That I have. And I've bedded a lot of women just like Jennie."

They stared at each other for nearly a minute before Boggs spun on his heel, turning toward his other sons. "You two go down there and cut the backstrap out of one of them cows. Might as well have a dinner off of 'em if nothin' else."

Daniel and Martin moved away in obedient silence, and Boggs watched them pull knives from their belts as they walked down the hill. "Now them's the kinda boys a man needs, Jake," he said pridefully. "Never say nothin', do what they're told, and don't ask no questions."

Barnes watched them as well, and nodded his agreement. "You're right and you're wrong, Hoss. Timmy's got more man in him than either of them, but the part about askin' questions is true for a fact. Seems like there ain't always time for answers."

Unseen by the two stockmen, lying flat on the adjoining prairie rise, a man moved backward in the grass and the single feather in his hair rustled with the breeze. A magnificent spotted pony stood patiently at the bottom of the hill on the far side of the rise, and when he knew he could not be seen, Black Wing stood and moved toward his mount in a hunched-over trot. When he swung onto the horse's back, he glanced once more toward the crest. There was hatred in his eyes combined with the defiant look of a warrior, angry and prepared for battle. There was a wild handsomeness about him, mixed with the deadly countenance of a rattlesnake coiled and ready to strike. Finally, Black Wing touched a moccasined heel to his pony's flank and raced across the plains toward the distant hills.

two ————————————————

"You sure this is gonna work, Stro?" a lanky, angular man asked from where he was seated by the small fire, picking his teeth with the tip of a buffalo knife.

Strother McFarland dipped two blunt fingers in the tin of bear grease by his side and continued waxing the bowstring trailing through his left hand as though nothing had been said. His face was covered with a long, unkempt beard that matched his tattered shirt, jacket, and pants, the legs of which were tucked into tall black boots with pull-straps dangling on either side. Four other men, dressed in mismatched clothing of equal disrepair, ate sullenly from tin plates and waited for Mc-Farland's reply. But McFarland, a relatively small man with a round, jovial face, continued his work in silence, with the exception of the soft tune he was humming.

Frank Laskey jabbed the knife into the sheath at his side and, snatching his coffee cup from the ground, swallowed a mouthful before tossing the black liquid to one side. "God, what awful-tasting shit! We got any whiskey left?" he asked the man nearest him.

"Nope. Drank it all last night."

"That's what I feared," Laskey said sadly. McFarland's humming continued in rhythm with his stroking of the bowstring, and irritation crossed Laskey's face. "I asked you a question, Stro, and I got no reply. Answer me now and knock off that goddamned humming! I don't like singin', especially bad singin', and if you're as happy as you sound, you gotta be crazier'n I think you are. Now, is it gonna work or ain't it?"

Ignoring Laskey, McFarland stood, hooked the heel of the longbow beneath his left instep, bent the wood artfully, and slipped the top loop into its notch. He snapped the taut string once before reaching down and taking an arrow from the ground, which he then casually nocked into the string. He worked the bow in several short, testing pulls, then turned and quickly pulled the string back to his chin, with the arrowhead but inches from the straining wood. The shaft of the arrow was pointed directly at Laskey's heart, and McFarland watched him with a cold-eyed delight on his face. Standing no more than ten yards away, Laskey stared at the quivering arrowhead before tearing his eyes away to search McFarland's face.

"Come on now, Stro," he said weakly. "If this is a joke, you'll notice I'm not laughing."

McFarland continued to grin, but there was a deadly glint in his eyes. "Neither am I. Last man I used this on," he said, his mouth barely moving behind the feathers, "died in thirty seconds. Bad thing was, when he fell over backward he broke my arrow, 'cause it was sticking out his spine."

Laskey's lips trembled openly now and his eyes went back to the arrowhead as he took two cautious steps backward. "All . . . all I did was ask you a question. Didn't mean no . . . no harm."

"Didn't mind the question, Frank. *Did* mind the way you asked it. Like you figure you're runnin' this outfit, 'stead of me. Can't be havin' none of that. You don't mean nothin' more to me than fresh buff shit. Same goes for the rest of ya." His grin widened and it was obvious that he enjoyed the terrified look on Laskey's face. "Frank, you're less than half a second from bein' a dead man."

Laskey's face twisted and contorted, and there was a tone of pleading in his voice. "Look, Stro, just a damned minute now. I'm . . . I'm . . . sorry if I riled ya. Forget what I said."

9

"I don't forget real good."

The others around the fire sat stock-still, some with their forks suspended in midair and others with unchewed meat bulging their cheeks. They were all familiar with the maniacal look in McFarland's eyes, and they knew the insanity he was capable of. They held their silence and waited for the arrow to slam into Laskey's chest.

Then McFarland suddenly lowered the bow, released the tension on the string in the same motion, and turned his back on Laskey. "Gonna let you live, Frank, and you'll be thankin' me for that, I'm sure. Need a good skinner right now, and you're one of the best." He turned back to Laskey and his face was as cold as his words. "But don't never push me again."

Wiping the sweat from his upper lip, Laskey nodded and sank down as though suddenly exhausted. "Thank you, Stro. Like I said, I . . . I didn't mean no harm."

"What you mean is one thing, what you do is another," McFarland said, laying the bow aside and taking up his plate as though nothing had happened. He talked as he ate, heedless of the grease on his beard and staring into the fire as if he might have been hypnotized by the glowing embers. "Took that bow off a dead Sioux. Mighty fine weapon. Quiet, don't attract no attention. Just what we need for what we're gonna do.

"Once was a time when buff hunters like ourselves could pick and choose. Them days are gone now, and we gotta keep what buff are left for ourselves. Stockmen killin' 'em on the left, featherheads killin' 'em on the right, don't leave much room for honest businessmen like us'ns. Way I see it, we got a year, maybe less, to take what we can. Only way to do that is to get the stockmen and the Indians at each other's throats. That'll keep that damned Matt Kincaid and everybody else in Easy Company busy and off our asses while we clean up."

McFarland laid his plate aside. Taking up a quiver full of arrows, he pulled two out and examined them carefully, turning them in his hands with gentle, almost loving care. "This arrow with the red markings here I took from that Sioux warrior. This one with the green stripes I took from an Arapaho who happened to turn his back one more time than was good for his health. It's the color that matters, like leavin' your name in a dead man's hat. Kincaid's scout, Windy Mandalian, he ain't no dummy. We do what we're gonna do with Sioux arrows, he'll know it's a setup quicker'n owlshit." Pausing, he looked up and grinned. "That's why we're gonna use the green ones. Everybody'll think the Araps done it."

"When we gonna do it, Stro?" a man named Jenkins asked cautiously.

McFarland's eyes were on him instantly. "When I say to. And that's right now. Get off your asses and on your feet, kick that fire out, and mount up. We want to hit just before daylight."

The buffalo hunters scrambled to their feet while McFarland carefully returned the arrows to his quiver, picked up the bow along with his Spencer, adjusted the revolver in its holster at his side, and walked toward his horse with a bowlegged swagger.

The prairie was dotted with them, longhorns grazing peacefully in the false gray light of dawn, but cold and stiff-jointed from the night's sleep on damp ground. They looked up as the six horses topped the ridge, then went back to their searching for tender shoots of grass. Having been driven up from Texas, they were used to men on horseback, and even though they didn't like them, they had grown used to them. They were an odd mixture of cattle, but the oddity could only be perceived by the discerning eye, the practiced eye, of a Texas cattleman. While the majority of the herd boasted an awesome horn span of nearly five feet, tip to tip, at least a fourth of them were less imposing, smaller in size and shorter of horn.

McFarland, a hide tramp and prairie opportunist, noted nothing unusual about the herd as he angled toward the nearest pocket of cattle, watching him now with heads raised slightly above the grass and mouths stilled. He and the others reined in their horses at a distance of thirty yards, and McFarland casually retrieved an arrow from the quiver attached to the pommel of his saddle, inspected its markings, nocked the arrow, and drew the string to his chin. The tip of the arrow centered on a huge steer with yellow-and-white-splotched markings, then moved up to a point just before the front shoulders, at the base of the neck. McFarland held the bowstring taut for a moment longer while his horse took a restless half-step, then the string snapped away from his chin with a sudden whir.

By the time the sound registered in the startled steer's brain,

11

the razor-sharp arrowhead had slammed home with a solid *thunk*. The animal's head jerked up sharply; it stepped sideways, stumbled, and pitched forward with the arrowhead protruding from the opposite side of its neck. McFarland was not watching the wounded animal's death ballet. Instead he had quickly nocked another arrow, which pierced the ribcage of a cow, nervous and moving away, and the animal bawled in pain before sinking to its knees and rolling onto one side. The other longhorns had begun to trot now, and the third arrow thudded into a steer's flank, while a fourth hit another animal in the upper neck, just behind the left ear. The remaining cattle in the pocket broke from trot to panicked run, and McFarland's fifth arrow bit flesh and buried itself in the fleshy hip of a brownish cow, which sagged to one side but continued to drag itself forward, its mouth open and its terrified bawl rattling on the thin morning air.

McFarland turned to his companions and grinned. "Be good for Boggs to find a few of 'em dyin' but not dead. Make him madder. Let's circle around to the other side and pick off a few more. Stick to the thick grass and don't run your horses. Don't want 'em to pick up any sign of iron-shod hooves. We got one more job to do afore we're finished with this bow."

When they rode cautiously away, half an hour later, two more longhorns lay dead on the prairie, two more were gutshot, and a fifth had an arrow lodged high in its back. The first pinkish-red rays of the rising sun were spreading across the High Plains, and the peaceful dawn of another day was shattered by the bawling moans of dying cattle and the wild laughter of Strother McFarland as he led his men away from the carnage. And then the laughter died and was replaced by a contented humming. Frank Laskey rode beside McFarland and made no mention of the quality of the music.

"What do you make of it, Jake?" Samuel Boggs asked, as he and the foreman stood on the front steps of the main house and listened with ears cocked to the southeast.

"Got some hurtin' cattle, Hoss, that's for sure. Sounds like four, maybe five. Too damned far away to tell. Must be down in the south draws." Jake Barnes paused to listen again. "Can't be wolves, they'd be happy with one cripple. Didn't hear no gunshots, either. Hard to say what the hell's goin' on."

12

"Let's bust ass on down there and find out," Boggs said, turning and stamping into the house, shouting as he moved and pulling up his suspenders at the same time. "Daniel! Martin! Get out to the barn and saddle up some horses! Timothy? Round us up some extra ammunition and throw my doctorin' tools in the bag."

The two elder Boggs boys stood up from the breakfast table and rushed out the door, but Timmy rose slowly and watched his father.

"What's gone wrong, Pa?"

"Don't know," Boggs replied, stamping into his boots and pulling them on with a groan. "Got cattle bawlin' their eyes out in the south draws. Might've got some bad weed, but don't know for sure. Now get them things I told you to get, and let's move out!"

"Sure, Pa," Timmy replied, stepping quickly toward the gun rack. "Won't take but a minute."

"Too damned long," Boggs growled. "Now where the hell's my hat?"

Even over the pounding of hooves of five horses moving at a dead run, they could hear the bawling lessen until only two cows continued their pitiful moaning. And when they pulled their horses to a sliding stop beside the first steer, four of the riders stared down silently with unmasked hatred in their eyes, while the fifth surveyed the scene with curiosity and calculation. In front of them lay a once-healthy longhorn, its mouth open in death and its eyes rolled upward. The shaft of an arrow—a green-striped arrow—protruded from just behind its front shoulders. There was silence except for the jangle of bit chains and the restless shifting of horses that had been run hard and were now cooling in the morning chill. Then Hoss Boggs broke the silence.

"Those filthy, murderin' sons of bitches!" His scream reverberated across the prairie and distant cattle raised their heads from grazing.

"That's an Arapaho arrow, Hoss," Barnes said flatly, without emotion.

"I know it, Jake, goddammit! And they're gonna pay for this, mark my words." His eyes searched the surrounding plains and he saw two more large mounds in the grass, and a fourth

13

cow standing hunchbacked, with its head drooping and drool dripping from the corners of its mouth. "Those featherheaded sons of bitches!" Boggs screamed again.

Barnes turned to the men behind him. "Daniel, you and Martin circle the herd. Find out how many more have been killed. If you see any more gutshot like that miserable cow over there, put them out of their misery."

"Yessir, Mr. Barnes," Martin said, and the two brothers galloped away.

"Timothy? Break the shaft off from that arrow. Your pa'll be wantin' to show it to Kincaid over at the outpost."

"Sure," Timmy replied, stepping easily from his saddle and moving to the dead animal's side.

"Hoss? I think I'd better put a final shot in that old girl over there. All right?"

Boggs' lips were tight as he continued to stare at the dead steer, but he nodded and Barnes pulled out his Colt and moved away.

Timmy broke off the shaft and studied it carefully before stepping toward his father's horse. "Pa? Doesn't it seem strange that the Arapaho would kill these cattle and not attempt to butcher them, or at least cut off a hindquarter or something?"

Boggs' grizzled head swung toward his youngest son and he paid no attention to the jarring explosion of Barnes' Colt, nor to the sudden movement of his horse. "What you gettin' at, boy?" he said sullenly.

Timmy shrugged. "Just seems strange to me that sensible people—"

"Sensible! The Arapaho, sensible? They're savages, boy! Nothin' more than savages, and don't you take up with defendin' 'em like you always do! We know they killed five head of stock and Christ knows how many more. That's all the proof I need, and sensible be damned!"

Timmy stood his ground and continued to watch his father. "But would they shoot our cattle with their own arrows, which immediately implicates them, instead—"

"Don't be usin' them ten-dollar schoolhouse words on me, boy! I don't care how much book-learnin' you got, you still wouldn't make a pimple on a cowhand's ass!"

"Sure, Pa, however you want it," Timmy replied with a shrug.

They heard two distant shots as Barnes reined in beside

14

them again, and Boggs fell into a silent glower at the horizon.

When the two brothers galloped up minutes later, Daniel held five broken arrow shafts in his hand, and both men wore sullen hatred on their faces. "Five more, Pa," Martin said. "Three dead and two dyin'. We finished them two off."

"I heard," Boggs replied without looking at his sons.

Nothing was said for more than a minute, until Boggs finally broke the silence. "I can't wait to see the look on Kincaid's Injun-lovin' face when I show him them shafts," he said, his words just above a whisper.

"Why don't we just go after them Arapaho, Pa?" Martin asked cautiously. "We got the right, don't we?"

Boggs nodded slowly. "Yeah, we got the right. But let's do this legal-like. Then, if Kincaid don't do nothin', then we'll pay 'em back in kind."

Timmy hesitated, drew in a half-breath, then looked up at his father. "We've already done that, haven't we, Pa?"

Boggs' head snapped toward his youngest son. "What do you mean by that?"

"Yesterday. Buffalo are cattle to them. We killed seventy-five of their stock yesterday. It was cold-blooded slaughter, just like they've done here. *If* they did it. We're no better than they are."

Samuel Boggs fought the urge to put the spurs to his horse and ride right over his son, and in doing so he pulled the reins back too hard and his horse backed away with a nervous snort, while rolling its lower jaw against biting iron.

"Damn you, boy! If I ever hear words like that come from your mouth again, I'll forget you're kin. Buffalo are varmints, not cattle, and Indians are savages, not white men. We got government permits and they don't. You're still shittin' yeller and your ears is greener'n a cookin' apple, and I'm beginnin' to wonder if you'll ever be a Boggs like your brothers and me. Damn your mother and her soft-headed thinkin'!"

Timmy opened his mouth and started to speak, but Jake Barnes shook his head and looked down with his hands folded over his saddle horn. "You'd best be holdin' your tongue, Timmy. Ain't wise to chase a bear long enough to catch it."

Timmy glanced once at the foreman, then back to his father, before stepping to his horse and swinging into the saddle. "Thanks, Jake," he said simply, before pressing his horse to a gallop and turning toward the ranch.

Boggs listened to the sound of retreating hooves until they were gone, then muttered, "Damn fool kid. Got the strangest notions about things I ever did hear. Daniel, you and Martin set to butcherin' a couple of these critters. I'll send some of the hands back to help. Salt 'em down good, 'cause that's gonna be a hell of a lot of meat to store. Jake? I got a couple of things to do back at the ranch, and you do too. After that, what say we make a set of tracks to Outpost Number Nine? I'll be curious to hear what the good lieutenant aims to do about our losses."

"Sure, Hoss, be glad to. Might make interestin' listenin'."

For the first time that morning, Samuel Boggs allowed a grin to spread across his lips. "Yeah, could be, at that. Let's go."

three ——————————

Outpost Number Nine was but a low silhouette on the prairie, with its cut-lumber-and-sod walls arranged in a square configuration and an American flag flying high on a pole in the center of the parade. The inner side of the continuous outer wall was utilized as the back walls of living quarters, stables, shops, and warehouses, and was parallelled by an inner sod wall; the two main walls were joined by a sod-and-tarpaper roof. There was a main gate leading into the post through the eastern wall, and directly opposite the gate was situated the post headquarters, with its back to the prevailing westerly wind. Inside the headquarters section, there was an orderly room and the captain's office, and inside the captain's office, four men had met that morning for a meeting of sorts.

Captain Warner Conway—tall, distinguished, with hair just beginning to show graying at the temples—sat behind his desk and leaned back casually in his chair. He was overage in rank. Even though he had served as a lieutenant colonel under General Grant during the Civil War, across-the-board demotions that were the result of governmental belt-tightening after the War, combined with the obscurity of his post assignment on the frontier, had caused him to be passed over by the promotions board. He was not embittered by this oversight, only slightly annoyed and more concerned with the welfare of his troops than with personal aggrandizement. In his mid-forties, and a Virginian by birth, he was army to the marrow of his bones and content with his station in life.

Seated in a chair to one side, First Lieutenant Matt Kincaid flipped the pages of a report he was perusing. There was a look of bemused incredulousness on his handsome face. Also overage in grade, Kincaid was a graduate of West Point and a veteran of two Western tours, and had been cited for bravery on the Staked Plains in the campaign against the Comanche. Thirty years of age and a Connecticut Yankee by extraction, he was tall, lean, and well muscled, and the cut of his uniform had caused more than one pretty girl's eyes to track him carefully on his infrequent trips into town.

Leaning against the wall and casually working a whetstone along the shining blade of the bowie knife in his hands, stood a man of entirely different character. While the others in the room wore blue uniforms, his compact frame was encased in fringed buckskin. There was an aquiline cast to his nose, and his dark features, accented by high cheekbones, caused travelers passing through to inquire whether he was of Indian origin. Invariably, Windy Mandalian replied dryly, "Armenian," and the inquirer would nod knowingly and move along. Although a friend of many "reconstructed" Indians, Mandalian was nearly a legend on the High Plains as an Indian fighter. As chief scout for Easy Company, he was without peer as a tracker and in possession of a sixth sense that made him nearly as much an Indian as the Indians themselves. Though he had open access to all the amenities of the post, Mandalian could more often be found with the squaws of the pacified Indians living nearby than bunking within the walls of the outpost.

Rounding out the foursome was a barrellike man, acting First Sergeant Ben Cohen. He too was due for a promotion that had not come, and as he sat there with his beefy arms folded across his chest, the white scars on his knuckles told of much behind-the-barracks discipline that he felt was not worth troubling the captain about. He was totally dedicated to the captain and the lieutenant, and God help the enlisted man who didn't carry out either of the officers' orders to the letter. On the other hand, he was willing to help any man who was trying his best to soldier properly, and had been known to place his stripes in jeopardy to give a good man another chance.

Matt Kincaid gave the last page one final glance, shook his head, and folded up the report.

Captain Conway watched him with an easy smile. "Would it be fair to assume that your opinion of that report is similar to mine, Matt?" he asked as he reached for a cigar.

"Only if your opinion is that that report is the biggest bullshit ever written by the hand of man, Captain." Kincaid shrugged and held his palms up in a helpless gesture. "So the inspector general, who spent most of his time while he was here trying to sober up, if I recall, says that Easy Company does not conform to the regimental directive on battlefield readiness. What the hell do they expect? We're armed with single-shot Springfields instead of repeating Spencers as we should be, we play hell getting spare weapons, such as they are, ammunition, supplies, pay, promotions, any of the things that we need just to survive, let alone stand parade inspection in Washington, D.C.—which, I need not point out, this is definitely *not*."

Conway chuckled and blew a stream of smoke at the match he held in his fingertips. "I see we concur, Lieutenant. In my opinion, if that thing had a nail driven through the upper left-hand corner and was attached to the wall of the enlisted men's latrine, it would then be serving a positive purpose for the good of this command."

"I don't think the men would even want to wipe their asses on that garbage, sir," Cohen threw in. "If you don't mind my saying so."

Mandalian looked up with an easy smile. "Maybe the *officers'* shithouse would be a better place, Captain. What with all the chewin' you fellers get, your asses might not be so tender."

Conway and Kincaid laughed openly. "Yeah, Windy, maybe you're right," Conway allowed. "Any way you look at it, it's a damned-if-you-do-and-damned-if-you-don't world." Then the captain's face sobered and he leaned forward to place one elbow on his desk. "But that report isn't why I asked you all to come in here this afternoon. Regiment has plenty of time to play around with paper problems, but we've got *real* problems to deal with. You're all familiar with General Phil Sheridan's philosophy toward the Indians, right?"

The others nodded and Matt looked up sharply. "Sure. 'The only good Indian is a dead Indian.' Try telling that to a ten-year-old boy standing beside his mama, with a hole blown through her stomach. Those big brown eyes tell a different story."

"We've all been there, Matt," Conway said softly, "and none of us is any less affected. But the disturbing thing is, Sheridan isn't the only one with that viewpoint. There is a growing school of thought that the 'Indian problem' can be resolved simply by making them wards of the state, totally dependent upon us for their existence on the various reservations we've established. The means by which they think this can be accomplished is the extermination of the buffalo. Since the Indians rely on the buffalo herds for nearly every facet of their existence, with the buffalo gone, the Indians will have no other means of survival than to peacefully acquiesce to our demands and stay on their reservations like good little boys and girls and wait for our handouts."

Kincaid tossed the regimental report on the captain's desk and shook his head in disgust. "That's another crock of shit, Captain. The Bureau of Indian Affairs, no matter how well intentioned some of the agents are, has been something less than a glorious success. Most of the time there aren't half enough supplies to meet the original promises made when the treaties were signed."

"No one could be more aware of that than I, Matt. But, as you well know, we are bound by orders issued on higher authority than either of us commands. And that brings us to the real problem at hand: the establishment of the Wahilla Reservation between the South Pass and the Powder River. The agency there is poorly stocked, as Matt mentioned, and the Wahilla tribe has been issued permits to hunt buffalo off the reservation until such time as the BIA can take better care of them. And that's the rub. Grazing permits have been issued to cattlemen on all sides of the reservation and, as is the stockman's nature, he also grazes his cattle on any other government land in that proximity and considers it his own by right of eminent domain. We are supposed to protect the settlers from the Indians and the Indians from the settlers. No small task by any means, and I would liken it to having a cat and a dog tied to the same tree on short ropes."

"Issuing repeating Remingtons to the Arapaho ain't helping matters one damned bit either, is it, sir?" Cohen asked. "It seems to me that's another flaw in General Sheridan's overall plan. He thinks the Indians will help in the eventual killing off of the buffalo. He doesn't realize that they, unlike some folks, take only what they need."

Windy Mandalian dropped a fresh wad of spittle on the stone and spoke as he continued to work the knife. "Feed 'em all winter and fight 'em all summer. That's a hell of a way to accomplish anything. Every man in this room knows that a lot of those bullets are going to settle old debts and hatreds against the white man. But unless you catch 'em at it, which is damn near impossible, then old Phil thinks everything is hunky-dory."

There was a feeling of impatience spreading through Kincaid's bones, and he stood and moved to the window without looking out. "Red Hawk is the chief of the Wahilla. He's a warrior and a man any of us can respect. I've fought against him in the past, but now I think he's really trying to live within the terms of the treaty. But you can't take a proud man and drag his nose through fresh cowshit too long before he says enough is enough. He sees the buffalo herds dwindling, and where the life's blood of his tribe once roamed in plentiful numbers, he now sees longhorns, which aren't intended to feed his people, but which will be shipped back East to fatten up white folks instead."

Kincaid paused to rub his eyes with the tips of his fingers before turning again to the senior officer. "Captain, I say that any longhorns that drift across reservation lines should be fair game for the Indians. That's the only way we can get these stockmen to police their own borders. The worst offender I can think of in this area is Samuel Boggs with his Double G stock."

The captain brushed a long white ash from his cigar and nodded. "I'm familiar with Boggs, Matt. Have you checked his grazing permits?"

"I have. Under the Homestead Act, he is entitled to a quarter section, one hundred sixty acres, which he has. But that's probably the place where you would find the least number of his cattle. The rest are on federal land. I've tried to evict him from that land in the past, but he's always had a grazing permit issued by the Bureau of Land Management of the Interior Department, and he even has receipts to show that he's paid the goddamned fees. You know as well as I do, Captain, that if he is allowed to use that land for any length of time, he will eventually come to regard it as his own and kill anything that takes so much as a blade of grass from 'his' land."

"Tell me, Matt," Conway asked, "do you think he has ever shot any buffalo on reservation ground?"

"I'm sure of it."

"Can you prove it was him?"

"No. With everybody in the country shooting buffalo right and left, it's kind of hard to pinpoint who actually pulled the trigger. But I'll tell you this for a fact—he's the most unscrupulous son of a bitch I've ever met in my life."

"So I've heard, from yourself and other sources. Still, until we can catch him at something illegal, we're stuck with him." Conway struck another match and held it to his cigar, saying, "I've never met the man, but I suppose I will someday."

"Consider yourself lucky, Captain," Kincaid said, moving away from the window. "The pleasure would have to be his."

Mandalian leaned forward and looked out the window, then wiped the blade on his pants leg, dropped the stone in his pocket, and sheathed the knife on his gunbelt, opposite a Colt .44. "Your luck just ran out, Captain," he said laconically.

"What do you mean by that, Windy?"

"Big poison just rode in with his foreman, a less-than-gentleman named Jake Barnes. They're heading straight for your office."

Sergeant Cohen stood, looked quickly out the window, then went into the orderly room and took a seat at his desk. He had less than a minute to wait before the door slammed open and banged back against the wall. Cohen looked up innocently.

"May I help you?"

"You're damned right you can, and you better, too," Boggs said, with a cursory glance around the room. "I'm Sam Boggs and I want to talk to whoever in hell runs this goddamned place."

"Would you be referring to Captain Conway?" Cohen asked with a hint of pleasure.

"Does he run it?"

"He's the commanding officer."

"That army talk don't mean shit to me, soldier boy. If he runs this fucking place, then he's the man I want to talk to."

Sergeant Cohen smiled politely. "Of course, my apologies. It was unfair of me to assume that you might know something about the military."

"Look, bucko, I pay my taxes and they pay your damned wages, so don't get uppity with me!"

"Wouldn't think of it, Mr. Boggs. I'd hate to have you fire me."

"Where is he?"

"Captain Conway?"

"The feller in charge of this shithole!"

"Captain Conway."

"Then dammit, boy, I want to talk to *Captain Conway*."

Cohen smiled again; he had gotten what he wanted. "May I state the nature of your business with the captain?"

"My business with him ain't no business of yours!" Boggs roared, holding up a clenched fist containing five broken arrow shafts.

Cohen glanced at the shafts as he stood and shook his head. "Those couldn't be ours," he said as he moved to the door to Conway's office. "We quit using arrows years ago." He opened the door and poked his head inside and noted the pleased grin on the captain's face. He knew the officer had heard his words with Boggs. "There's a taxpaying citizen out here to see you, sir. A Mr. Boggs?"

"Thank you, Sergeant. I have a few important matters to take care of just now, but tell Mr. Boggs I will be happy to talk with him in half an hour."

"Very good, sir," Cohen replied, backing away and pulling the door shut while he turned to Boggs. "The captain said—"

"I heard what he said, goddammit! I haven't got half an hour to waste. I want to see him now!" Boggs shouted, taking a threatening step toward the door.

Cohen squared away with his massive arms folded across his chest, and there was an unmistakable look in his eye. As he spoke, he emphasized each word. "The captain said half an hour. You'll see him then, not before."

Boggs hesitated, thought a moment, then backed away. "Have it your way, soldier boy. Anyplace where I can get a drink around here while I wait for his majesty?"

23

"The sutler sells beer in his store just across the parade. I assume he would serve you."

"He damned well better," Boggs snarled as he stomped from the office.

In exactly a half-hour, Boggs slammed his way into the orderly room once again.

"Well?"

"Mr Boggs?" Cohen said, looking up from his paperwork. "Good to see you again. I trust the sutler was properly hospitable?"

"Cut the bullshit. Where is he?"

"I'll see if he has time for you now," Cohen said, moving to the captain's office door. "But please make your visit brief, he's a very busy man."

"*He's* busy? Do you think I raise *chickens* for a living?" Boggs asked with a snarl.

"And you do well at it, I'm sure," Cohen replied, smiling almost sweetly. "One moment, please."

"Oh, Christ!"

"Captain? Mr. Boggs is here to see you."

"Send him in, Sergeant."

Stepping to one side, Cohen held the door open and invited Boggs to enter with a sweep of his hand. "The captain will see you now, Mr. Boggs."

"It's about time," Boggs replied, turning sideways to squeeze past Cohen's barrel chest.

Captain Conway was signing some papers on his desk, Mandalian continued to stand by the window, and Matt Kincaid had resumed his seat on the opposite side of the room.

Boggs brandished the arrow shafts in the air with a flourish of his hand and spoke in the same instant. "Do you know what these are?" he demanded.

Conway glanced up from his work, then down at the papers again. "Good day, Mr. Boggs. One moment, please, and I'll be with you. Have a seat, if you wish."

The firm, commanding tone in the captain's voice silenced Boggs and he looked first at Kincaid and then at Mandalian. Windy glanced at the shafts and offered laconically, "I'll try a guess. They're short arrows?"

Boggs' cheeks puffed out and the bristly red hair seemed to become spikes in his face, but he offered no reply.

24

Captain Conway signed the last paper with a flourish, shoved the pile to one side, then looked up at his visitor.

"Now, Mr. Boggs. It is Boggs, isn't it?"

"Yeah, it's Boggs."

"We haven't had the pleasure. I'm Captain Conway." He gestured toward Kincaid. "And this is my adjutant, Lieutenant Kincaid."

Matt nodded, but Boggs didn't return the courtesy, choosing instead to step to the captain's desk and throw the arrow shafts onto the polished wood in a scattered splash. "Know what those are?"

Windy looked at Kincaid and shrugged. "So I was wrong?"

"I thought you had it all the way, Windy," Matt said with a chuckle. "Now we'll have to wait and see, I guess."

Conway glanced once at the offering, then back to Boggs. "I think it's fairly obvious what they are, Mr. Boggs, and I haven't got time for word games. Please state your business."

"Do you have any idea where those shafts came from?" Boggs demanded.

Windy tried to hold back the remark, but could not contain himself. "Got you this time, Boggs. From your hand?"

Boggs whirled and his eyes flashed with renewed rage. "I know who you are, you squaw-lovin' son of a bitch, and I don't need any of your shit!" Turning back to Conway, he said, "I demand to speak with you in private, Captain."

Conway's eyes were level and cold. "You make no demands here, Mr. Boggs. With Windy and Matt in my presence, you *are* speaking in private. Now get on with it."

"All right, we'll play it your way," Boggs said as he contemptuously rested a filthy boot on one of the leather-covered chairs before the captain's desk. "Ten of my cattle were killed this morning. Seven dead on the spot and three gutshot, which we had to destroy. Ever' damned one of 'em had an Arapaho arrow stickin' out his side. You remember the Arapaho, don't you, Captain?" Boggs asked derisively. "Those miserable thievin', lyin', murderin' bastards what was supposed to be so peaceful and content on that reservation you carved out of a piece of my ground?"

"Are you sure it was Arapaho who fired those arrows?" Conway asked, ignoring the remark about ownership of federal land.

"Sure as hell wasn't the Ladies Quilting Society, I'll tell you that for damned sure!"

"Then that leaves only the Arapaho, doesn't it, Mr. Boggs?" Matt said quietly.

Windy shifted to a more comfortable position against the wall. "What kind of sign was there, at the place where you say your cattle were killed?"

"Where I *say* they was killed? Maybe you ain't familiar with livestock, feller, but when a cow ain't breathin' no more, it's dead."

"Fine. But what kind of sign?"

Boggs hesitated before waving a hand toward the shafts. "Well . . . them arrows right there . . ."

"Besides the arrows."

"What . . . whaddaya mean?"

"Hoofprints, iron or bone. Direction of travel. Formation of the riders, if there was more than one of 'em. Depth of the arrows in the cows' hides, accuracy, angle of entry, that sort of thing," Windy concluded with a barely perceptible grin.

Boggs was obviously flustered now. "Well, I mean, we didn't have time to look for all that stuff. We—"

Windy watched Boggs closely. "Didn't have time? Once a cow is dead, or quits breathing, it's going to be that way for quite a spell, ain't it?"

Conway picked up a pencil and held it between his fingertips while he spoke slowly, calculatingly. "What you mean is, you didn't have time to try to investigate the circumstances because you were in such an all-fired big hurry to get in here and have us send a detachment to the Wahilla Reservation and arrest any Arapaho who happened to have arrows of this description in his posession, which happens to be every Arapaho in the Nation, by the way."

Boggs' frustration turned to indignation. "Who the hell's side are you on, anway? A pack of thievin' Arapaho come onto my ground, shoot my cattle with their own damned arrows, and you're askin' me who done it?"

"Correction," Conway said, continuing to turn the pencil. "That is federal land deeded to you, the remainder of which you supposedly have legal grazing permits for. I am not disputing what you saw, nor am I taking sides with the Arapaho. I am, however, a firm advocate of the philosophy that there

26

are two sides to every story."

Captain Conway turned toward Kincaid. "Matt, you and Windy take First Platoon and ride out to Mr. Boggs' property. Windy? You check those cattle over carefully for the things you mentioned earlier, as well as the surrounding area. Then ride over to the reservation and have a talk with Red Hawk." His eyes drifted back to Boggs. "Will that be all right with you, Mr. Boggs?"

Boggs shifted his massive bulk uncomfortably and hitched his boot against the chair, which moved sideways with a squeak. Conway's gaze darted once to the chair and then locked on the stockman's face. "And get your boot off that chair. I'll not tolerate the defacing of government property."

Boggs tried to match the captain's icy stare, failed, and dropped his boot to the floor.

"Thank you, Mr. Boggs. Now, I'll ask once again, is my proposed course of action suitable to you?"

Boggs nodded sullenly. "The part about sending your army boys over to the reservation is right fine. But there ain't no need in coming to the place to look over the dead cattle." He swallowed hard, and it was obvious that he was becoming increasingly uncomfortable. "My boys butchered 'em this mornin'. And as for tracks and such like that, the rest of the hands rounded up the herd and moved 'em closer to the home place."

Windy stepped quickly away from the wall and snatched up a handful of shafts. "So this is all you have to prove that the Arapaho killed your cattle? A handful of broken arrows that any Arapaho squaw would trade for a sack of tobacco?"

"Looks like that's it."

"Well, Mr. Boggs," Conway said, "that isn't enough proof to prosecute the entire Wahilla tribe. We will investigate and do our best to bring the responsible parties to justice. That's the best we can offer on what we have to work with."

"That's the best you can offer, huh?" Boggs shouted, his indignation returning in full measure. "Well, that ain't quite good enough. I know damned well my cattle were killed by some stinkin' Arapaho, and if you don't do nothin' about it, me and my boys will. Any Injun I see on my homestead, or the ground I got legal permit right to, is gonna be shot on sight. And if I find any more of my cattle with arrows stickin'

27

out of 'em, we won't wait for them Arapaho to cross our land, we'll go find 'em and do the job you were supposed to've done."

Indignation had given way to fury, and Boggs' face was livid with rage as he turned and nearly jerked the latch handle from the door. But he stopped with the captain's softly spoken words.

"Mr. Boggs?"

"Yeah?" he replied without turning.

"The law applies equally to everyone within my district. Break that law and you'll pay the price, same as the next man."

Boggs turned his head halfway toward the captain, hesitated, then stamped out through the orderly room.

Windy, Matt, and Captain Conway heard Sergeant Cohen say, "Good day, sir."

And they heard Boggs reply—"Fuck you, soldier boy!"— followed by the violent slamming of a door.

four

"You sure this is gonna work, Stro?" Frank Laskey asked as he crouched behind McFarland, shielded by the jutting stone of the rimrock.

McFarland didn't look at Laskey, but his words were equally as piercing as his eyes might have been. "If you ask me that one more time, Frank, you won't have to worry about the answer."

Laskey studied McFarland's response, rubbed his chin, and fell silent. In the three years they had been together as buffalo hunters, he had never really crossed the small Scotsman. He knew little of McFarland's past, except that he had spent two years in an insane asylum, from which he had escaped after feigning recovery and then slitting the throats of three guards. But he also knew that McFarland was a hunter who took more hides annually than any three other men put together. And now, with times as tough as they were, he was wise enough to know that, as a skinner, his only future lay with the best in the business. So he fell silent and watched the solitary figure approaching them from the southwest.

Spike Dowler was a relatively young man, maybe twenty-six, who had been orphaned as a child and had thrown his lot in with the Boggs family because there seemed to be none of the rules and restrictions he had known as a young man in the orphanage. Sure, he admitted to himself often as he rode the prairie alone, there was a lot wrong with Hoss Boggs, and some of the things he did wouldn't stand a whole lot of inspection in full daylight, but overall, if a man did his job and kept his mouth shut, he got paid regularly and was pretty much left alone.

Dowler turned to study the lowering sun. There was but an hour—maybe an hour and a half—left until darkness, and so he decided to make one last sweep along the rimrock for strays before turning his horse toward home. He felt good; the horse between his legs was a strong, sturdy animal and there was a sense of contentment in knowing he had worked hard and well throughout the day in compliance with the boss's wishes. With the flaming ball behind him, his shadow stretched across the darkening grass and he yawned expansively and thought little of anything other than the bunkhouse, a warm meal, and a few drinks of whiskey.

Shielding his eyes against the dying sun with one hand, McFarland held the bow and arrow beside him with the other and judged the distance of the approaching rider. He blinked, rubbed his eyes with the back of his hand, then moved the weapon up sharply. The nocked arrow caught on an unnoticed rock and, gripped tightly between two fingers, the long shaft snapped and hung limply by a sliver of wood. Dowler was in range now and McFarland blinked his watering eyes.

"Goddammit!" he muttered, knowing the arrow was shattered. "Laskey?"

"Yeah, Stro?"

"Grab me another arrow from the quiver," McFarland hissed. "Quick, he's face-on now!"

"Sure, Stro," Laskey said, watching Dowler and reaching blindly for the quiver at the same time. His fingers closed over an arrow and he handed it quickly up to McFarland, who fixed the arrow to the string without taking his eyes off Dowler. His eyes constantly locked on his prey, McFarland continued to lay on one side, pulled the bow back, and then twisted to his knees and straightened. Dowler was no more than twenty yards away, and a startled expression crossed his face at the sight of a man rising before him. He died with that same look on his face.

Sailing downward, the arrow slammed home through the right side of his ribcage and lodged against his hipbone. The rider's mouth dropped open and his body twisted to one side, and he slowly toppled from the saddle to thud against the ground with one foot entangled in the left stirrup. The reins dropped in front of the horse and it stopped and stood still with the dead rider staring sightlessly up at the darkening sky.

"Good shot, Stro," Laskey offered as the two men scrambled away from the rimrock and down to where their horses were tied.

"Shitty," McFarland grunted, "I was aimin' for his neck."

Laskey tried again. "Still, he's dead with an arrow through him. That's all we want."

"Yeah," McFarland replied, swinging into his saddle, pulling the horse's head up and turning toward Laskey. "Hey, Frank?"

"What?" Laskey grunted, swinging a leg over his horse's rump.

"What color was that arrow you handed me?"

"What color? Hell, I don't know. Same as the other one, I guess."

"That damned sun was right in my eyes and I couldn't tell for sure, but I thought I caught a flash of red when I turned 'er loose." McFarland studied Laskey more closely, and there was a changing look in his eyes. "You sure you handed me a green one?"

Laskey smiled nervously and tried to sound positive. "Yeah, Stro, I'm sure. It was a green one. No question about it."

"There better not be, Frank," McFarland said ominously. "For your sake, there better not be."

"There ain't, Stro, all right? Now let's get the hell out of here."

After one last long glance at Laskey's uncertain face, McFarland turned his horse south and galloped across the plains.

Dowler's mount stood there until well past dark before thirst overwhelmed its training to stand when the reins were dropped,

31

and finally, with its head cocked to one side to keep the leather strips from beneath its front hooves, the horse began to work its way home, the stiffening body dragging behind with a boot twisted in the stirrup.

Samuel Boggs' rage slowly increased with each drink from the whiskey bottle, and when he slammed his hamlike fist against the tabletop, glasses jumped and the bottle tilted at a crazy angle.

Seated at the table in the cluttered kitchen, his three sons and Jake Barnes watched him silently and waited for the outburst they knew would come. They had not long to wait.

"Those sons of bitches! They treated me like a cow thief instead of an honest rancher tryin' to make a livin' in this godforsaken place. Them arrow shafts might just as well of been toothpicks as far as they were concerned. And that damn squaw-lover was the worst of the bunch, what with all his bullshit about looking for tracks, angle of entry, and all that other garbage. What the hell was I supposed to do, just leave them beef to rot in the sun?"

"We got 'em butchered and salted away like you said, Pa," Martin offered with a conciliatory gesture.

But he might as well not have spoken, because Boggs didn't appear to have heard him, choosing instead to stare at the tabletop before snatching the bottle and pouring another shot. "Them blue-legged sons of bitches! They ain't worth the powder to blow 'em all to hell, where they damn well belong, and I ain't never goin' to them for help again."

"I heard most of it through the window, Hoss," Barnes said, "and it sounded to me like they were gonna check it out."

"Check it out?! Check *what* out, Jake? Maybe Kincaid wants to ask them beefers who shot 'em? Bullshit! There ain't nothin' to check out. We saw what we saw and there ain't nothin' more to it."

Timmy had been watching his father impassively, but suddenly he cocked his head toward the window and listened to a sound the others hadn't heard. Standing quickly, he moved toward the door.

"Where you goin', boy?" Boggs demanded.

"No place, Pa. Just outside for a minute." Timmy looked around the smoke-filled room and smiled. "Maybe get a little fresh air. For a feller who doesn't smoke, I'm pickin' up the habit real quick in here."

32

"Can't trust a man who don't smoke or drink," Boggs growled, striking a match beneath the table and holding it to the stump of the cigar clenched between his teeth. "Even if he's your own damned son, which I'm beginnin' to wonder more about ever' damned day."

"Ma's the only one who could tell you about that, Pa, but she's dead," Timmy said softly before stepping onto the porch.

"Damned whelp!" Boggs yelled at the retreating figure of his son.

A dirty yellow glow from the lamps spilled through the kitchen windows and spread dull shafts of light across the packed earth of the yard. But the moon was full, a beautiful silver disc in the star-sprinkled sky, and Timmy could clearly see the creature that had aroused his attention. A horse, saddled and bridled, stood at the water trough and sucked noisily through the steel bit in its mouth. And stretched on the ground, his arms trailing behind his head, lay a man who was obviously dead.

"Pa! Better get out here!" Timmy yelled as he started to run across the yard. He could hear the almost instantaneous pounding of boots on wooden planking, and by the time he had knelt beside the body, the four other men were crowding behind him. Timmy carefully turned the man's head to the light, then looked up at his father. "It's Spike, Pa. He's dead."

Shoving his other sons roughly to one side, Boggs dropped stiffly to one knee and ran his hand up the side of Dowler's chest. His hand closed around the arrow shaft and his face went as cold as a frozen stone, while his head rose slowly to stare at nothing in the darkness.

"They'll pay for this," he murmured, his lips barely moving. "They'll pay for this," he said again, the volume and viciousness rising in his voice with each spoken word. "They'll damn well pay for this! Cows is one thing, but my men is a whole 'nother kettle of fish! At first light tomorrow, I want you boys to spread out, take all hands, and search every damn square inch of my property. If you find an Arapaho, I don't care if it's old or young, man or woman, shoot the son of a bitch and send him back to them, just like old Spike here, deader'n a fart under water. Make sure it's on legal Double G land, 'cause I don't want no truck with Conway. But we're gonna get even if we can find us a trespasser, and then, if them featherheads want to push it, the war is on."

Timmy rose and looked to the north and his mouth moved

33

in a silent prayer, which went unnoticed by the others. Then he turned and walked quickly back to the house.

The wolf lay at his feet and the young Indian brave felt pride swelling in his chest as he stood there with the bloody knife in his hand and looked down at the dead animal. He felt no pain from the claw marks across his chest, because this was no time for pain, but only triumph.

"I shall be known as Gray Wolf," he said softly, thinking of the rites of passage that would give him his manhood, the right to choose a warrior's name; those rites were now in progress at the Wahilla Reservation. "I have killed a she-wolf in her own den with my knife, a thing so brave only an Arapaho warrior could accomplish. Heya, my father will be proud of me and I shall ride beside him as a man."

The sixteen-year-old boy knelt beside the wolf and rolled back her upper lip to expose the long white fangs. "And her fangs will hang around my neck and all will know why I am called Gray Wolf." Gray Wolf listened to the yelping of pups in the dark recesses of the den, and he knew they were nearly weaned and old enough to survive on their own. "And you, little ones, will grow strong, and one day my son will meet one of your children as I have met your mother. Then we will know if my blood is pure and strong."

After wiping the knifeblade on a tuft of grass, Gray Wolf began skilfully to strip the hide from the she-wolf, and then severed the neck before standing with the pelt and head in his hands. He could visualize the magnificent robe it would make as it hung down his back on those cold days of the coming winter. Then he heard the snorting of a horse, and he whirled quickly in the mouth of the cave.

Daniel and Martin Boggs sat their horses, with rifles raised waist-high and casually trained on the young brave's chest.

"Well, well, what have we got here, Martin?" Daniel asked with a leering grin. "Looks like a junior featherhead to me."

Martin chuckled cruelly. "Sure 'nuff, brother. Guess he couldn't catch no cows, so he had to kill that poor old wolf in there."

Gray Wolf glanced down instinctively at the pelt in his hands before his eyes went back to the two brothers. There was no fear in his voice as he said, "My name is Gray Wolf. I am an Arapaho warrior on Arapaho land. What do you want with me?"

"Arapaho land?" Daniel echoed. "There ain't no Arapaho land 'round these parts, boy, 'cept six feet under."

"I have done nothing to you. What do you want with me?"

"Nothin' more'n your hide, boy," Martin said, "even though I don't think you'll skin out as nice as that old lobo there."

Gray Wolf's dark eyes went first to one brother and then the other. "I am an Arapaho warrior," he said, his voice firm and unwavering. "I fear no white man."

"Maybe you don't," Daniel replied with a pleased chuckle, "but you will pretty soon. Time you featherheads was taught a lesson. You're as good a place to start as any."

With his fingers closing more tightly around the knife in his hand, Gray Wolf carefully tossed the pelt aside and lowered himself into a wide-legged crouch, with the blade held before him. He would not beg or back away, and his eyes were locked on Daniel's throat. Moving cautiously forward, he swung his upper body from side to side and approached the two white men with fearless determination. When Gray Wolf was halfway between the mouth of the cave and Daniel's horse, Daniel raised his rifle to his shoulder and squinted down the barrel.

"Let's take him, Martin," he said simply.

Gray Wolf lunged and the two rifles exploded simultaneously. Twin slugs of heavy lead crashed into the Indian's chest and stopped him in midair before throwing him backward to slam against the hard earth. He was dead before he hit the ground, and the knife fell from his hand with a clatter upon the rocks.

The two brothers showed no more emotion than if they had shot a coyote, and Daniel yawned as though bored with the whole affair. "We seen his pony tied down in the draw, Martin. You get it and bring it back here, then we'll tie him across it and send him home to his pappy. Let's throw that hide on for good measure."

In fifteen minutes, Gray Wolf was lashed across the horse's back with the hide wrapped around his chest. Martin checked the lashings one last time before slapping the pony across the rump, sending it galloping toward the north with its cargo bobbing on its flanks.

Daniel heard the yelping of the pups in the rear of the cave, and nodded in that direction. "Let's kill them whelps too. We've got enough vermin roamin' our land as it is. Then let's go home. I'm gettin' sort of hungry."

five ─────────────

It was nearly noon and the sun was high in the emerald-blue sky when First Platoon, Easy Company, reined in at a respectful distance from the Indian encampment on the Wahilla Reservation. With Matt Kincaid and Windy Mandalian in the lead, the soldiers were strung out in a column of twos behind them and their horses shifted restlessly in the piercing sunlight.

"You've taught me well, Windy," Matt said as he watched the tipis in the distance. "The Arapaho respond better to courtesy than they do to force."

"That they do, Matt," Windy replied, "and Red Hawk in particular. For a chief he's kind of young, but his people respect him for his wisdom. Here he comes now."

Three ponies were approaching from the village with lean, bronzed men upon their backs, and each man wore twin eagle feathers in his hair. Their horses moved at a leisurely pace until there were but ten yards separating the two groups, and Red Hawk pulled up on the hackamore in his hands.

"Hello, Lieutenant Kincaid," the Arapaho offered in a controlled voice. "The Wahilla people welcome you."

"It's good to see you, Red Hawk. Thank you for allowing us this visit. Do you remember my scout, Windy Mandalian?"

Red Hawk's calm eyes shifted to Mandalian's face, and what might have passed for a smile crossed his lips. "I remember him, but to us he is known as "the snake." We have met before in circumstances other than these. Welcome to Wahilla land."

"Thanks, Red Hawk," Windy replied with a grin. "It's true, we've looked at each other over a rifle barrel a time or two, but now we meet in peace."

Knowing no business matters could be discussed until the chief had been given the opportunity to offer hospitality, Kincaid waited for Red Hawk to speak again.

"Would you do us the honor of joining us?" the proud-looking Arapaho asked. "We are having the initiation for our young men, and it might be of interest to you. There is one young man yet to be put to the test."

"It would be our pleasure, Red Hawk," Matt replied. "Thank you for the invitation."

Red Hawk nodded, and in unison the three warriors turned their mounts and rode back to the village.

Sergeant Gus Olsen, a veteran of numerous Indian campaigns, and the NCO in charge of First Platoon, spoke up from behind Kincaid. "If you'll pardon my sayin' so, sir, ain't it gonna seem a little strange, breakin' bread with these Arapaho instead of breakin' heads with 'em?"

The troopers behind him chuckled their agreement while Kincaid nudged his horse forward. "Yes it will, Sergeant. But I find the former preferable to the latter. Move the platoon out. Find some shade near the encampment and put the men at ease. We will be leaving in approximately one hour."

"Yessir."

When Windy and Matt dismounted, their horses were led away to be watered and they joined Red Hawk, who was standing near two rows of warriors, perhaps fifteen to a row. The Indians stood five feet apart facing each other, with curved sticks in their hands. A sixteen-year-old youth stood at one end of the line, and there was a mixture of determination and consternation on his face. Red Hawk leaned toward the two white men.

"The trials go on for two days, as they have done already, and he is the last to go through. He must run between the lines

37

and the others will swing their sticks at his lower legs. He must jump over them or be hit or tripped. If either happens, he is all right unless he falls. Should he fall, he must go back and start over until he successfully makes it to the other end."

Red Hawk paused and pointed toward the far end of the line, where two mounted warriors held a barebacked pony between them by twin hackamores. "When he makes it, if he does, the two braves waiting for him will take his horse away from him at a gallop. He must catch them and mount between the two running horses. There is a lance stuck in the ground a short distance away, which he must retrieve with his pony at a full run. If he does so, he will then go out onto the plains to prove his manhood. Armed only with a knife and his lance and bow, he will not return until he has successfully killed a wild creature equal to the stature of an Arapaho warrior."

"And I thought basic training was hard," Matt commented with an approving smile. "How many young men have been put to this test so far, Red Hawk?"

"There have been nineteen before him." There was unmistakable pride in the chief's eyes as he added, "My son was the first to go through. He has been on the plains for three days and nights now."

"When will he be back?" Windy asked.

"When he is a man," the Arapaho said, while raising his hand in the air.

The warriors in the twin lines began to chant and swing their sticks with threatening motions, then the young Indian drew in a deep breath and darted between them. When he was a third of the way down the line, a stick broke across his shin and he stumbled; another was thrust between his legs and he sprawled flat in the dust. Red Hawk's face was impassive while the boy glanced at the chief, raced back to the starting point, and sped between the lines again. Several more sticks smacked against his shins, but he maintained his balance this time, leaping high in the air, twisting, landing, and leaping again. His chest heaved from the exertion as he sprinted toward the horses moving away, first at a trot, then a full gallop. He slipped between the churning hooves of the pony on the right side, grasped his horse's mane, and vaulted onto its back. The woven-hair ropes were dropped and he leaned forward and pulled them in while lying low across his horse's withers. The

38

animal was now moving at a dead run. Suddenly he leaned low to the right side, snatched the lance from the ground, and brandished it high over his head as the pony pounded away across the plains.

Red Hawk allowed a tiny smile to touch his lips. "That is good," he said, turning away. "He has failed before. Come, we will eat and drink and then we will talk."

Kincaid chewed the final bite from his strip of pemmican in silence, took a long drink from the container of cool spring water, then looked across at Red Hawk, who had been watching them eat.

Red Hawk nodded; it was obvious that the time for business was at hand.

"What do you wish of me, my friend?" he asked.

"First of all," Matt began, "is there anything I can do for you?"

Red Hawk smiled openly now. "There are many things. We have not been given the supplies we were promised with the signing of the treaty. We hunt for buffalo as we have in the past, but they are no longer plentiful." A pained look came into his eyes and he glanced away. "They are being slaughtered, and soon there will be none left for the Arapaho people."

"As you know," Matt began, "the agency here on Wahilla land is new and not yet complete, and the agent, Larry Watkins, is quite inexperienced in the ways and needs of your people. But he is a good man and will one day represent your people well to those back in Washington."

"One day? What of today, my friend? Another winter is coming, and we must prepare for it or die."

"You have been given permits to hunt for buffalo off the reservation until we can better serve you. Has that not been of any assistance?"

"Not when your people come onto our land to kill our herds." The chief shook his head sadly. "Yesterday, my oldest son, Black Wing, watched five white men kill a herd of seventy-five buffalo in the northwestern corner of the reservation. They took nothing and left the carcasses to rot."

Windy's eyes darted to Kincaid's face. "Then they weren't hide hunters, Matt. It must have been some of the men that Sheridan regards so highly."

Red Hawk nodded. "I have heard of Sheridan and his views

39

on the Indian tribes. He has said that every buffalo hunter should get a medal with the impression of a dead buffalo on one side and a dejected Indian on the other. Is this the way the white leaders intend to honor the peace treaty?"

"Not all white people, Red Hawk, only a few."

"They may be few, but their voices are loud and their power great."

"Could Black Wing identify the white men if we brought them before you?"

"Of course," the chief said with a tired smile. "But what good would that do? When an Indian pits his words against those of a white man, there is little question who will be considered the liar."

Matt knew the chief was right. He was certain the men in question were Boggs and his sons, but to have them prosecuted, they would have to be brought before the senior officers at regimental headquarters, which was staffed by firm backers of Sheridan's policies. Red Hawk accurately read the look on Matt's face.

"I see even you agree with me, Lieutenant Kincaid. It is useless. We will soon be forced into a decision: to accept starvation with the coming snows, or to take what we must. The time for talking is nearly past. And that is why our young continue to be initiated into manhood in the traditional ways of our people. They may have to fight for the survival of their tribe."

Kincaid lifted his hat and ran a hand wearily through his hair. "I'm sure we both hope these things can be changed before that decision must be made. But we have other problems right now, which are working against you and your people."

Red Hawk nodded again. "And it is these problems that have brought you here?"

"Yes."

"Tell me about them."

"There is a stockman named Samuel Boggs who has a homestead about a day's ride from here. Yesterday he claims to have found ten of his cattle shot." Kincaid studied the chief carefully. "They had been shot with arrows. Arapaho arrows."

Impassively, Red Hawk watched the two men across from him. "And you think my people did this?"

"No, I'm fairly certain they didn't."

"Then why are you here? You should be looking for the ones who did it."

"Only to make certain that *none* of your people were involved. Is there any chance that some of your young men, those taking part in the manhood ritual, perhaps, might have shot those cattle?"

"No, there is no chance," the Indian said without equivocation. "That would be cowardly, which is exactly the opposite of that which they are sent to prove. They want to be warriors, not squaws."

Matt fell silent, studying the alternatives. "I'll take your word on that," he said finally. "But I would ask you one favor both for the sake of your people and in the interest of bringing the guilty ones to justice. Make certain that none of your tribe leave the reservation until I have found the men who have done this."

"Why? We must hunt to survive."

"I know that, and it won't be more than two weeks at the most. There has been a threat made by Boggs, that any of your people will be shot on sight if found on the land he has a legal deed to. I wish only to avoid bloodshed."

Red Hawk watched Kincaid for long moments with dark, fathomless eyes. "It is too late to stop the young ones. They will range wherever they must and as far as necessary to accomplish their goal, and they will not come back until they are successful. But the others, I will—"

The tipi flap was thrown to one side, and a grim-faced warrior stooped and spoke quickly in the chief's ear. The bronze mask that was Red Hawk's face became even less expressive as he listened to the warrior's words. Then he nodded and abruptly rose and left the tipi without looking at, or saying a word to, his guests.

Kincaid understood only a few words of Arapaho, but he knew Windy was fairly well schooled in the language and he looked at him questioningly. "Any idea what that's about, Windy?" he asked.

Windy pursed his lips in concentration and tried to reconstruct what he had heard. "My long suit is Cheyenne, Matt, but I did pick up a few words. I think he was saying something about a dead man on a horse outside."

Kincaid sprang to his feet and ducked through the opening, with Windy following close behind.

The warriors who had participated in the gauntlet had gathered about a brown and white spotted pony, but now they stood back as their chief approached. Matt caught a glimpse of a

41

young warrior strapped across the horse's back, with a wolf's head dangling across one shoulder. His pulse quickened and he pushed his way toward the mount, paying no attention to the sullen looks directed at himself and Windy.

Red Hawk gingerly touched the boy's face and lifted one eyelid, which he then slowly lowered again. He spoke some commands in Arapaho, and the young man was cut free from the horse and laid gently upon the ground. There was a dark red hole above either breast, and his chest was caved in on both sides. The wolf pelt was laid beside him and there was complete silence in the Wahilla camp.

Red Hawk's eyes found Kincaid's face, and there was a tremor in his voice. "Is this a fair trade for ten dead cattle, Lieutenant? One young man's life for ten animals we did not even kill?"

"I'm sorry, Red Hawk," Matt said with deep sincerity. "Very sorry. With Windy's help, we will track the young brave's horse back to where he was killed, and from there we will find those who did this terrible thing."

"No! The Arapaho will avenge their own. We have tried to live within the terms of your treaty. We have not broken our word, but we are the only ones who have not."

"Listen to me, Red Hawk. This boy was sent to you as a message from those who killed him. They will be waiting for you to come to them. They *want* you to come to them. They know you do not stand a chance in our courts of law, and you will be providing them with the one thing they seek—the complete destruction of your tribe."

"Again, we have no choice, Lieutenant. The young man laying there"—he gestured helplessly toward the blood-smeared youth—"had only set out to prove his manhood. What was proven is that the white man is even more treacherous than the timber wolf. He was victorious over the wolf, but the white man? He was slaughtered, as are our buffalo. How many more promises must we be asked to believe before we no longer hear your words?"

Windy stepped up beside Kincaid, and when he spoke there was a strange sort of communication between himself and the Indian chieftain—that of men who live by their wits on the prairie. "Hear me, Red Hawk. We both survive only because we are too cunning to fall prey to our enemies. This boy, like many children, red and white, was not given the chance to learn what we know. He was brave, the same as you, or the wolf pelt would not lie beside him. But bravery ain't enough. Where once we all roamed free, there are now laws that kind of tie us down. If either one of us breaks those laws, we will be hunted and killed. The men who killed this boy will be found and put on trial, but while that's happening, there just ain't no sense in you or any of your warriors getting killed in the process. Trust the lieutenant here. I promise you, he's a man of his word."

Red Hawk looked first from Matt to Windy, and then back to Kincaid again. Matt stole the moment of indecision to drive his point home.

"Red Hawk, just give me a little time."

"How much time?"

"Two weeks."

"Three days."

Matt shrugged helplessly. "I would like more, but if that's all you can give, I'll have to accept it. If, within three days, I have not given you satisfaction, I'll not ask you to trust me anymore. At that time, if you choose to leave the reservation and seek revenge, I will not ask any different of you. But if that happens, we will be enemies once again."

Red Hawk looked down at the boy, but refused to allow the impassive expression on his face to change. Then he looked again at Kincaid. "It is agreed. You have your three days. Nothing will bring this young man to life again, but I do not wish to see others die. If, after that time, your justice has not worked, we will be at war." His eyes swept the plains and his voice became distant. "There are nineteen other young braves out there. If another meets death at the hands of the white man, our agreement is concluded. We will take up our weapons and face the inevitable."

A tall young warrior stepped forward; hatred was written plainly on his face. "Listen no more to the white man's promises, my father. They are made only to be broken. We must avenge this death in our own way against the white man, just as we would have against the Cheyenne or Sioux. For each Arapaho warrior killed, two whites must die."

"No, Black Wing. I have given the lieutenant my word that we will wait three days, no more. Until he has broken his word to me, I cannot break mine to him."

Black Wing glared at Kincaid and spat viciously upon the

43

ground. "He has no word, only false promises," the warrior said before pushing his way through the surrounding braves.

Kincaid offered his hand, and he and Red Hawk clasped forearms in solemn agreement. "Thank you, Red Hawk. You are truly a great chief. I only hope I am as good a soldier."

"We will see," Red Hawk said flatly. "You have proven yourself in battle against my people. Now we must wait to see how well you do against your own kind."

"I won't let you down," Matt said, turning away.

"Lieutenant Kincaid?" The words were soft, like smoke drifting from a campfire.

Matt turned and his eyes went to Red Hawk's somber face. "Yes, Red Hawk?"

"Do you know who this boy was?"

"No, I'm afraid I don't."

Red Hawk's gaze drifted to the lifeless form. Then slowly, ever so slowly, his head turned again toward the army officer. "He was my youngest son, Black Wing's brother," he said softly. "Before the ritual began, he said his name in manhood would be Gray Wolf. To earn that name, he had to prove he had slain a wolf using nothing more than the traditional weapons of our people."

Now Kincaid's eyes went to the silent figure. "I am truly sorry, Red Hawk. He would have been a great warrior and a leader of his people. His name to me is Gray Wolf. I shall remember him by that name. He proved himself a man and honored your traditions; now I must do the same. There are many bad whites on the plains right now, but there also are many good ones. I will prove to you that your trust in me is not misguided."

"Do that, Lieutenant, and for the sake of my people, as well as your own, do not fail."

"I won't, Red Hawk. And thank you." Kincaid looked up to where the platoon stood watching with weapons holstered but ready. "Sergeant Olsen?"

"Yessir!"

"Mount the troop and prepare to move out!"

"Yessir. P'*tooonn!* Mount 'n' form ranks!"

The echo of his command drifted over the silent Indian encampment.

• • •

44

"What do you make of it, Windy?" Kincaid asked as he peered into the cave, with the sun sinking heavily toward the horizon behind his back to the west.

"This is where it happened, all right," Windy replied as he stepped into the opening in the wall of the butte. "There's four dead pups back there, heads bashed in by something, probably the butt of a gun. Had to be white men that did it, 'cause no Indian would've killed young'uns like that."

Matt knelt and ran his fingers over the congealed blood on the approach to the wolf's den. "This must be where they shot him, huh?"

"I'd say so. From the looks of things, Gray Wolf knew he was done for and decided to go out like a warrior."

"Which he did. Have we got enough light to follow those tracks?"

Windy squinted at the horizon. "Not much. But one of the two horses has throwed a shoe. Tracks should be just as good in the mornin' as they are right now."

"Right, we'll bivouac here, then. If we're after who I think we are, they shouldn't be hard to find in the morning."

Windy grinned in the fading light and spat at a rock off to his left. "Yeah, but I think you better sleep with your ears covered tonight, Matt. They're gonna need some rest for all the lies you're gonna hear tomorrow. Catchin' 'em is one thing. Provin' they did it is a whole 'nother story."

"Yeah, I know. Boggs is too smart to leave a trail leading straight back to his place, but we'll follow as far as we can and see what happens."

"We better come up with something pretty damn quick, Matt. The Arapaho are famous for their blood revenge, and I'm sure Red Hawk ain't no exception. If they can't find the exact person that crossed 'em, they'll find somebody, and Lord help the poor bastard they choose."

Matt watched the sun slip beneath the horizon and waited in silence for a moment before speaking again. "I'm aware of that, Windy. We just might have a war on our hands unless we can bring the guilty parties to trial. I don't relish the thought of warring against Red Hawk's people in defense of the likes of Boggs. But we've got no choice."

"Strother McFarland and his bunch ain't what you'd call a real big improvement over Boggs, either, Matt," Windy offered as they walked toward the platoon waiting at the bottom of the hill. "He still hangin' around, shootin' whatever buff are left?"

"I'm afraid so. He's just the kind of scum Sheridan would like to see decorated with his goddamn medals. I check his permits every damned chance I get. He's always legal, at least on paper. But I wouldn't trust him as far as I could throw an artillery piece."

Windy chuckled. "That ain't a very long toss, Matt. And even then, it's more trust than he deserves, I 'spect."

"He'll fuck up one time too many someday, Windy. Then we'll have him. But right now we've got to concentrate on the killers of Gray Wolf."

"You think maybe McFarland had a hand in it? He ain't been known to exactly love the Arapaho himself."

"Hard to say. What happened to Gray Wolf was just cowardly enough to match McFarland's methods. After we talk to Boggs, we'll hunt the bastard up and have a chat with him. By this time tomorrow we should have a better idea what in hell's going on."

"Either that or we'll still be chasin' our own tail. 'Night, Matt."

"'Night," Kincaid replied, watching Windy take his horse and lead it a short distance away on the plains to camp by himself, as was his habit when on maneuvers with a military unit. Matt had tremendous respect for the buckskin-clad scout, and he was damn glad to have him on his side.

They had heard the distant shots earlier that afternoon, and now, with the sun nearing the horizon, Jake Barnes reined in his horse and looked across at Timothy Boggs. "Not much sense in us lookin' any farther today, Timmy," he said. "What say we turn tail and head for home?"

Timmy looked first at Barnes and then toward the north, and there was a faraway look in his eyes. "That sounds fine, Jake. But you go on back by yourself. I'm gonna ride alone for a while. I . . . I got some thinking to do."

"Suit yourself," Barnes replied, pulling his horse's head up and turning the animal. "But don't be too late. Your pa worries about you."

"He doesn't have to worry about me, Jake, and neither does anybody else. I'm man enough to take care of myself."

"I know that, Tim, but your pa don't. Take care."

46

"See you later, Jake," Timmy replied as he watched the foreman jig his horse to a gallop and ride back in the direction from which they had come.

He waited for nearly five minutes before turning his own horse and angling at an easy lope toward the northwest. As he rode, he constantly searched the plains before him and on either side, with an occasional glance over his shoulder. And the farther he went, the more excited he became. A thrill of anticipation passed through his lean frame. He knew she would be there, waiting for him as she had over the past few months.

Kita Wak, the daughter of Chief Red Hawk, stared at the reflection cast back to her from the dark pool of water at her feet. At eighteen years of age, her face was indeed beautiful and her figure bore the ripe maturity of a young lady blossoming into womanhood. Firm breasts pressed against her buckskin dress, which was pulled tight across a flat stomach and then followed the rounded contours of her hips and bulged enticingly across sculpted buttocks. Absentmindedly, she touched her jet-black hair, woven into a single braid and trailing across her left shoulder, and hoped he would say she was beautiful, as he always had before. And, she wondered, what kind of present would he bring her?

Her pink tongue moistened her full lips and she could taste the unfamiliar flavor of rouge, the gift he had left behind at their last parting. Her father would have forbidden her to wear white women's paint, but she wore it for her young man, and there was a delicious excitement in waiting for him now in their secret meeting place in a sheltered grove beside the river. Buried in an earthen container, beside a large boulder, were a lace handkerchief, a silk scarf, and other offerings, which she sat and stared at when he was gone, because those beautiful gifts reminded her of him. And now she had a gift for him that would be even more precious, more beautiful than any other single thing in the world. But a troubled look marred her dark beauty as she looked one last time into the pool. Would he want her gift? Would he hate her for it, or would he take her into his arms and thank her with a kiss before doing the wonderful things he did to her body? Then she heard the clatter of hooves on stone, followed by the flutelike warbling of a meadowlark, and her heartbeat quickened. Cupping her hands around her mouth, she mimicked the call, smoothed the dress across her thighs, and turned her back to the rising moon.

Timothy Boggs smiled softly in the twilight when he heard the answer to his call, and he stepped down from his mount and tied the horse securely to the roots of a fallen tree. His hands went quickly to the saddlebags and his fingers closed around a tiny package, which he pulled out and dropped into a vest pocket. There was a strange ache in his throat as he moved cautiously toward the cove, and he remembered again how they had met.

He had come upon Kita Wak's secret hideaway quite by accident, and their first meeting had been quite an embarrassment for both of them. It was early morning and Timmy had camped by the stream after having trailed a stray cow and her calf for the better part of the previous day. Having gone to the stream to wash, he heard water splashing just around the bend and, taking his rifle for protection, he crept to the spot and peeked around the corner of a huge boulder beside the stream bed. And when he saw her, his breathing stopped for a moment; he thought she was the most beautiful woman his eyes had ever touched.

She was standing there in the water, which reached up to her thighs, with the sunlight glinting off the ripples and turning her bronzed skin a golden hue. He could do nothing but stare unblinkingly at her. The black hair of her pubic region, moist and shining as she stood with her legs slightly apart, was the pivotal point of his gaze, and then his eyes went up to her drum-tight stomach, to her navel, then to her delicately rounded breasts, arching upward, their pinkish nipples hard and well defined, with cold water cascading over them as she threw her head back and massaged her scalp. She was lovely and innocent, and Timmy had been immediately ashamed of violating her privacy. Yet, he could not tear his eyes away. Then his horse nickered from back in the grove, and the girl's eyes were upon him before he could duck back behind the rock. They stared at each other for long moments, and a red flood of embarrassment crept up Timmy's neck and his face became flushed and hot.

There was a glint in her dark eyes that he mistook for anger, but when she smiled, the whiteness of her teeth was startling against the darkness of her skin.

"Well," she had said quietly, without attempting to cover

her body, "you have seen all of me now. There is no further reason to hide."

"Sorry, ma'am," Timmy replied, conscious now of the heavy rifle in his hands. He lowered it to his side. "I didn't mean to sneak up on you."

She smiled again. "You didn't? Why?"

"Why, what?"

"Why not? I would have done the same to you."

"You would have?" Timmy asked incredulously.

"Of course. Men aren't the only curious ones in the world," she had said before walking from the stream to dry off while saying over her shoulder, "let me get dressed and then I will introduce myself."

That was how it had begun, their beautiful, tender love affair, and now neither of them were virgins anymore, and heat flashed through his loins as Timmy stepped from the bushes and into the moonlight.

"Hello, my little Kita," he said quietly.

She stood before him, back arched and head held proudly. "Do you still love me, my Timothy?" she asked almost breathlessly.

"I love you more with each passing day, Kita. And when I think I can love you no more, I always do."

"And I worship you. You are my white god and master."

Tim smiled shyly and looked away. "I am not your master, Kita, and I wish you wouldn't say that. We love each other and we are equal in that love." He stepped forward and took her into his arms, and their lips met in a searching, hungry kiss. Kita moaned and the tenseness drained from her body as he held her. Finally he pushed her away slightly and pulled the tiny package from his vest pocket.

"I have a surprise for you."

A squeal of delight escaped her throat, and her face glowed with excitement and anticipation. "What is it?" she asked as he pressed the box into her hand. She had never known an Indian woman to receive a gift of any kind from her man, and now she had yet another.

Timmy grinned happily. "If I told you, it wouldn't be a surprise. Go ahead, open it."

Working carefully, so as not to make even the slightest tear in the brightly colored paper, Kita opened the box and lifted a tiny bottle from the container. She stared at it curiously, then looked up at Timmy. "What is it?"

"It's perfume."

"What do I do with it?"

"You take the top off, put your finger over the hole, tilt the bottle, then put just a tiny bit behind your ears, on your neck, and . . . anywhere else you like."

"Why?"

"Because it's exciting and the fragrance is wonderful. Go on, take the top off."

Kita's delicate fingers twisted the tiny cap and she held the container to her nose. "That is beautiful, Timmy," she sighed, sniffing again. "It's like all the spring flowers across the meadows have been put into one tiny bottle. Please, show me again how to put it on."

Taking the bottle carefully, Timmy touched his finger to the opening and gently placed a drop behind each ear, then trailed his fingers down her neck and loosened the thongs at the top of her dress. His hands moved inside to caress first one breast, then the other, before he dabbed with his fingers again. Kita's breath was coming faster now, and she arched her head back in the moonlight. Timmy held the bottle to one side and his mouth closed over her nipple and the girl moaned in ecstatic delight. He managed to get the lid back on the perfume before they sank to the blanket spread across the grass and their clothes fell away, the victims of urgent tugging. Then he moved to enter her, slowly, gently, while nibbling at her neck and breasts. The white heat rose in them and they were as one with the meandering gurgle of the stream coursing beside them, and the brilliant moonlight washing across their bodies and contrasting the whiteness of his skin against the brownness of hers.

Later, satiated, they lay quietly, her head cuddled against his shoulder while he gently stroked her hair. They were entirely content merely to have their bodies touching one another. Finally, Kita rolled to her stomach, rested her upper body upon her elbows, and trailed her fingers through the hair on his chest.

"Timmy?"

"Yes, Kita?"

"I have not been to my village since noon. I came here to bathe and wait for you. It seemed the night would never come."

"I felt the same way, hon. I thought I'd never get away. But won't your father be concerned about you?"

"No. Today is the final day of our initiation for the young braves. They do not wish to have women present during the ceremony. My little brother was the first to go through."

"What's his name?"

"He will be known as Gray Wolf when he becomes a man. You would like my brother."

"I'm sure I would. Perhaps we will meet one day."

"You will. He is much like you, gentle, honest, and kind."

Timmy smiled and arched his neck to look down at her. "That doesn't make him much of a warrior, does it?"

"It makes him a man. That is more important." She watched him now, and there was a mysterious depth to her dark eyes. "Thank you for the beautiful present."

"You're welcome. I only wish I could bring you more."

"You have brought enough. More than enough. I have a present for you, as well," she said, speaking cautiously.

"You have? You didn't need to do that."

"Yes I did. It is our present."

"*Our* present? What is it, let's see it."

Kita watched him closely. "You can't see it."

Timmy rose up on one elbow. "What in the world are you talking about, Kita?"

"This," she said simply, taking his hand and pressing it against her belly, just below the navel. "Our present is in here."

"What? Do you mean..." Timmy held his hand perfectly still and stared at her. "Do you mean...?"

"Yes. I mean we're going to have a baby."

"We are? Are you sure?"

"I am sure."

"Well, I'll be damned!"

"Does that make you angry?" she said, continuing to watch him.

"No, honey," Timmy said quickly and with great tenderness. "Not at all. I love you, and that is the finest present you could have given me."

Kita lowered her head to his chest again, and tears glistened at the corners of her eyes. "Thank you, Timmy. I was afraid you would not want our baby. I was afraid you would not want to be known as... as a squaw man."

His hands went to her hair and he kissed the top of her head. "You are the most beautiful person I know, and where either of us comes from doesn't matter to me."

"But your father—he hates the Arapaho, you have told me yourself. Will there be trouble?"

Timmy stared up at the stars and his chest heaved with a heavy sigh. "I suppose, but he doesn't matter where you and I are concerned. We'll go away if we have to, start over and live as we choose."

"Can we do that, Timmy?"

"Yes, but it will take time and some planning. We'll need money, a house, some land, and some cattle. Hey, we're going too fast here! What are we going to have, a boy or a girl?"

"Which do you prefer?"

"Hell, I don't care!"

Kita smiled at him. "I do. I will have a boy for you. He will be fine and strong, just like his father. And I will wish him to have blue eyes."

Timmy's arm went around her and he pulled her tightly to him. "So I'm going to be a father? How long is this going to take?"

"He will be born in the Moon of the Snow-blind."

"Let's see, that's . . . February or so, right?"

"Yes. We have six months to go. I'll start showing pretty soon."

"And I'll be the proudest man in the Territory when you do." Timmy scrambled to his feet and stood naked before her as he reached down for her hands, which she offered, and he pulled her to her feet. "Come on, let's have a swim, and then let's make love to celebrate. Okay?"

Kita grinned happily. "I'll race you to the water!" she squealed, bolting for the stream.

Timmy laughed and chased her, and they dove in side by side, then swam with powerful strokes, like two young otters in the night.

six _____

"Where the hell were you last night, boy?" Boggs demanded as his son stepped into the barn.

Timmy shrugged. "I just took a ride. Felt like being alone."

"You and that 'alone' bullshit! You're takin' to wantin' to be alone quite a bit at night of late."

"That's the way I am, Pa. Is Martin's horse the only one we're going to shoe?" Timmy asked with a wave of his hand toward the animal tethered to the post.

"Only one I got time for," Boggs grunted as he turned his back toward the horse, grasped a leg between his knees, and began rasping the hoof down with long strokes. "Threw a shoe a while back. First time I've had a chance to get to it."

"Did Dan and Martin find any Arapaho yesterday? Jake and I heard a couple of shots."

"Nope. Said they just shot a pair of coyotes. Seem to be a lot of 'em on the place these days."

"Yeah, Pa," Timmy said with relief. "Seem to be."

53

Boggs looked up from his work and brushed the sweat from his brow with his sleeve, then hammered a shoe in place. "Look, boy, the sun's been up for damned near three hours now. Better get aboard that horse of yours and trail on out to help your brothers with the herd. I only let you sleep 'cause I didn't have time to throw your night-crawlin' ass out o' bed."

"Sure, Pa. And thanks a heap."

"Don't backtalk me, boy!" Boggs snarled, then he fell silent and the hammer was motionless in his hands. They both heard the sound of voices and the restless shuffling of several sets of hooves. "Now who the hell you suppose that is?" he asked, directing the question at no one.

"We'd best find out, I guess," Timmy said as he walked to the barn door. Boggs dropped the hoof, hurriedly picked up his tools, led the horse to a stall, and locked it inside. Then he untied the leather apron from around his waist, hung it up, and hurried toward the voices outside.

"Good morning, Lieutenant," Timmy said, looking up at Kincaid and sheltering his eyes from the sun with one hand. "What brings you around so early in the day?"

"Good morning, Tim," Matt replied. He had always liked the younger Boggs and wondered how he could be so different from his father and brothers. "Your pa around?"

"Yeah, sure. He's in the barn now, sh—"

"Timothy!" Boggs yelled as he stepped from the building. "I told you to get on out and go to work! Now git, afore I find me a board and blister your backside!"

Timmy smiled up at Kincaid and shrugged his shoulders helplessly. "Sounds to me like he wants me to go to work. See you later, Lieutenant, Windy."

"See you, Tim," Matt said, and Windy added, "Don't want to get your ass too close to any boards, Tim."

The young man grinned again and walked toward the barn.

"Do anything about them Indians yet, Kincaid?" Boggs demanded without observing cordialities.

"Yes, I spoke with them yesterday afternoon. They claim that none of their warriors fired the arrows that killed your cattle."

"Well, what in the jumped-up Jesus did you expect them to say, goddammit! Maybe 'Hell yes, we shoot cows all the time'?"

"I think Chief Red Hawk is a man of his word. If he knew

54

any of his people were guilty of a crime, he would bring them forward."

"In a pig's eye!"

"Perhaps," Matt said calmly, as he rested his gloved hands on the pommel of his saddle. "But Red Hawk has even more reason for anger and revenge than you have now, Mr. Boggs."

"Yeah? How so?"

"His son Gray Wolf was killed yesterday. Two shots in the chest," Kincaid said, watching the stockman closely. "He was sent back to the reservation, tied across his horse's back."

Boggs snorted and spat in the dust. "So? What's that got to do with me?"

"Maybe nothing, maybe everything. We tracked the boy back to a wolf cave about half a day's ride from here. That's where he was killed. Then we picked up the tracks of two iron-shod horses and followed them in this direction until we lost them in a dry stream bed." Matt's eyes narrowed. "One of them had thrown a shoe. Would you mind if we took a look at your stock, Mr. Boggs?"

"Are you sayin' somebody from my place done it?"

"No. This is merely a routine part of the investigation. But you did state yesterday, in Captain Conway's office, your intention to shoot any Arapaho you might find on your homestead. That, and the death of Gray Wolf, seem strangely coincidental. Like I said, would you mind if we took a look at your stock?"

"Hell no," Boggs said, flinging a massive hand toward the barn door. "There's one inside there. Start with it."

"Thank you," Matt said as he and Windy stepped down. "Sergeant Olsen? Have the men dismount and stand at ease."

"Yessir. P'*tooonn* . . . diss*smount*!"

Leather creaked behind them as the soldiers stepped heavily in their stirrups while Matt and Windy followed Boggs into the barn. Timmy stood beside the door with his horse's reins in his hand. There was a troubled look on his face, which Boggs ignored, but it caused Matt to stop beside him.

"Is something wrong, Tim?"

"What?" Timmy asked, looking up with clouded eyes.

"I said, is something wrong?"

"Oh. No . . . no. I'm just fine."

"Mind if I take a look at your horse?"

"No, not at all."

Matt lifted each hoof in turn, while Windy moved into the stable to inspect the other horse. When Kincaid lowered the last hoof, he patted the horse's flank and looked at the young man again. "That's a fine animal you've got there, Tim. But he's going to need new shoes before long."

"Yeah, I know. Thanks, Lieutenant. Can I go now?"

"Sure, Tim," Matt replied, while they both heard Windy talking to Boggs.

"When did you shoe this horse, Boggs?"

"Uh . . . day before yesterday."

Timmy's eyes wavered and he glanced once at Kincaid, who had noticed the falter, before he looked down at the floor.

"Hasn't been out of the barn yet, has it?" Windy continued. "Look like brand-new shoes to me."

"Hasn't been ridden since I changed iron."

"Why not?"

"This ain't the only horse I got on the property."

Matt continued to watch Timmy's face, and could see the bunched muscles working along his clenched jaw. "Did you say an Indian named Gray Wolf was killed yesterday, Lieutenant?" the young man asked in a low voice.

"Yes he was, Tim. Coldblooded murder. Why? Did you know him?"

Boggs' searing eyes had fallen upon his son's face. "Goddammit, boy! Get on to your work now. Just 'cause the army's got all day to stand around jawin' don't mean we have! Now, git!"

"Sure, Pa," Timmy replied as he moved toward the door.

"Tim," Matt said gently, "is there anything you want to tell me?"

Timmy's eyes went to his father's face, back to Kincaid, then down to the floor again. "No, Lieutenant. I haven't got anything to say."

"Well, if you ever need to talk or need any help, you know where to find me."

"Thanks, Lieutenant," Timmy mumbled before swinging into the saddle and galloping away.

"Fine boy you've got there, Mr. Boggs," Matt offered cordially.

"He's a pain in the ass," Boggs snarled. "They's some more horses in the corral. You wanta take a look at 'em?"

Matt shook his head. "No, I don't think that'll be necessary.

I don't think we'll learn any more than we know already."

"Suit yourself. But if you're finished, I've damn well got something to tell you."

Pulling the gloves from his fingers, Matt leaned against the barn wall and studied Boggs' face. "Go ahead. I'm listening."

"You come in here cryin' about some Injun buck that's been killed and just as much as accuse us of doin' it. Are you gonna do the same to them Arapaho when a white man dies?"

"Of course, if there is reasonable cause to assume the Arapaho did it."

There was a look of triumph in Boggs' beady, piglike eyes. "One already has."

Matt glanced at Windy, then turned his gaze back to Boggs. "When?"

"Night before last."

"Who?"

"One of my hands. A feller named Spike Dowler. Put him in the ground yesterday morning."

"How was he killed?"

"Same as my goddamned cows. With an arrow through his chest. His horse drug him in here around ten o'clock at night."

"Why didn't you report this to the outpost?"

"Because you wouldn't do a fucking thing about it, that's why!" Boggs snarled. "Them Arapaho done Spike just like they done my cattle."

"Are you sure it was Arapaho?" Windy asked.

"Let's not go through that shit again, feller. He was shot from above by somebody who bushwhacked him. Arrow went in through the upper side of his chest and came out the right side of his ass."

Windy watched Boggs closely. "Where's the arrow?"

"What the hell difference does it make?" Boggs asked with an impatient snort. "An arrow's an arrow."

"Not to me. I'd like to see it."

"Aw, hell, I couldn't get the whole damned thing out of him. Just broke off the shaft, like I done the other ones."

"Then where's the shaft?" Matt asked with a hint of impatience.

"Layin' behind the shed, over by the well. Leastwise, I guess it is. I threw it there that night."

Windy was moving toward the door before Boggs finished speaking, with Matt following close behind. He searched the ground for nearly a minute before stooping and picking up the broken shaft, which he studied briefly before handing to Matt.

Kincaid turned the broken piece of arrow slowly in his hands and looked at Windy.

"Does this tell you what it tells me, Windy?"

"No question about it, Matt."

Boggs shuffled up beside them and glanced once at the shaft. "See you found it," he said without concern. "Shoulda burned the damned thing."

"No, you shouldn't have," Matt corrected. "Did you examine this arrow closely?"

"Naw. It was dark and I was a mite riled at the time. What about it? Spike wasn't gonna get any deader."

"That's true, but I think this shaft tells us there's a third party involved, and that maybe the Arapaho haven't had anything to do with the slaughter of your cattle or the killing of your hand."

Boggs looked at the shaft with more interest now. "Whaddaya mean by that?"

"This is a *Sioux* war arrow, Mr. Boggs. The yellow and red markings confirm that. There isn't an Arapaho alive that would kill a man with another tribe's war arrow. Someone other than the Arapaho killed your rider."

"Then who?"

"That I don't know. But I'll find out." Kincaid's eyes were cold on the stockman's face. "And while I'm at it, I'll find out who killed Gray Wolf. And when I do, the man—or men—responsible will hang."

Boggs stared sullenly at the ground while Kincaid and Windy moved past him to their mounts. Matt hesitated with one foot raised to the stirrup. "Have a good day, Mr. Boggs. Oh, and one more thing. Gray Wolf wasn't killed on your property. He was killed three, maybe four hundred yards away, on the Wahilla side of the line. Just thought you might like to know that."

There was a deeply disturbed look on Boggs' face, and he didn't reply as the platoon mounted up and rode away.

Dressed in a black coat, he was a lean, tall man who sat erect in his saddle and looked disapprovingly about the interior of Outpost Number Nine. Although his shoulders were broad, there was a hunched sunkenness about him, as though he suffered from a hidden pain of which he could not determine the origin. Deep green eyes peered out from beneath his wide-brimmed felt hat, and they too had a restless, burning quality about them, as though they could not be dulled even in sleep.

His white shirt, with a black string tie encircling his collar, was dusty, as were his black boots and striped gray pants. A long, cadaverously white hand held the reins while the other massaged the back of his neck. When challenged at the gate, he had announced himself as the Reverend Thomas Pope, and the guard on duty had quickly given permission to enter after having been stared down by the righteous, almost scathing eyes.

The Reverend Pope dismounted like a prairie windmill slowly toppling onto its side, and led his horse to the nearest trough. Slung low across his narrow hips, and mounted in cross-draw fashion, hung a pearl-handled "Buntline Special," with its ten-inch barrel sticking through a hole cut in the bottom of the holster and pressing out against his coat. And as the horse walked, a walnut-stocked Winchester Seventy-seven bobbed in its saddle scabbard.

Pope dipped a hand in the trough and rubbed the coolness across the back of his neck while watching aimlessly as Sergeant Cohen dressed down a squad of soldiers.

"You men are a disgrace to the uniform!" Cohen raged as he strode back and forth before the beleaguered troopers. "Especially you, Callahan!" he shouted, and turned with his finger pointed directly at the face of a young, slightly built soldier. "The seven of you came here for disciplinary reasons, and its discipline you'll get! I don't want to hear any more out of you reconstructed Rebels about the War Between the States, who won or who lost. We all know the answer to that! You are here—and being paid, I might add—to soldier for the United States Army, Mounted Infantry Detachment, Easy Company, Outpost Number Nine. And one more fuck-up from any of you and you'll do your soldiering in the stockade. Is that clear, you miserable, motherless sons of bitches?!"

The seven stood in a single rank and stared straight ahead like waxworks, with the exception of the man named Callahan. He twisted his head slightly toward Cohen and said in a heavy Southern drawl, "If the good sergeant will pardon my saying so, the North didn't *win*, the South just *lost*. Save your Confederate money, Sarge"—he grinned—"the South will rise again."

"Callahan! Fall out here!"

"Shore, Sarge," Callahan said, stepping forward.

Cohen closed on the soldier, and the blue veins bulged in his neck as he pressed his face within inches of the young trooper's. "You, Callahan, are an ignorant asshole! Your goal seems to be to prove that, since you claim to be from Texas, everybody in Texas is as ignorant and stupid as you are, which I won't argue with. But you are not in Texas now! You're on Outpost Number Nine in the Territory of Wyoming, and as long as you wear that uniform, you're damned well going to wear it with pride! Now, these here stripes on my sleeve come off every night, right along with my shirt. And when they're gone, I'm a man just like any of the rest of you scum. Tonight, at six o'clock, you'll report to the paddock area. I'll be waiting for you there. At that time I'll prove to you once and for all that the War Between the States, as you call it, is over and done. You will be the last Reb to fall. Is that understood?"

Callahan grinned again. "The part about me fallin', or settlin' the War 'Twixt the States?"

"Both. Now fall back in! The seven of you are assigned to permanent patrol with Lieutenant Kincaid when he gets back. You are denied all privileges. There will be no passes, no access to the sutler's store, and permanent stable duty when you are not on assignment. Now fall out. I will inspect your barracks in fifteen minutes, and I'd better not find a single fucking glove out of place. Dissss*missed*!"

The six other soldiers turned quickly and trotted across the parade, but Callahan took his time, walking slowly, holding his rifle by the barrel, upside down across his right shoulder.

"Callahan!"

"Yeah, Sarge?" Callahan said without turning.

"Make that *five* o'clock. I don't think I can wait until six."

"Suit yourself, Sarge. I'll be there."

"And you damned well better be! Now hold that rifle at port arms and double-time back to your barracks."

Callahan slowly lowered the rifle and continued to shuffle toward the barracks.

"Now, goddamn you, soldier!"

The searing bite of the first sergeant's words jolted Callahan into a run and he hastily tilted the rifle across his chest.

Cohen watched until all seven of the troopers were out of sight before stalking toward the orderly room. He hadn't noticed Pope, and his step faltered with the reverend's castigating words.

"You will pay in hell for that, Sergeant."

"Huh?" Cohen said, startled and turning as his step slowed. "What's that?"

"I said you'll pay for that in hell."

"Pay for what, mister?"

"For taking the Lord's name in vain."

"For *what*?"

"Your use of profanity will be your downfall, young man."

"Well, thank you for the 'young' part, but I'll say whatever in hell I fuckin' well please. What's your business here?"

"I am here to carry out the Lord's work," Pope said, a sepulchral rumble in his voice.

Cohen's eyes went to the Buntline and then to the Winchester. "Mighty strange-looking equipment for a man of the cloth, ain't it?"

"The Lord cannot always react in time to protect even His most faithful servants."

"Not always a lightning bolt handy, huh, Reverend? Since you claim to be on the Lord's payroll, what's the nature of your business, if you don't mind my asking again?"

"Don't mind at all." His eyes never wavered and he might well have been intoning a prayer. "I am here to kill a man."

"A soldier?" Cohen asked, watching Pope more closely now.

"I doubt it."

"Then who?"

"Don't rightly know just yet."

"Does he have a price on his head?"

"Yes he does, the Lord's and that of the Granada Grande in Mexico."

"Then you're a bounty hunter?"

"Bountiful is the lot of those who follow the pathway to heaven, my friend. The reward on this man's head will only serve to make this earthly bondage a mite less troublesome."

Never having darkened the door of a church in his life, except for the day he married his wife, Maggie, Cohen fell silent and contemplated the man across from him. The conclusion he drew was obvious: the Reverend Pope had apparently caught some of the bats from his church's belfry, and was carrying them around in his own.

"Fine, however you want to go," the sergeant said. "What brings you to Outpost Number Nine?"

"Would that be the name of this establishment?" Pope asked, looking around once more.

"It would."

"Then I am in the right place. I have come to purchase provisions and in the profound hope that there might be a chapel here where I might fall to my knees and bare my soul to Almighty God."

With a slight shake of his head, Cohen pointed across the parade toward the sutler's store. "Pop Evans over there should be able to help you with some supplies, but you're out of luck on the fallin'-on-your-knees part. Any prayin' that goes on around here is usually done under the workin' end of a gun."

"Communion with the Lord, however it comes, is a blessed thing."

"Yeah. Look, I've got a lot of things to do. My name's Cohen and our CO's name is Captain Conway. If we can be of further help to you, let us know." Cohen nodded cordially and stepped toward the orderly room.

"The Lord is my shepherd, son, I shall not want. My only concern is those who have strayed from the flock."

"That's a pretty fair-sized herd in these parts, Reverend. Good luck."

Cohen stepped into the orderly room and, turning to close the door, watched the Reverend Pope amble toward the sutler's, like a stork making a bad landing. He shook his head again, more vigorously this time, and turned just as Captain Conway stepped from his office with a piece of paper in his hand. Conway noticed the strange look on his first sergeant's face.

"Have you seen a ghost, Sergeant?"

"Nossir. Just the keeper of ghosts. That fellow's a real peculiar duck."

"What fellow?"

"Some old beanpole callin' himself Reverend Pope."

"What's his business here?"

"Says he's doin' the Lord's work," Cohen replied as he moved behind his desk. "Says he's going to kill somebody."

"That's the Lord's work? Should tickle the hell out of General Sheridan to hear that."

Cohen chuckled appreciatively. "That it would, sir. I guess the man he's lookin' for is wanted in Mexico. I think he's more interested in collecting bounties than souls. What have you got there, sir?" the sergeant asked with a nod toward the paper.

"I've just been going over the service record of that squad of new recruits we got in here the other day. Pretty scruffy lot, in my opinion."

"Did you expect anything else, sir?"

"Not really. But it looks to me like one of them at least, Private Callahan, should be serving his time at Leavenworth instead of here."

"Yeah, I agree, but we'll shape 'em up just like we've done all the others." A glint came into Cohen's eye—one with which the captain was entirely familiar. "As far as Callahan is concerned, he's first-sergeant property. I think he'll have a different attitude very shortly."

Conway nodded. "Yes, I suppose he will. Remember that battlefield-readiness report we went over the other day with Matt and Windy?"

"Yessir?"

"I think we can expect a little visit from the inspector general's office in the not-too-distant future. Best keep that in mind, I suppose."

"I have already, sir. I'll be inspecting the new men's quarters in approximately ten minutes, if that's all right with you."

"You've got it, Sergeant. Do whatever's necessary." Conway moved toward his office and, turning in the doorway, added, "Within reason, of course."

Cohen grinned. "Within reason, sir."

Conway smiled and closed the door.

The seven privates stood before their bunks in ramrod-stiffness, with the exception of Callahan, who affected an air of nonchalance even though standing erect, while Sergeant Cohen stalked before them like a tiger on the prowl. Actually, he was quite pleased with the layout of their equipment, again with the exception of Callahan, but he allowed no indication of approval to appear on his face.

"I've seen better-looking dungheaps than this display of

equipment, men," he said, turning and clasping his hands behind his back. "When you're assigned to Easy Company, you learn to soldier and you learn damned quick. You will be inspected again tomorrow morning, and I'll expect to see those blankets tight enough to make the regimental drummer envious, your boots polished to a fare-thee-well so's a blind man could see to shave in them, and your weapons clean enough to make a flyspeck look as big as a horse turd. And speakin' of horse turds, there's a stable needin' muckin' out, which you'll set to the second we've finished here. That facility, as well, will be inspected in the morning, and I'll expect to see those mounts wearing diapers, if that's what's required to keep the fucking place clean. Are there any questions?"

There was no response, with the exception of a laconic smile from Callahan. Cohen glared at each man in turn for nearly a minute before shouting toward the doorway.

"Malone! Get your butt in here!"

A huge, rawboned man stepped inside, and the easy grin on his face belied the awesome power of his wide-shouldered, barrel-chested physique, with thick, muscled arms exposed beneath rolled-up shirt sleeves.

"You'd be callin' me name, Sarge?"

"Is your name Malone?" Cohen asked with impatient derisiveness.

"That it is."

"Then I called you," Cohen replied, turning again to the new recruits. "This somewhat poor facsimile of a soldier is Private Malone. He is the master of the shit detail, a position he has earned through dedication and application. He knows every aspect of disciplinary life at Post Number Nine, and he constantly strives to improve by fucking up at the drop of a three-day pass. He will be in charge of your stable detail. And he has my personal permission to take whatever steps might be necessary to ensure that my orders are carried out. If the stable fails to pass my inspection in the morning, Private Malone here will be the man held responsible. He is due for another pass sometime within this decade, and I'm sure he doesn't want to see that opportunity screwed up by some new recruit. Isn't that correct, Private Malone?"

Malone glowered at the recruits. "Sure, an' you said it prettier than a red-haired schoolmarm, Sarge. Me gal, Rosemarie, would be gettin' a mite lonely in town, and I won't be wantin' to sit here and stare at some ugly spalpeen when me next pass is due. What say we get crackin', fellers?"

The replacements filed toward the door, with Callahan going out last.

"Private Callahan?" Cohen said softly.

"Yeah, Sarge?"

"I'll be seeing you at five o'clock. Please don't make Malone damage the merchandise too much before I have a chance to get to it."

Callahan grinned easily. "Never fear, Sarge. I'm all yours."

"Good. Now move it out!"

The sun was hanging but an hour from the horizon when Ben Cohen walked to the paddock area and dropped his suspenders, then unbuttoned his shirt and hung it on a post. Rolling up the sleeves of his woolen longjohns, he turned to see Callahan trotting toward him from the direction of the stable. Cohen hitched his suspenders up again and stood spraddle-legged, with his hands on his hips and the muscles rippling in his forearms.

Callahan's step slowed as he neared, and a pensive look came over his face. "Sorry . . . sorry I'm late, Sarge. Malone kinda kept me after school."

"You're here, that's all I care about. Take off that tunic, and that way neither of us will have any uniform to hide behind."

"Look, Sarge, I—"

Cohen's fist shot out and cracked across Callahan's chin, and the private sprawled in the dirt. "Don't backtalk me, soldier. Now get it off!"

Callahan struggled to his feet and stripped the shirt away, then stood before his sergeant.

"All right," Cohen continued, noticing the red weal puffing up along Callahan's jaw, "now repeat after me. I am a private in the United States Army. When Sergeant Ben Cohen says jump, I ask how high."

Callahan hesitated, and there was a lingering look of hatred in his eyes. But that lasted only until the scarred knuckles on Cohen's left hand slammed into Callahan's stomach and the right came down in a crashing blow along his left temple. The private spun and tumbled facedown upon the earth, packed solid by thousands of hooves.

Cohen's face was expressionless. "Get up, Private, and repeat after me," the sergeant said as Callahan stirred to life once again. "I am a private in the United States Army . . ."

Callahan touched the trickle of blood running down the side of his cheek and mumbled, "I . . . I . . . am . . ."

Cohen's left fist cracked across Callahan's jaw and he went down a third time, while the sergeant moved up to stand over him. "That wasn't loud enough. We're gonna do this till we get it right. Get up and repeat after me, but make it loud enough to set the hounds of hell to hollerin'. I said get up, goddammit!" Cohen shouted, grasping the man's shoulders and fairly throwing him to his feet.

"One more time," Cohen said. "I am a private . . ."

"I am a private!"

"In the United States Army . . ."

"In the United States Army!"

"When Sergeant Ben Cohen says jump . . ."

"When Sergeant Ben Cohen says jump . . ."

"Louder, goddammit!"

"When Sergeant Ben Cohen says jump!"

"I ask how high."

"I ask how high!!"

Cohen stared at the reeling soldier. "Jump," he said quietly.

"What?"

Again, Callahan went down, this time from a right to his ribcage.

"You don't learn real good, Private. Get up."

After several failed efforts, Callahan again managed to crawl to his knees and then force his legs to stand.

"Jump."

The private watched Cohen through glazed eyes. "How high?" he said weakly.

"That's better. Jump and I'll tell you when it's high enough."

Callahan made a desultory leap, but Cohen shook his head.

"Not high enough."

The beaten man made another attempt, then a third and a fourth. His legs were weak, and he stumbled and staggered after each landing, and his breath was coming in tortured gasps. On the fifth try, Cohen finally nodded his approval.

"Piss-poor, but good enough, Private," the sergeant said,

turning and pulling on his shirt. As his hands worked the buttons, his eyes were locked on Callahan's face.

"You're in Easy Company now, soldier, and you'd better give your soul to God, because your ass belongs to me."

As Cohen stalked away, he passed by the Reverend Pope, who was leading his horse across the parade from the direction of the sutler's store.

"I just gave the Lord most of one fucked-up private, Revered," he said with a jerk of his thumb over his shoulder, "but leave his ass alone. That belongs to me."

Confused, Pope stared at the red-faced sergeant before gazing at the soldier leaning limply on the fence rail.

seven _____

It was nearly nightfall when Daniel and Martin Boggs, Jake Barnes, and the six hired hands rode up to the Double G and swung down from weary mounts. Samuel Boggs looked up from the rope snubbed to a fencepost and stretched tight in his hands. He looped the final braids together, snipped away the trailing ends with his knife, and coiled the rope slowly as he walked toward his sons.

"How'd it go, Martin?" Boggs asked.

"Okay, Pa. Reckon we oughta be able to finish the castratin' and brandin' by tomorrow night, maybe. Wouldn't mind some help from little brother, if he could ever find the time," Martin added sullenly. "He's got just as big a piece of this pie as me and Dan have."

Boggs' eyes searched the group of men, and a surprised look crossed his face. "Timothy? Didn't he come out to give you a hand?"

"No. Was he supposed to?"

"Damn right he was. Shoulda been out there by midmorning at the latest."

"Midmorning, Pa?" Daniel asked. "Ain't quite the same as sunup, is it? We didn't see hide nor hair of him."

"Well, where the hell could he of went?"

"Don't know," Martin grunted while dragging the saddle from his horse's back. "But I do know he didn't turn one goddamned lick a work today. Seems ta live in a world of his own nowadays, and sweat, brandin' irons, and cuttin' knives ain't part a that sweet little life of his."

"Think somethin' might've happened to him, Hoss?" Jake Barnes asked as he draped a stirrup over his saddle horn and loosened the cinch strap. "After what happened to Dowler and them cattle, he'd best not be ridin' around here too damned much by himself."

"If he gets hisself killed, he's got it comin'," Boggs said without emotion. "But not showin' up for work when I tell him to, that's a different matter." He looked toward the darkening horizon and there was a menacing tone in his voice. "He'll come trailin' in here sooner or later, and when he does, there'll be a lesson waitin' for him. Get some dinner now, boys, and turn in. Tomorrow's gonna be another big day."

"Saw a troop of soldiers ridin' east about noon today, Hoss. Looked like they come from this direction. See anything of 'em?" Barnes asked, tossing his saddle over his shoulder and holding it by the horn.

"Yeah, I seen 'em. Kincaid and that scout of his, plus the others. Said somethin' about an Injun kid what got killed the other day. Said a horse lost a shoe and they trailed it toward my place until they lost the sign in a dry creek bed." Boggs' gaze swept slowly over his sons and the rest of the crew. "Any of you boys know anything about a dead featherhead?"

To a man, with the exception of Barnes, the riders all looked away with a negative shake of their heads and grunted disclaimers. Barnes watched Sam Boggs closely.

"You think they're onto something?"

"Naw, not really. Just playin' a hunch that didn't pan out."

Barnes nodded his satisfaction. "That's good. Market's gonna be up this fall, and I've got quite a bit at stake with this herd. Hate to see it all go to hell because of one dead Injun."

"I know you have, Jake, and nothin's gonna go haywire. But we can't let ourselves be pushed around, either, with things like what happened to Dowler and those cattle. Kincaid did say one thing, though, that made me kind of curious."

"Yeah? What's that?"

"Said Dowler was killed with a Sioux arrow, not Arapaho. Wonder who in hell did it, if they didn't?"

"Beats the shit out of me, but somebody did. We'd best keep an eye out for a while. And you'd better tell Tim to keep his ass a little closer to home."

"For damn sure. Seems like that dead kid was Red Hawk's son. I just imagine he's gonna be a mite pissed, and could be wantin' a little revenge. Let's be ready for 'em when the time comes."

Barnes grinned in the closing darkness. "When it comes time for a fight, you've never seen this hand to be slow, have you, Hoss?"

"No. And I'll be countin' on you again, just like always. I'd just as soon have it out with them Injuns once and for all, and make it so the government don't need no reservation on our land. For now, though, we'll have to just play it one card at a time. Kincaid and his scout are gonna be watchin' us pretty close from now on, I'm thinkin'."

Barnes started toward the bunkhouse and spoke over his shoulder without turning. "Let 'em watch."

"You know, Jake," Boggs said, moving toward the house, "that dead kid and Dowler, plus a few of my cattle, might work to our advantage. Give the army somethin' else to think about."

Now Barnes stopped and turned. "Did you say 'my cattle,' Hoss?"

Boggs scratched the thick hair at the nape of his neck with a dirty, blunt finger. "Yeah, Jake, guess I did."

"But what you meant was 'our cattle,' didn't you?"

"Sure, Jake, sure, that's what I meant. Just a slip of the tongue. Nothin' to get riled about."

Barnes watched the larger man closely, and there was a flash of cold indifference on his face. "I'm not riled, Hoss," Barnes said, moving away again. "Only makin' sure you remember the facts, that's all. 'Night."

Boggs didn't reply, and watched his foreman's back momentarily before walking quickly to the house.

After he left his father, Timmy had ridden hard, turning toward the north and pushing his horse at a steady gallop. It was early afternoon when he pulled the lathered mount up beside the

70

grove and jumped from his saddle. Having heard his father lie about shoeing the horse, remembering the gunshots of the previous day, and hearing the mention of Gray Wolf's death, he had been greatly disturbed and concerned about Kita Wak. One question, to which he thought he knew the answer, raged through his brain in revolving circles, and a deep anger boiled in his chest. Had his brothers killed the brother of the woman he loved, the woman who now carried his child within her womb? If so, there would be grave trouble, and he was concerned for Kita Wak's safety. He knew that if she was disturbed, or hurt, she would come to the bend in the river to be near him through the gifts he had brought.

Ignoring their customary signal, and realizing it was foolish to come to their meeting place in broad daylight, he stepped quickly through the brush and foliage with both anticipation and dread in his heart.

Kita Wak was there, staring into the water and holding the silk scarf pressed to her cheek, while smelling the perfumed fragrance. At the sound of a snapping twig, her head jerked toward the alien noise while she leaped to her feet. Her dark eyes were troubled and her beautiful face was drawn tight with sorrow. But when Timmy stepped into the clearing, the relief that flooded over her brought a tiny smile to her lips and she rushed toward him. His arms were reaching for her and she threw herself against his chest and pressed her cheek against his shoulder.

"Kita, thank God you're all right," Timmy whispered as he pulled her to him and gently massaged the small of her back with his left palm. "I had to come to make sure nothing had happened to you."

"I'm glad you did, my Timmy," she said, pulling slightly away, tears glistening in her eyes. "I needed to be near you."

"We're together now and everything will be all right," Timmy said, pulling her to him again. "I love you, Kita. More than anything on earth, I love you."

"I love you, my Timmy. My heart would burst without you."

"Soon, very soon, we will never be apart again."

"I long for that day," Kita replied, and then fell silent. Tim could feel the gentle throbbing of her breast, and he knew she was crying openly now. "Please, Kita, please don't cry."

The young woman tried to hold back the tears, but without

71

success. "The women of our people are not supposed to cry, but I cannot help it when I am with you. Do you remember my telling you of my brother Gray Wolf?"

"Yes, I remember."

"I loved him too. In some ways more than you. We played together as children, and he was very special to me. When it was time for him to be a man, we could no longer be so close, but we still loved each other deeply. He would have been a great warrior and leader of our people."

Timmy held his breath and waited for the words he dreaded, but knew would come.

Kita drew in a deep breath and exhaled slowly. "But now he is . . . he is . . . dead. He was killed yesterday and sent to us with two bullet holes in his chest. It was a terrible, terrible thing and now there will be great trouble between our people. The death of my brother must be avenged." She paused to pull away and look up at him. "He was killed by some white men during his manhood rituals."

Timmy nodded. Heartsick, he turned away and sank down on a log. "I know, Kita," he said softly. "And I think I know who did it."

Kita sprang forward and dropped to her knees before the log and looked up at him. "You know who did it? You must tell me and I must tell my father. He will go after the killers and avenge the loss of my brother, which is fair and honorable. If they are caught, maybe bloodshed can be avoided between your people and mine."

The excitement in her voice only saddened Timmy all the more, and he shook his head sadly. "I can't do that, Kita. At least not in the way that you ask. I must be certain, and when I am, I will kill them for what they have done."

"No, Timmy! You might be hurt or killed. It is the responsibility of my father or my other brother to avenge the loss of Gray Wolf. Tell me, Timmy, please tell me."

Timmy watched her with tenderness in his eyes. "I can't do that, but I will tell you who I think it is, if you promise not to tell anyone else until I am sure. Do I have your promise?"

Kita hesitated and her gaze wavered before she nodded her agreement, then watched him silently, waiting for his words.

Timmy said nothing for long moments, staring at her and knowing she would hate him after he said what he knew he must say. Finally he took her face in his hands and looked deeply into her eyes. "Do you love me, Kita?" he asked.

"Yes, I love you so very much. More than anything in the world."

"Good. Because it will take all your love to keep you from hating me after I tell you who I think killed your brother."

"I could never hate you, Timmy. Not ever."

Timmy nodded, drew in a deep breath, and exhaled as he stood, pulling Kita to her feet in the process. "This is very difficult for me, but it must be done. I am almost certain that the killers of Gray Wolf are . . . are my brothers, Daniel and Martin."

Kita's eyes darted across his face, searching for another meaning to the words she had just heard, but finding nothing. Her mouth fell slightly agape and she struggled for words, while slowly turning her head from side to side.

"No, Timmy, please tell me this is not true. I have your child—*our* child—within me, and I could not stand to think that the blood of those who killed my brother would be in the veins of my son. Please tell me it's not true. Please?"

"I can't, Kita, because I am almost certain that it is true. I could not lie to you," Timmy said, reaching out to draw her to him.

A terrified wildness came into her eyes; it clouded their darkness and made her appear almost hypnotized. A slight cry escaped her throat while her head jerked from side to side in disbelief. When Timmy's hands touched her shoulders, her right hand flashed out and snatched the big knife from his gunbelt while she darted away.

"No, Kita!" Timmy yelled as he lunged toward her, grasping her hand as the knife blade flashed downward. It was too late. The glancing blow of his hand had diverted the knife from its target, which was the center of her stomach, but the blade slammed home, hilt deep, in her left side, just below the rib-cage.

"God, no! Kita!" Timmy shouted as she tried to pull the blade out to strike herself once more. His hand closed around her wrist while she sank to the ground with a sad, weak smile on her face. Timmy was over her instantly while the flow of blood turned the buckskin leather of her dress to deep crimson. Her hand fell away from the knife handle and she looked up at him as he cradled her head in his hands.

"I am sorry, Timmy, but I could not bear the shame. I love

you and I love our child, but he would have been an outcast forever. It has to be this way."

"No, Kita, it doesn't. You can't die. You'll have to live for our son. When you're well, we'll go away to where no one knows us and start..."

Kita smiled up at him tiredly. "That won't work, Timmy, because I will know forever. It has to be this way."

Helplessly, Timmy stared down at her while her eyes fluttered and slowly closed, but her head remained erect and he felt a glimmer of hope. Working quickly, he stripped his shirt off and tore it into long strips of cloth. Gently, carefully, he knelt down and pulled the knife from her side and quickly pressed a piece of cloth deep into the wound. He watched as the flow of blood decreased before wrapping the strips tightly around her waist and cinching them down. As he stood and looked about him, wondering what he should do, where he should take her, Lieutenant Kincaid's words that morning rang through his ears and he sprinted toward his horse.

"If you ever need any help, Tim, you know where to find me." That was what he had said, Timmy recalled, voicing the words as he ran. "I need your help, Lieutenant," he muttered through clenched teeth as he untied his horse and led it back to where Kita Wak lay. "I need your help now more than I ever will again in my entire life."

After checking the makeshift bandages one more time, he took the unconscious girl in his arms and lifted her onto the saddle before climbing up behind her. He took up the reins and urged the mount forward while holding her around the waist with his free arm and pressing his palm firmly against the wound. His fingers turned red, but he did not notice. His eyes were locked firmly on the eastern horizon and his mind was on the terrible distance between them and Outpost Number Nine.

Matt Kincaid placed the coffee cup down carefully on the edge of Captain Conway's desk while listening to the bustling sounds of the fort coming to life. It was 7:00 A.M., and he knew First Platoon would be forming ranks on the parade at that very moment, while waiting for the lieutenant to get his final instructions from their commanding officer.

"Captain," he began, "I can't tell you in absolute certainty that Boggs had anything to do with the killing of Gray Wolf, but I can tell you we don't have much time to find out. Red Hawk gave me three days, no more, to bring his son's killers in, and he will not wait a second longer. If I don't succeed, we'll have another full-scale war on our hands."

Conway sipped his coffee in silence before nodding and holding the cup before him in both hands. "I know that, Matt, but we have no real evidence against Boggs, only a threat made in the heat of anger. Remember, one of his men is dead as well, along with those cattle, and I'm sure he feels he has justifiable cause for revenge as much as Red Hawk does. Do you think any of those scruffy buffalo hunters hanging around here might have had a hand in any of this?"

Taking up his cup again, Matt took a drink and stared into the black liquid. "I can't say for sure about that, either, Captain. About the worst of the lot are Strother McFarland and his bunch. I intend to find him today and put a few questions to him. He sure as hell isn't above killing a man, but I can't understand his reasons, if he has any in this case."

"Do you have any idea where to find him?"

"I think so. He's probably working that federal land between Boggs' homestead and the reservation. At least that's where I intend to start looking. The bigger herds of buffalo seem to be bunched in that area."

"Good. What do you make of that Reverend Pope that Cohen told you about this morning? According to Ben, he was about as peculiar as they come."

"Yes, sir, it sure sounds like it. I don't know where he fits, but if he's a bounty hunter, I'm sure there are plenty of candidates out there for his services."

"No doubt about it," Conway replied, leaning forward to set his cup down. "If you come across him, try to find out what he's up to. His appearance on the scene seems a little bit too coincidental to me."

"I agree. We'll be on the lookout for him. About those new recruits I'm taking with me today. Do you have anything special in mind for them, sir?"

"Just good old hard, sweat-stained soldiering, Matt. Ben seems to think they need a little shakedown work."

"How about that Private Callahan? When I saw him this morning, it looked to me like he'd walked through hell backward."

"He's a young runaway from Texas who wanted to fight

in the Civil War—on the Confederate side, I might add—but who missed the action because of his age at the time. For some strange reason I can't really put a handle on, I have the notion that he probably wants to be a good soldier if only he could get that chip off his shoulder and be accepted as a contributing member of this unit. It's our job to find the means to extract his qualities, whatever they might be." Conway smiled with a glance toward the closed office door. "As for his wrong-way trip through hell, I think he got the wrong person's dander up. You know Cohen as well as I do, and while he can be a soldier's best friend, he can also be his worst enemy. I rather suspect that Callahan found that out yesterday, but as usual, I don't involve myself in discipline meted out by the first sergeant unless asked to do so."

Kincaid grinned and reached for his hat and gloves. "Ben hasn't been wrong yet, to my knowledge. If a man won't listen to reason, then he'll sure as hell be listening to a ringing in his ears, not to mention having a fuzzy look at the world for a while. If you'll excuse me, sir, I'd better get on patrol. We have to use what little time we have as effectively as possible."

"Right, Matt," Conway said, returning Kincaid's salute. "I'm sure that if there's a sane solution to this whole mess, you're the man to find it."

"Thank you, sir. We should be back in a couple of days."

Sergeant Cohen looked up from the duty roster spread before him as Matt paused to pull on his hat and gloves in the orderly room. "Have a good patrol, sir."

"Thank you, Sergeant. It would be to my advantage to know what, or who, I'm looking for, but it's a damned good bet I'm not going to find them here." Then a thought struck him as he stepped through the doorway. "What was the name of the outfit that that Pope fellow said he was working for down in Mexico?"

Cohen rubbed a hand across his wide jaw in contemplation. "I think it was Grand Granada, something like that. Mind if I ask why, sir?"

"Yes, at this point anyway. Something just flashed through my mind and I'd like to think about it a bit more before I discuss it."

"Certainly, sir, I understand. Like I said, have a good patrol and I hope those new men work out for you."

"Thanks again," Matt said, stepping outside. "I hope I don't have a reason to test them too thoroughly this first time around. See you in a couple of days, Ben."

Kincaid was halfway between the headquarters building and the mounted platoon when he heard the sentry's urgent call.

"Lieutenant Kincaid?"

Turning toward the main gate, Matt squinted against the rising sun and shielded his eyes against its brightness. Yes, Private? What is it?"

"Riders comin' in, sir! Two of 'em on one horse, and it looks like one of 'em is hurt."

"Let 'em in!" Matt called back, turning toward the main gate and crossing the parade with long strides.

Timothy Boggs' horse, flanks heaving and mouth frothing, trotted through the gateway and stopped, exhausted, before Kincaid. Instantly recognizing its owner, Matt stepped forward and touched Tim's leg. "What's the matter, Tim? Who is this girl?"

There was a grim tightness about Tim's face and he leaned forward to peer down at the girl before responding. His arm was clutched to her waist and his hand was caked with congealed blood.

"I think she's still alive, Lieutenant. At least I pray to God she is. You told me to come to you if I needed help, and I sure as hell need it now."

"You've got it. What's her name?"

"Kita Wak. She's Red Hawk's daughter."

"What happened to her?"

"Can I explain that to you later, sir? I'd like to get her help as fast as I can. We've been riding all night."

"Of course," Kincaid said, whirling toward the orderly room. "Sergeant Cohen?"

There was a momentary pause before the door opened and Cohen stepped into the warming sunlight. "Yessir?"

"We've got a girl here who's badly hurt. Could you ask Maggie to give us a hand?"

"Yessir!" Cohen snapped, breaking into a run for his quarters.

Maggie Cohen, the first sergeant's wife, was a matronly type, thick of body and slightly plump, but not unattractive. Among the enlisted men's wives, she was the den mother, midwife, and Mother Superior, and she never hesitated to step

77

forward with help or encouragement. On the other hand, being Irish, she was also a force to be reckoned with when crossed by the unsuspecting. In less than a minute she was bustling across the parade with her skirts clutched about her knees and a deeply concerned look on her face.

Passing off to one side of the parade and just leaving the officers' quarters, another woman stopped and watched the scene before her with great interest. In her late thirties and exceptionally beautiful even after all her arduous years as an army wife, Flora Conway, the captain's lady, had the physical attributes of which most men only dream, and a sense of kindness that transcended her station as wife of the commanding officer. If help was needed, she would be the first one on the scene if called, and now she also ran toward the Indian girl who was being carefully lowered into Lieutenant Kincaid's arms.

"Be careful with her now," Maggie Cohen called as she neared. "Carry her to my quarters and let's have a look at the lass!"

Kincaid nodded and stepped away from the horse, to be followed by Tim Boggs, who jumped down from the saddle.

"Please don't let her die, Lieutenant," Timmy said softly as he walked beside Kincaid and watched Kita's ashen face. "We just can't let her die."

"We'll do our best, Tim. Tell me how she got hurt."

"Stab wound. Deep in the left side."

"That's the *where*. Now tell me the *how*?"

There was hesitation in Timmy's step as he glanced up at the officer. "She did it to herself, Lieutenant. But can I tell you why later? I'll be honest with you when I do."

"Sure, Tim. Let's take care of her first," Matt replied, turning sideways to step through the doorway of the Cohen quarters and gently laying the girl down on the bed.

"Can I be of any help, Maggie?" Flora asked.

"You sure can, ma'am," Maggie replied, taking a washbasin from the bedside and offering it across. "If you wouldn't mind. We'll be needin' water quick as scat to clean the poor dear up."

Flora took the basin and raced toward the well while Matt leaned over and listened to Kita's chest for breathing and heartbeat while holding a finger against her pulse.

"Is she . . . she ain't . . ." Tim tried to ask breathlessly.

Matt's face was grave when he turned toward the young man after feeling the pulse a moment longer. "No, she isn't dead, Tim. Not quite. But her pulse is very weak and I'm afraid she's lost quite a bit of blood. Where and when did this happen?"

Maggie moved in between Kincaid and the girl, with a pair of scissors in her hand, and began stripping away the bandages. "If you'd be so kind as to step back, Lieutenant, I've got work to do here."

"Certainly, Maggie. I'll be just outside if you need me. Come on, Tim. There's nothing you can do that Maggie and Mrs. Conway can't do better."

Timmy followed Matt to the door and they both stood to one side as Flora stepped inside, moving quickly, but carefully balancing the water in the basin held before her.

"Good morning, Lieutenant," she said cordially, without looking at Kincaid.

"Morning, ma'am," Matt replied, dragging the hat from his head. "Thank you for the help."

"Oh, posh! Nothing to be thanked for. This girl's hurt and needs help. There certainly aren't any thanks necessary for that."

"Yes, ma'am," Matt replied and steered Tim through the doorway with a hand on his elbow.

"Could you use a cup of coffee, Tim?" Matt asked as they stepped onto the parade. "And maybe some breakfast? Old Dutch is a mighty fine cook."

"Well, Lieutenant I . . . I thank you, but . . . but maybe I'd better stay here close to Kita, just in case I'm needed."

"You won't be, not right now, anyway. Maybe when she comes around. How long has it been since you've eaten?"

"Yesterday morning."

"Then that's settled. I'll have a trooper take care of your horse and then we'll get you some hot coffee and something to eat. Then I'd like to hear what happened and how you happened to be with Red Hawk's daughter."

Timmy glanced away for a second and then looked Matt straight in the eye. "Thank you, Lieutenant. I'll tell you everything."

"Fine. Private Dahlman! Take care of that horse. Double ration of grain, not too much water, and have it curried and cared for."

"Yes, Lieutenant! On the double!" returned a soldier as he swung down and left the platoon waiting in the middle of the parade.

"Sergeant Olsen?"

"Yessir?"

"Dismount the platoon and wait for further instructions."

"Yessir! P'*tooonn*...diss*smount*!"

Kincaid placed an arm around Timmy's shoulders while they walked toward the mess hall, and he could feel a quivering beneath his hand. "Just calm down, Tim. Everything that can be done for the girl will be done. Just try to get it off your mind and concentrate on keeping your strength and presence of mind intact."

Timmy offered a nervous, almost shy smile. "I will, Lieutenant, and thanks for the help."

"You're welcome," Matt replied, opening the door to the mess hall and holding it to one side for Timmy to enter first. "Dutch?" Kincaid called as they stepped inside.

Upon hearing his name called, a fat, florid-faced man, with the stubble of the night's beard still bristling along his jowls, stamped from the kitchen with obvious irritation in his eyes, waving a gigantic spoon menacingly in his hand.

"Now what the hell do you want?" he asked, before recognizing the lieutenant. "Oh! Sorry, sir. I thought it was some damnable KP wastin' my time with his damfool questions."

Kincaid smiled easily. "That's all right, Dutch. Sorry for busting in on you. Could you fix my friend here up with some breakfast, and I'll have a cup of coffee if you don't mind. We'll sit at this table over here."

"Comin' right up, sir," the mess sergeant replied, turning immediately toward the kitchen.

When the breakfast was served, Matt drank his coffee in silence while Tim alternately ate and toyed aimlessly with the food on his plate in contemplative lapses of interest. Finally, with only half the potatoes left uneaten, he pushed the plate aside and leaned back in his chair.

"Thank you, Lieutenant, I guess I needed that more than I thought. But I'm afraid I can't finish the whole thing."

"Quite all right, Tim, quite all right. While Dutch isn't the most pleasant person in the world, he does make certain the men eat well."

A brief smile flashed across Timmy's face, but then his

features became serious again as he looked at Kincaid. "I love her, Lieutenant," he said simply.

"Kita Wak?"

"Yes, Kita Wak."

"Isn't that a little strange, with your father hating the Arapaho the way he does?"

Timmy sighed. "My love for Kita is not strange, Lieutenant Kincaid."

"How long have you known her?"

"For six months," Tim replied with an upward glance, before looking down at the table again. "I'm going to be the father of her child. She's three months pregnant right now."

Matt nodded and stirred his coffee aimlessly. "Does your father know about this?"

"No."

"Does Red Hawk?"

"No, I'm sure he doesn't."

Matt took a sip of coffee before asking his next question. "Why did she stab herself?"

"To kill the baby. After her brother's death at the hands of white men, she said she would be ashamed to have the child. She said it would be a disgrace to have white blood in her veins."

"Do you know who killed Gray Wolf?"

"I . . . no . . . no, Lieutenant, I don't."

"Do you have any idea?" Matt asked, his eyes narrowing at the boy's evasiveness.

"No. And if I did, I couldn't tell you."

"Why?"

"I can't tell you that, either."

"All right, Tim," Matt said without rancor, "you don't have to tell me anything that might go against your conscience. Do you intend to marry Kita Wak? Knowing the hatred your father and Red Hawk have for each other, that might be a difficult thing."

There was an unwavering earnestness in Timmy's voice when he spoke again. "Yes, I intend to marry her. We'll go away to someplace where nobody knows us, if we have to." Then his voice lowered into dejection. "That is, if she will have me."

"And if she survives. She and the baby, that is."

"She has to survive, Lieutenant. I consider the people who

are responsible for her brother's death to be responsible for what Kita did to herself. And I will get even for that. But the baby? I would marry her even without the child."

"Even knowing that your father would probably kill you if you did?"

"I know he'd probably *try*."

Matt nodded and his tone softened. "You must love her very much, Tim, and I congratulate you for that. She's a beautiful lady, and one of whom any man should be proud."

"I am that."

"You know that someone will have to tell her father about this injury and your involvement with her, don't you?" Matt asked, finishing the cooled coffee in a single gulp.

"Yes, I'm aware of that, and I will tell him myself," Timmy said with conviction. "But first I have to do something."

"What's that, Tim?"

"I can't tell you, Lieutenant. I have to do it on my own."

"Fine, have it your way. There's a very dangerous situation between your father and Red Hawk, and other innocent Indians and white people might become involved. I would ask you to think about the consequences of your actions before you do anything rash."

"I've thought about it all I have to, Lieutenant. All night last night, as I rode here with Kita in my arms, I thought about it. I will do what I must."

"I'm sure you will. You are a fine young man, Tim, and if the baby lives, someday he will be proud to have you for his father. As I'm sure you noticed, I have a platoon standing by for morning patrol, and I have to go now. If anything comes up relative to the deaths of either Gray Wolf or Spike Dowler, I want you to get in touch with me immediately."

Their eyes met and held briefly before Timmy glanced away, saying weakly, "I'll do that, Lieutenant. If I can."

"That's all I ask. Let's check in on Kita before I leave. You're welcome to stay here as long as you like."

"Thanks, but I'll be leaving too. My business won't wait any more than yours will."

"Fine. Let's go, then."

As they passed out of the mess hall, Timmy poked his head into the kitchen. "Thanks for the breakfast, Dutch."

The grizzled cook turned and offered what was supposed to pass for a smile. "Never heard that word before, son, but

82

if I remember right, I'm supposed to say you're welcome. So, you got it."

When they stepped back into Sergeant Cohen's quarters, the two women were standing beside the bed and looking down at the wounded Indian girl. The covers were drawn to her neck, and Maggie dabbed at the beads of sweat on her forehead.

"How is she, Maggie?" Kincaid asked.

"She's weak from loss of blood, and it's too soon to tell." Maggie glanced at Timmy, then back at Matt. "The girl's pregnant, Lieutenant. I·thought you should know that. The baby's still alive, and if the girl lives, the baby might as well. But she's going to have to be taken good care of for a week or two if she has any chance at all."

"Thank you, Maggie. I know about the baby. Timmy here is going to be the proud father. Make sure she is comfortable, and arrange any conveniences for her that the post might have to offer under the circumstances."

"She will be taken care of, Matt," Flora said with a sweet smile. "Dear Maggie here and I will see to that."

"Good, and thank you both. I have to go now." He offered his hand to Timmy, who accepted it firmly "Take care of yourself and remember what I asked you to do. It's proper that you should tell Red Hawk about your involvement with his daughter, but I'm going to have to tell him she's here. Is that all right?"

"Sure, Lieutenant. I'm sure he'll be worried about her. And thanks for everything."

After Kincaid left, Timmy moved up to the bedside and looked down at Kita Wak. There was tenderness in his eyes as he reached out and trailed the tips of his fingers over her lips and mumbled something that might have been a silent prayer. Then his mood suddenly changed, as though he had been slapped by an unseen hand, and his face became tight, his eyes went hard, and he spun on his heel and stalked out the doorway. The platoon was mounted and heading out the gate as he crossed the parade, and he stopped and stared momentarily at the receding blue shirts before breaking into a run in the direction of the stable.

eight ———————————

Mounted on a magnificent bay-and-cream-colored pinto, Black Wing, at twenty years of age, sat tall and proud as he faced the nine other braves fanned out before him in a casual semicircle. A green stripe of warpaint ran in a broad swath from his upper right forehead across the bridge of his nose and down to the lower left side of his chin. In matching arcs, one above his left eye and the other below his right cheekbone, white paint contrasted with his bronzed skin, and twin eagle feathers dangled from his knotted black hair. Across his bare chest and stomach, muscles rippled in the early-morning sunlight, and buckskin pants clung tightly to his firm thighs. The others wore green-and-white warpaint as well, each with his own individual design, and they waited now for Black Wing to speak. They held rifles across their laps, and a slight breeze caused the feathers in their hair to wave restlessly.

Black Wing held his silence while his dark eyes touched each of the faces of the warriors ranged before him. They were several miles from the village, and when Black Wing spoke, his words were strong and clear, with no fear of being over-heard.

"Hear me. Today we will avenge the death of my brother, Gray Wolf. My father, Red Hawk, has had his ears closed by the lies of the Blue Sleeve chief, and it is up to us, the young warriors of our tribe, to seek revenge for this injustice. He and the other old ones have signed an unfair treaty that the white settlers see only as a means for them to steal our land and kill our buffalo. Especially the red-haired demon and his two sons, and it is my belief that they are the ones who killed Gray Wolf. I have personally watched them slaughter seventy-five animals in one group and leave them lie to rot on the plains. There are more buffalo, even though they grow fewer daily, but there was only one Gray Wolf. He is gone, never to return. So too will be the buffalo, if this slaughter is not stopped. And with the death of the buffalo comes the death of the Arapaho people as proud, fierce warriors. The Americans will have what they want, the Arapaho eating out of their hands, when and if they choose to offer us food."

"Our brother speaks of things that we all know to be true," said a young brave named Crooked Nose, "but won't the deaths of two white settlers bring the Blue Sleeves down on our tribe, like what happened to the Southern Cheyenne at Sand Creek?"

"No, Crooked Nose, it will not. We will strike from am-bush, as the white men do, and no one will know who was lying in wait. We know where they will pass. Crow-in-the-Rain is following them now, and we will go to that place on foot and leave no tracks. Our ponies will be held on our side of the reservation line, and it will not be unusual for our hoofprints to be seen. After we have done what we must, we will return to our ponies on foot, then mount and leave. And justice will be done."

Black Wing paused to stare at the others before his gaze shifted to hold on Crooked Nose's face. "Are we squaws and root-eaters?" he demanded, his voice rising in anger. "Do we allow one of our brothers to be killed during the proof of his manhood and not take revenge for his death? Do you, Crooked Nose, wish now to wash off your paint, put away your rifle, and follow the old women to the white man's agency for a handful of corn? If you do, do so now. We are Arapaho warriors and we do not wish to have the weak among us."

Crooked Nose fairly withered under the intense stare and

scathing remarks, and he glanced nervously at the others who watched him with open contempt. "No, Black Wing. I do not wish to leave. I will gladly follow you and do my part in this thing of justice."

"That is good, Crooked Nose," Black Wing said with a final, appraising look at the brave, before turning to listen to the distant sound of a horse running. "That will be Crow-in-the-Rain," he said with a satisfied nod. "The time for revenge is at hand. I have spoken."

A black and white pony crested the rolling prairie swell at a dead run, with its rider leaning low to the side of its neck. When Crow-in-the-Rain pulled the lathered mount to a stop, there was wild jubilation on his face, and he turned the mount beside Black Wing. "They are coming to us, my brother. In half an hour they will cross the stream where the big trees grow. They are dead now, but don't know it."

"That is good, Crow-in-the-Rain. Are you sure they suspect nothing? They have no idea you were following them?"

"They suspect nothing. There are two of them, and it is obvious their hearts are not in their task. They glance around occasionally, but they have little interest. Even though they are close to our boundary, they feel safe on the land they have taken."

"Good. Manitou is with us. We must move quickly now. It will take us the time of a few breaths to run from where we will leave the ponies to where we will wait for them." He looked around at the rolling prairie and nodded approvingly. "It is a good day to die, but I think we will not be the ones to do the dying." He dug his moccasins into his pony's flanks, and the animal surged into motion, followed by the rest of the band.

Eleven young warriors, resplendent in their paint, raced across the plains. There was pounding excitement in their chests, and the desire to scream a war cry was nearly uncontrollable in their throats.

Daniel and Martin Boggs rode side by side, and wore identical desultory scowls on their faces. The sun was becoming hot on their backs, and Daniel pulled his hat from his head and wiped his forehead on his sleeve.

"Dammit, Martin," he said, "I'm gettin' just a little sick

86

of this shit. We not only have to do the little bastard's work for him, now we gotta ride all over hell's half-acre tryin' to *find* the son of a bitch."

"Yeah, me too," Martin replied with a nod of agreement. "That goddamned Tim don't do half the stuff we do for the old man, but still he gets on our ass as much as his."

"Damned right he does. Seems like he ain't figured out Tim ain't a baby no more. A coward maybe, but he sure ain't no little kid."

"Hell no, he ain't. But let me ask you this. Do you think little brother would have shot that thievin' Arapaho like we did to square away Spike's murder? Not on your goddamned life! Dowler was a good feller, a drinkin' buddy, but that don't make no never-mind to Tim. Just like them cattle the featherheads shot. The little bastard said he didn't think it was them what done it. Who the hell else would have?"

Daniel dug a match from his vest pocket and scrubbed vigorously at his yellow teeth. "He's always sidin' with the Injuns anyhow, so what he says don't matter. Like the time when I told him if the Arapaho didn't like the way things were around here, why the hell didn't they go back where they came from. 'Member what he said?"

"Yeah. He looked at ya kinda sassy-like, and said, 'This *is* where they came from.' Ain't that a crock of shit! That's a fairly new reservation they're squattin' on."

"Fuck the little son of a bitch. I'm almost as tired of talkin' about him as I am of lookin' for him. What say we cross the stream, take off our boots, and lay in the shade awhile. Then we'll go back and tell the old man we couldn't find him. Pa won't know the difference anyway."

"Sounds good to me," Martin replied, breaking into a satisfied chuckle. "Speakin' of things the old man don't know about, what do you think he'd say if he knew we'd dropped that little Injun bastard with the wolfskin coat? Think he'd be pissed?"

"Can't say for sure, that's why I ain't told him. But he did say he'd shoot any Arapaho he found on our property. So what if that wasn't quite on our land? It was close enough."

"Yeah, he was mad when he said that, but he coulda meant it. Just the same, we'd better keep it to ourselves."

Daniel tossed the match away and looked at his brother with

a dirty grin. "Was worth it, though, wasn't it? Watchin' them two slugs lift that little redskin up and slam him down on his ass? Funniest thing I ever did see."

"Sure was. And the look of surprise on his face," Martin agreed with a hearty laugh. "You'd think that wolf had come to life and bit him right square on the balls."

Their uproarious laughter rattled across the vacant prairie, and tears rolled down their cheeks. Finally, Daniel gained control of his mirth and pointed toward the grove of cottonwoods lining the creek bank. "Almost there," he said. "Got that pint with ya?"

Reaching backward, Martin dug in his saddlebags until he found the flat rectangular bottle and held it to the sunlight. "Sure do, and she's more'n half full."

"Good. We'll polish 'er off and then take a little snooze. This lookin' fer Tim might not be so damned miserable after all."

With Martin's horse in the lead, they entered the trail through the tall grass. Mud sucked at their mounts' hooves as they neared the creek bank. There were no frogs croaking and the birds were silent in the trees, but the two brothers had whiskey on their minds and didn't notice the unusual quiet.

The first booming shot that broke the stillness slammed into Martin's chest, and he jerked upright in the saddle while the whiskey bottle fell from his hand and he clutched at the hole in his chest, blood spurting between his fingers. His horse reared, spinning sideways, before it went down with a bullet through its neck while more rifles fired almost simultaneously. Two more slugs ripped into Martin's body as he tumbled from the mount and splashed facedown in the stream.

With the sound of the first shot, Daniel jerked his horse's head up and around in a twisting turn, but the alarm had sounded too late. A bullet crashed into his spine, another shattered his ribcage, and a third tore through his thigh. The horse fell to its knees with a bullet through its chest before toppling sideways on top of the dead rider sprawled in the trail.

As quickly as it had been broken, the silence was restored. But there was an ominous heaviness about the calm, and the smell of burned gunpowder drifted on the breeze. Daniel lay motionless beneath the horse, but Martin slowly drifted downstream, turning the water crimson around him. Ghostlike shapes flashed through the timber, crouched in a trotting run and leaping over fallen logs and brush. After five minutes a single bird made a testing call, and was answered by a second, then a third. A frog croaked its mating call, which was echoed by a challenger, and the stream came to life once again.

Strother McFarland and Frank Laskey looked up at the sound of rifle fire in the distance, as did the other skinners who stopped their work and looked around with bloodstained knives in their hands. Scattered about them lay thirty-five buffalo, some skinned, with white fat glistening in the sunlight, and others still unskinned and destined for the knife.

"Whaddaya make of it, Stro?" Laskey asked in a hushed voice, as he remained hunched over the animal at his feet.

McFarland listened intently for several seconds before wiping his knife on the hide in his hands and slipping it into the sheath at his belt. Taking up his rifle from where it lay propped against the buffalo's massive head, he straightened while continuing to stare into the distance.

"Don't know for sure, Frank. How many rifles you make that out to be?"

"Ten, maybe eleven."

"Same count here," McFarland replied with a nod.

"Couldn't be buff hunters, shootin' all at once like that. Sounded more like an ambush."

"Musta been purty damned good shootin', if it was. Only one round of shots."

"Yeah. Either that or the numbers weren't quite even. Let's leave the rest of the boys here while you and me mosey on over for a little look-see."

Sheathing his knife as McFarland had done, Laskey picked up his rifle and they trotted toward their horses, tethered beyond a low rise. When they neared the creek at the place where they estimated the sound of shots had come from, they reined in and listened closely once more.

The cacophony of nature's calling creatures drifted to them and McFarland spat to one side and spoke from the corner of his mouth with his gaze directed toward the river. "There's a trail crosses just up ahead. You go downstream a bit and I'll go upstream, then we'll work our way along the creek until we get to the crossing. It's pretty tangled in there, except for the trail, so we'd best go on foot. You know the signal if you see somethin' 'fore I do, so let me know. I'll do the same."

After tying their horses to the roots of a fallen tree, they worked their cautious way along the stream, darting from stump to log to tree. After pausing to listen, they moved forward carefully, rifles cocked and held before them. When he was nearly at the trail, McFarland saw something tangled in a low-hanging branch and he took it down and examined it carefully. It was an eagle feather decorated with string and beads. A cunning grin crossed his face as he moved forward again with less caution than before, and after watching the trail from behind a log for better than a minute, he stood up and cupped a hand to his mouth. The call of a prairie hawk drifted through the trees and was greeted by a matching call, then McFarland moved into the open and walked forward to examine the two dead horses and the single dead man. Five minutes later, Laskey splashed through a shallow inlet and stood beside McFarland.

"Found another one downstream, Stro. Caught up in some branches and deader'n a goddamned doornail," Laskey said without concern. "Know who this feller is?" he asked, pointing at the dead man beneath the fallen horse.

"Yup, sure do," McFarland replied as he began to dig through the saddlebags. "Name's Boggs. Daniel Boggs. The other one down there'd be his brother Martin. Their pa runs a spread called the Double G, and he's just the feller we been tryin' to rile. Looks like the Injuns are gonna do it for us."

"Injuns? How do you know they done this?"

McFarland grinned and pulled the feather out from his shirt-front. "Belongs to an Arapaho. One that just left here," he said, glancing around again. "Wind woulda blown it out of that tree if it'd been there long."

"We gonna tell Boggs about this?"

"Sure we are. When the time is right. This is the kinda thing I been tryin' to get started all along. But we gotta bide our time and use this information when it'll do us the most good. Them Injuns won't be back, and these here boys won't be found for a day or two. Give us time to get our skinnin' done and hides salted away. Then we'll pay a little visit to Mr. Boggs, and with all that's been goin' on lately, he'll be on them Arapaho's necks like stink on shit. We'll have a little war goin' on, with every damned body too busy killin' each other to pay any attention to what we do with the buff. We'll have a free hand to take what we want."

"Gotta hand it to ya, Stro, you ain't nobody's fool." Laskey chuckled as he took a step down the trail. "When it comes to dirt work, you're—" His foot struck something in the mud and he looked down, then stooped to retrieve it. He pulled up the pint whiskey bottle Martin had dropped, and wiped it clean on his pants leg. "Well, lookee here! These boys musta been plannin' to have a little drink when they got jumped. Ain't this our lucky day?" He pulled the cork free and tilted the bottle against his lips.

After watching Laskey's Adam's apple jump twice, McFarland jerked the bottle from his hand and drank thirstily. When he lowered the bottle, a whistling breath escaped his lips and he heaved a contented sigh. "Now that's a slice of pure heaven, Frank. After we take care of what buff are left in these parts, we'll have all we can drink of that."

Laskey licked his lips and reached for the bottle, which McFarland again jerked away. "You've had enough, Frank. You got skinnin' work ta do."

"That ain't fair, Stro," Laskey whined. "I'm the one that found it."

"And I'm the one that took it away," McFarland growled. "Now get on back to yer work while I look these fellers over and see what's worth takin'."

Laskey chanced a sharp glance at McFarland before moving down the trail, his shoulders drooping in disappointment.

"And don't be tellin' none of them other fellers what we found here, ya hear me, Frank?" McFarland called after the retreating figure.

Laskey simply waved a hand behind him in disgust and kept on walking without reply.

nine ─────────────────

Larry Watkins had just sat down to his evening meal at the makeshift table in the rear of the equally makeshift agency building situated on the southeast corner of the Arapaho Reservation. He was lonely and felt terribly isolated from the rest of the white world, and he wondered at that moment, as he often did, why he had sought to become an employee of the Bureau of Indian Affairs. It had sounded so exciting and romantic at first, not to mention the fact that it provided a much-needed social service for the downtrodden red man, but somehow the glamour had not been there. Instead, he had found an unsympathetic army on one side, while the profound shortage of supplies had kept the reservation Indians hostile toward him on the other. And Watkins, in his ramshackle cabin, was caught in the middle.

The Arapaho had been a constant bafflement to him, and no matter how hard he tried, he could not break through the stone wall of impassiveness that surrounded them. He could speak only the most rudimentary of their words. They spoke to him in English only when they came to complain about the lack of promised rations that didn't ever arrive, and he felt like a hostage in his own agency.

Watkins shoved the salt pork around on his plate with his fork and watched the trail of slick grease it left behind. A growl of revulsion rose within his stomach. The fork searched out a boiled potato, worried it around the plate for a few moments, then clattered down onto the tabletop as Watkins leaned back in his chair, thoroughly disgusted with the whole affair. He thought about his girlfriend back in St. Louis, whom he was sure was no longer his girlfriend, but even the memory of her could not soothe his troubled mind.

"I can't take any more of this," he said to himself as his gaze wandered throughout the agency, now dimly lit by the dying rays of the sun. "They can get somebody else to..."

The clatter of numerous hooves and rattle of bit chains startled him from his reverie. "Now who the hell could that be?" he asked no one as he stood and hurried toward the door.

Just as he stepped outside, Matt Kincaid swung down from his saddle. It was obvious from the dust caking his uniform that he had been on patrol for some time.

"Hello, Lieutenant!" Watkins called, delighted at the sight of a white face. "Good to see you. You're just in time for dinner—if you can call it that."

Matt smiled and offered his hand. "Nice to see you, Larry, but thank you, no on the dinner. I'll eat with my men." He turned toward the sweat-stained and equally dusty column of twos and said, "Sergeant Olsen, have the platoon dismount. We'll bivouac here tonight. Have the horses watered and fed, then issue rations to the troops."

"Yessir."

Windy Mandalian stepped from his horse in his characteristic fluid manner, and moved toward the agent. "Howdy, Larry. How goes it with the bureaucrats?"

"Not worth a shit, if you don't mind my saying so."

"Good. Situation normal, then," Windy replied with a smile.

"Too damned normal, Windy. Come on inside, I've got some hot coffee going and a little something to lace it with. Glad you two showed up. I get tired of drinking alone."

Matt watched Watkins walk ahead of them, and thought about the agent as they moved toward the door. He had always liked Watkins, even though he was young, inexperienced, and

93

totally ignorant of the ways of the frontier. He was well intentioned, did the best he could with what he had to work with, and complained only when he could stand no more of governmental bungling. If he survives another two years without a nervous breakdown, Matt thought as they stepped inside, he might make a decent Indian agent.

Matt and Windy pulled out chairs and sat down while Watkins poured the coffee and added a generous dollop of whiskey before handing the cups around.

"What brings you here this time of day, Matt?" the agent asked while taking a seat. "Surely we're not at war again, are we?"

"Damned near, Larry. I've come to ask some help from you."

"Help?" the agent echoed with a hopeless gesture. "What the hell can I do to help? I can't even take care of the Arapaho, much less the United States Army."

Matt took a cautious sip of the hot coffee. "The same favor will help both sides, Larry. Things are going to hell in a handcart and we haven't got much time to change that around. That's why I'm here."

"I'd be curious to know what's going to hell that isn't already there?"

"I know you've had it tough," Matt said with a kind smile, "but then, nobody said it was going to be easy. Good coffee, huh, Windy?" Kincaid concluded with a glance toward the scout.

"Yup. Somewhere around a hundred proof, I'd say."

"As far as easy goes," Watkins said, "the only easy thing I can think of around here would be for me to get my hat and walk out that door."

"That wouldn't be easy, Larry. That would be quitting. Never took you for that kind of man."

Watkins knew Kincaid had hit upon the one thing that kept him at his post, and he breathed a weary sigh while leaning back in his chair. "Okay, Lieutenant, you've got me. You know you have, so there's no use in playing games. What can I do to help?"

"Thanks, Larry. I knew I could count on you. You knew Red Hawk's son was killed?"

"Hell no. Nobody tells me anything."

"How about the murder of Spike Dowler over at the Double G?"

"No."

"Then you wouldn't know about the cattle, either," Matt concluded, sipping from the tin cup again.

"Let's assume I don't know anything," Watkins said with a derisive smile. "Which is more fact than assumption. So why not begin from the beginning?"

"Fair enough. Gray Wolf, Red Hawk's youngest son, was killed by two rifle shots. Spike Dowler was killed by an arrow, as were ten of Boggs' cattle. Red Hawk has given us three days to find the killers of his son before he goes on the warpath. Boggs is already mad enough to fight a bear with a willow switch, and Easy Company is caught in the middle."

Watkins arched an eyebrow. "*You're* caught in the middle, Lieutenant? In case you haven't noticed, I'm not exactly over-protected around here."

"I know you're not, and that's why we have to act fast," Matt said. "There are a lot of young hotheads among the Arapaho who would rather fight than eat, and the same goes for Boggs and his sons, as well as his hired hands. Everybody is spoiling for a brawl, but I think there's a third party involved somewhere along the line, who's just laying back, waiting for the fun to start."

"And who might that noble person be?" Watkins asked.

"I don't know for sure. But we've spent the whole day looking for Strother McFarland and his men, without success. We'll be at it again at first light in the morning. I honestly think he's the key to this whole mess."

"I've never heard of the man, but I'm curious anyway. Why do you think that?"

"Late this afternoon, Windy went out to do a little scouting on his own. He had some time to think and he came up with something we had both forgotten. Once, about a month ago when we were checking McFarland's hunting permits, Windy saw something sticking out from under a buffalo robe that caught his eye, but he didn't think much about it." Matt paused and watched the agent closely before speaking again. "It was a quiver full of arrows."

Watkins shrugged. "So? A lot of souvenirs got taken on both sides during the late conflict."

"True, but this one contained arrows with both red-and-yellow and green-and-white markings."

"If I may ask this intelligent question one more time," Watkins said with a confused look, "so?"

"So the cattle were killed with arrows striped with green and white, while Dowler was killed with a red-and-yellow one."

Watkins smiled. "Can you stand a third 'so'?"

"Yes I can. Green and white are the preferred colors of the Arapaho for their arrows and warpaint, but yellow and red are customary to the Sioux. There are no Sioux in this region, of course."

Comprehension glimmered in Watkins' eyes. "I see. So your assumption is that someone is shooting various things with arrows and hoping the blame will fall on someone else. Is that it?"

"Like I said, I don't know, but it's worth looking into. We haven't got anything else to go on."

"Then where does the murdered Indian boy fit in?"

"I haven't any idea. Boggs did make the threat that he'd shoot any Arapaho found on his land, but Gray Wolf was killed on land that doesn't belong to Boggs. Now, Boggs is one of the most foul-mouthed, miserable people I've ever met in my life, but that doesn't mean he would stoop to shooting a virtually unarmed Indian lad. There has to be a tie-in somewhere among all these killings, but I need more time to figure it out."

"And I would be delighted to provide you with that time, Lieutenant," Watkins said with a shrug, "but I don't really have a tremendous amount of influence over anyone, including the people I'm supposed to be in charge of."

"You have all the influence you need for our purposes. Red Hawk's daughter is lying on what might be her deathbed with a stab wound—"

"What?" Watkins asked, perplexed.

"—in her side, and his oldest son, Black Wing, has already threatened retaliation for the death of his brother. Tonight is the end of the time Red Hawk has given me to find the killers—"

"This is all so confusing."

"—and tomorrow he'll be on the warpath, as I assume his son already is."

Watkins blew on his steaming cup and tried to think. "I

see," he said before looking up with another confused gesture. "Correction. No, I don't see. How can I help in all of this?"

Matt inched forward on his chair. "You are the key to stopping all-out war before it starts."

"I am?"

"You are. I want you to be in Red Hawk's camp tomorrow by sunup, and tell him about his daughter."

"Me?" Watkins asked with an incredulous snort. "Lieutenant, there could only be one man in this whole country that he might hate more than he hates me, and that would have to be the man, or men, who murdered his son. I am not his favorite person, please be assured."

"But you are a representative of the United States Government, and he respects that. Go to him and tell him that Kita Wak is being treated for a stab wound, self-inflicted, at Outpost Number Nine. Tell him that she will be returned to him as soon as she has recovered, if she recovers, and—"

"*If* she recovers, Lieutenant?" Watkins asked, swallowing hard. "And what if she doesn't?"

"We'll have to worry about that when the time comes. But if you can convince him that his daughter wants to see him— say that she's calling for him and her mother—he might just postpone this quest for revenge until we've had time to find McFarland and maybe get some answers."

"I'll do it, of course," Watkins said, unconsciously massaging his neck as though a noose had suddenly slipped around it. "I won't be liking it, but I will do it."

"Good. Now, there's another man on the scene who calls himself the Reverend Pope. If he should come by here at any time asking questions, I want you to get to me and fill me in on whatever he might have to say or ask."

"Good God! And I was hating this solitude!"

"If we can't stop this thing before it starts, then you won't have one damned bit of solitude to worry about for a long time," Matt said before draining his cup. He turned and looked at Windy. "Have you anything to add?"

Windy shifted in his chair and crossed his legs. "Well, Matt, you covered it all pretty good, but there is one thing that Larry here should know."

Watkins watched the scout nervously. "I'm not sure I want to hear it."

"If Kita Wak dies, and the killers of Gray Wolf ain't found

97

quicker'n babies shit yellow, it's very likely that Red Hawk, his son, or any of his braves might kill the first white man they can get their hands on." Windy smiled pleasantly and hoisted his cup in salute. "Way it sounds to me, you just might be that man." Rising, the scout finished his coffee and walked toward the door. "'Night, Larry. Have a good sleep."

Watkins watched Mandalian's casual departure before looking sharply at Kincaid.

"He doesn't mean that, does he, Lieutenant?"

"Sure he does, Larry. He knows these Arapaho better than any other white man I've met. But don't worry about it," Matt concluded, rising and walking toward the door.

"Don't worry about it? Why the hell shouldn't I worry about it? As a matter of fact, I have every damned intention of worrying about it!"

Matt turned in the doorway and smiled. "Worry if you want to, Larry, but it isn't going to do a damned bit of good. If they go on the warpath again, you'll be the first man they'll kill anyway. Like you said, there is no love lost between them and the Bureau of Indian Affairs. Good night."

Kincaid stepped outside and closed the door while Larry Watkins stared at it in silence. Finally he slammed his fist down upon the table, and the salt pork jumped in a flopping twist on the tin plate. "Fuck you," Watkins snarled, glowering at the meat. "You're already dead anyway." His face dropped to his hands and he asked in a moaning voice, "Why in hell didn't I accept that job as baggage inspector at the Port of New York?"

They could see the dead buffalo, white and bloated, from some distance away, and Windy looked across at Kincaid. "We're gettin' closer to McFarland, Matt. Those buff must of been killed sometime yesterday."

"How do you know that, Windy?"

Mandalian studied the hard blue sky. "No vultures around yet. They usually like to let the meat rot a little bit before they dig in. Must have somethin' to do with the flavor."

"Yeah, I can imagine. Well, at least we shouldn't have much trouble picking up their trail. Must be thirty or forty dead animals over there, and those hides represent quite a bit of weight. They'll need at least three pack animals to haul them away."

Windy nodded. "At least. The hooves will sink deep, and there's no way that McFarland, even as rotten and devious as he is, can do anything to hide that. Let's cut across toward that rise over there. He's probably headin' for town now."

The hoofprints of nine horses, three of them obviously heavily laden, were easily found leading away from the site of the slaughter, and Windy knelt down to study them carefully. "Looks like he's got about a three-hour start on us, Matt," Windy said as his foot hit the stirrup again. "Must've left at sunup like we did. Strange thing, though. They seem to be headin' south, instead of east toward town. Wonder what the hell he's up to?"

"Hard to say, Windy, but we're damned sure going to find out. Those horses were walking, weren't they?"

"Yup. Them pack animals wouldn't make it far at a run."

"Good. At a run, with a couple of rests, we should be able to catch them in less than two hours," Matt said, studying the surrounding plains. "We're not very far from the reservation line, Windy, and we both know I haven't got any real hard evidence against McFarland, even though I'm certain he's guilty as sin. Why don't you take a little look around here and see if you can't dig up a little something in violation of his permits. Like maybe some hides taken on the reservation side with the carcasses being dragged across the line, a place where he camped on Wahilla ground, anything that I can hold him on."

"Sure, Matt," Windy replied, chewing the plug of tobacco in his cheek thoughtfully. "He's a pretty smart old bastard, but maybe we can dig up something. Shouldn't take more'n half an hour, maybe an hour at the outside. Ridin' alone, I can catch up with you mighty quick."

"That's what I was thinking. I'll take the platoon and go after McFarland. Even I can follow the trail he's leaving."

Windy spat and grinned. "Now that's a left-handed compliment if I ever heard one, Matt. See you in an hour or so."

Kincaid watched the scout gallop away before raising his hand and signaling the platoon to move out.

It was nearly noon when they caught up with McFarland's group. The hunters had stopped in the shade provided by an oak grove to rest the pack animals, and they looked up in mild surprise from where they were seated on the ground at the sight of the mounted infantry unit. They bay coloring of the army mounts had taken on a dark brown luster, glistening with sweat, and it was obvious that the animals had been ridden hard in pursuit.

"Wonder who's chasin' them fellers, Frank?" McFarland asked with a knowing grin, as he hunched to his feet.

"Looks like they been ridin' a trifle hard, don't it?" Laskey agreed. "Might be they want to palaver with us a little bit."

"Might be," McFarland said, watching the platoon move forward from where they had stopped on the rise and ride directly toward the grove.

Kincaid's gloved hand flashed above his right shoulder and the unit stopped behind him while he looked at McFarland.

"Afternoon, Lieutenant. We'd offer ya tea, but we done run out of cakes," McFarland said with a careless shrug.

"That's a real shame, McFarland," Kincaid replied. "Guess now all we've got to do is talk business."

"Business? What business would you and me have with each other?"

"First I think we'd better have another look at your hunting permits."

"Come on, Lieutenant! Them permits is good fer a whole damn year, and you've checked 'em a dozen times in the last goddamn six months!"

Matt smiled easily. "Then this will make thirteen, won't it? Get them out, McFarland."

"Well, I'll be go-to-hell," McFarland mumbled as he dug in his saddlebags and produced a grimy wad of folded papers and handed them up to Kincaid. "Read 'em and weep, Lieutenant."

Matt snapped the papers open and his eyes skipped over the printing before he handed them back down. "They're legal, all right. For hunting buffalo. Doesn't say a damned thing on there about hunting cattle, though."

"About what?" McFarland asked, his eyes narrowing.

"Cattle. Double G longhorns, to be specific."

"Now you know I ain't a real smart man, Lieutenant, so maybe you could explain what you jus' said a little better for these old ears to hear."

"Certainly. Ten longhorns were shot a few days ago on the Boggs spread. They were shot with Arapaho war arrows."

McFarland indicated his innocence by a confused look and

100

a helpless shrug. "So? Don't get me wrong, I'm mighty damn sorry to hear about that, but like I always tell the boys here, you just can't trust them damn Arapaho. What's all this got to do with me?"

"You're a pretty handy man with a bow and arrow yourself, aren't you, McFarland?"

"Me?" McFarland asked with a chuckle. "I been knowed to notch an arrow or two in my time, but always just for fun and sport."

Kincaid watched McFarland closely now. "Fun and sport? Tell me, what category did putting that arrow through Spike Dowler's chest fall into? Was that fun, sport, or both?"

"Never heard of the man."

"And he hadn't heard of you. But he did hear *from* you, on the receiving end of an arrow." Matt hesitated, watching the tightening look on McFarland's face. "A Sioux war arrow at that."

No matter how hard he tried, with the mention of the words, "Sioux war arrow," McFarland couldn't prevent his eyes from drifting to Laskey's face. Laskey flinched, and the corner of his mouth began to twitch uncontrollably. Kincaid had missed nothing, watching both men and waiting for McFarland to speak again.

Instantly, McFarland gained control and grinned up at Kincaid with a motion of his hand toward the shade, saying, "You'd better get in here out of the heat, Lieutenant. Way you're a talkin', you been out in the sun too long."

"I know exactly what I'm talking about. All I have to do is prove it."

"That's gonna take a heap of provin', Kincaid. 'Lessen you want to frame an innocent man. What makes you suspicion me of some low-down treachery like that in the first place?"

"The fact that it *is* treacherous makes you a prime suspect, McFarland."

There was a pleased, almost gloating tone to McFarland's voice, as though he were enjoying their cat-and-mouse game. "I don't believe what I'm hearin', Lieutenant. I'm a law-abidin' citizen, my permits are always legal, I don't take nothin' that don't rightfully belong to me, and I've got five fucking witnesses right here that will swear I never touched a piece of Boggs' ground."

"I'm sure you have," Matt said, gazing at the scruffy lot.

"And there isn't one of them that wouldn't push his own mother off her deathbed."

McFarland laughed. "Looks to me like you've got your butt hangin' over a mighty shaky limb, Lieutenant. And now, unless you got enough facts to arrest me—which we both know damn well you don't—I got work to do." He turned and started toward his horse, but stopped when Kincaid called his name.

"McFarland?"

"Yeah?"

Kincaid crossed his arms and shifted his weight on the stirrups. "You know, I got to wondering the other day who would benefit most from a war between the stockmen and the Arapaho. Certainly not Boggs, he's got too many cattle spread over too much land, and an all-out war would likely cost him most of his herd. The Arapaho? No, they've been beaten once, and now desire only to live in peace on their reservation. Not that they're happy, mind you, but they haven't got any choice. But what about a buffalo hunter? An unscrupulous buffalo hunter who would stop at nothing to make sure he got the lion's share of whatever hides are left to be taken. If the Indians and the stockmen were at each other's throats, then he would be the one to gain the most, wouldn't he?"

McFarland stared impassively up at Kincaid. "What's your point?"

"I think you're the one who killed Boggs' cattle and his hired hand, but where you screwed up was using that Sioux war arrow. If it hadn't been for those red-and-yellow markings, I probably would have had to press charges against the people of the Wahilla tribe. But Dowler being killed by a different kind of arrow than the cattle were puts a little different light on the matter. Sort of looks like someone, maybe the person trying to frame the Arapaho, used the wrong arrow by mistake." Kincaid's cold stare held on McFarland's face.

Again, McFarland's gaze drifted unconsciously in Laskey's direction, and the twitching at the corner of the skinner's mouth became more pronounced. Laskey tried once to return McFarland's hard look, but failed, and turned his back to the Scotsman. There was no doubting the insane hatred in McFarland's eyes when he looked at Kincaid once more.

"So? Whoever done it fucked up. That don't mean I had a hand in it."

"I think it does. Windy Mandalian, my scout, has one hell of a memory when he wants to use it, which he did yesterday. When we last checked your permits, about a month ago, he remembered having seen a quiver full of arrows sticking out from beneath a buffalo robe. His eye is pretty keen, and he said that quiver contained both Arapaho and Sioux war arrows." Kincaid smiled almost pleasantly. "Now doesn't that seem interesting to you?"

McFarland grunted and spat on the ground. "Hell no, it don't. He was seein' things, just like you're dreamin'. I ain't got no arrows of any kind, be they Arapaho or Sioux."

"Then you wouldn't mind if we took a little look at your equipment?"

"I sure as hell would!" McFarland snapped. "You got the legal papers what says you can search my belongings?"

"No, as a matter of fact, I haven't. But I can inspect and count your hides to make sure you haven't gone over your permit limit."

Matt was almost certain that McFarland wouldn't be stupid enough to keep the bow and arrows, if indeed he had used them, but he had to try some ploy to keep McFarland close at hand until Windy arrived with some sort of evidence to indicate a permit violation.

"I want all those hides unpacked and spread out for inspection, McFarland."

"What? That'll take at least an hour, dammit! I haven't got all day to fuck around with—"

"I said unpack those hides, and do it now or I'll confiscate the whole damned lot."

McFarland kicked a dirt clod in disgust as he turned toward his men. "All right, unpack the damn things. Kincaid's givin' us the runaround, but there ain't a damn thing we can do about it."

The hunters set to their work in silence, with an occasional surly scowl in the direction of the army unit, who sat their horses and patiently waited.

Matt had just finished counting the last stack. Even though he had carefully scrutinized McFarland's equipment as he worked, he had seen nothing of the bow and arrows, and McFarland watched him with contemptuous eyes as Kincaid straightened.

"You satisfied?"

"Thirty-five hides, just like you said. Your permit's good for a hundred, so I don't see any problem."

"You don't see any problem? Well, I by damn do! You knew there couldn't be more'n a hundred green hides on three horses, dammit, and I'm gonna turn in a complaint to—"

The pounding hooves of a single running horse silenced McFarland, and all eyes turned as Mandalian pulled his mount to a stop. Kincaid studied the scout for some indication of success, and noted the tiny shake of Windy's head. Matt turned toward McFarland, and there was a sinking feeling in his chest.

"Very well, McFarland. You can go. Turn in whatever—"

"Matt?" Windy said. "Can I talk to you alone for a minute?"

"Sure, Windy," Matt replied, moving off to one side while Mandalian stepped from his horse to follow. When they were out of earshot, Kincaid turned to the scout. "What have you got, Windy?"

"Nothin' we can hold McFarland on, but I'm afraid that war we been tryin' to prevent is about to bust wide-assed open."

"Why's that?"

"I went lookin' for that sign like you wanted me to, and found two dead men instead."

"Dead men? Did you recognize them?"

"Sure did. Daniel and Martin Boggs."

"Are you sure?"

"Hard to mistake anybody as ugly as those two. Looks like they were taken in an ambush, and from the looks of things, I'd say it was done by Arapaho. There's a few moccasin prints in the soft dirt, and I found where they held their horses on Wahilla land. Be tough to prove, but I'd bet my last hunk of cut-plug that it was Indian work."

"Black Wing?"

"That'd be my guess."

"Goddammit," Matt said softly. "When Boggs finds out about this, there won't be any stopping him."

"No, I don't think so. And don't forget, right now we're one day over the three that Red Hawk gave us."

"Yeah, I know. We'd better go back there and check out that ambush a little more closely and hope that Boggs doesn't find out about his sons until we've had a little more time."

Windy smiled and shook his head. "Don't think you're

gonna have a hell of a lot of time, Matt. From the direction McFarland's travelin', I'd say I know exactly where he's headed."

"Where?"

"Boggs' place."

"Goddamn," Matt said again, before pursing his lips and staring silently toward the horizon beyond which the Wahilla Reservation was located.

ten _____

Frank Laskey watched the platoon move out, and as he continued to gaze at them until they were lost from view, a look of dread came into his eyes. He chanced a snap glance at McFarland while pretending to tighten his cinch strap, but the Scotsman appeared to have forgotten about him.

"Right, boys," McFarland was saying to the others, "let's get them hides loaded one more time and get the hell out of here. Damn that Kincaid anyway!" Then his eyes drifted to Laskey. "Gonna give the boys a hand, Frank?"

"Sure, Stro, sure," Laskey said quickly, moving to help. "Be glad to."

"Didn't think you'd have it any other way, Frank. Bet you're glad I got rid of that bow and them arrows, huh? One little fuck-up with the damned things and a man could get in trouble."

Laskey glanced over his shoulder with a nervous grin as he leaned down to pick up a hide. "Sure 'nuff, Stro. Mighty good thinkin' on your part."

"Somebody's gotta do the good thinkin' 'round here, Frank. Sure as hell ain't gonna be you, 'pears to me like."

Laskey started to reply, thought better of it, and directed his full attention to loading the hides. There was merely a trace of sweat showing on the others while they worked, but Laskey's shirt rapidly became soaked, and the twitching continued at the corner of his mouth. When he thought McFarland wasn't looking, he would steal a peek in his direction, but the Scotsman's eyes were constantly on him, while his thumb absently caressed the long knifeblade in his right hand. And when the hides were nearly loaded, with maybe five left on the ground, McFarland waved the others away from the pack animal.

"Just leave the rest of 'em for old Frank there, lads. He's a purty fair-sized piece of the reason why we gotta go through all this bullshit in the first place."

Laskey straightened and pawed the sweat from his brow. "Look, Stro, I—"

"Ain't got time for talk, Frank. Now get them last hides on there!"

The other hands backed away, glad to quit their labors, and in the realization that any piece of ground near Laskey might be a very poor choice of real estate.

After several hesitant glances at the men now watching him from a semicircle, Laskey stooped over and clutched the heavy hide taken from a huge bull and started to lift. McFarland's boot caught him squarely in the ribs and sent him sprawling on the ground.

"Gotta work faster'n that, Frank," McFarland said with a leering grin. "We're all runnin' out of time, some faster'n others."

Laskey grimaced as he rolled to his knees, stood, and lifted the hide toward the packsaddle. "I'm . . . tired and . . . and I think you mighta broke a couple o' my ribs."

"Ain't that a shame, lads?" McFarland asked, without taking his eyes off Laskey. "Old Frank there, the man what brought Kincaid down on us, got a little hurtin' in his side. Move it, Frank, goddammit! And no more talkin' 'lessen you wanta try it with a broken jaw!"

"Sure, Stro, sure. Sorry," Laskey managed, running toward the next hide, stumbling to one knee, and struggling up again with a snap glance over his shoulder toward McFarland. The others watched Laskey in silence, with compassionless eyes, and none of them risked taking a long look at McFarland. To a man, they were glad it was Laskey and not themselves upon whom McFarland was directing his rage, but there was a hint of disgust in the air, a feeling of contempt as they watched a man who had been their friend being turned into an animal.

Apparently oblivious to the ominous tension, McFarland continued to stare at Laskey. The wild, crazed look was upon him again, glazing his deep blue eyes, and the rate of his breathing increased as though he could barely contain some hidden excitement.

"Faster, Frank! You've got two more to go! Come on, lad! I can't wait much longer!"

"I'm movin' . . . fast . . . fast as I can . . . Stro . . ." Laskey gasped. He picked up another hide, this one smaller and taken from a yearling, and moved in a stumbling run toward the packhorse. "Please don't . . . please don't . . . kill me, Stro," he moaned while attempting to spread the hide across the others, but it slipped to the ground in a brown heap. The flies swarmed over Laskey's face as he stooped to pick it up, and the sweat ran into his eyes, and he was beet-red from his neckline to his hatband.

When the hide slipped from the packsaddle, something snapped in McFarland. He lunged toward Laskey and kicked him squarely in the face with a heavy black boot, and the skinner catapulted onto his back with blood streaming from a broken nose.

"Can't you do anything right, Frank?" McFarland asked in a voice that might be used to scold a child. "All I asked from you was to load the hides onto that horse there. That's all, Frank. Is that too much to ask?"

Laskey clutched his broken face, and his terrified eyes rolled in his head. "I'm hurtin', Stro, hurtin' real bad. I can't . . . I can't do no more. Please . . . please don't make me do no more."

The insanity deepened in McFarland's eyes, and the tip of his tongue touched cracked, chapped lips. "You ain't no good, Frank. Know that? You ain't no good, just like them others a while back, you ain't no good. You're tryin' to put old Stro away, but old Stro was too smart for them and he's too smart for you." He was advancing on Laskey and caressing the knife the way a lover might fondle a woman's breast, while Laskey's heels dug into the prairie sod and he tried to inch away on his back.

"I didn't do nothin' wrong, Stro! Pickin' the wrong arrow was an honest mistake! I didn't mean no harm by it!"

"But you *did* harm, Frank. You did harm to others, and that ain't no good. You're gonna have to pay for that, lad."

McFarland was standing over him now, and as Laskey looked upward, the twitching at the corner of his mouth became a full-fledged convulsion and his face twisted in hideous contortions while the blood and sweat ran into his mouth.

"Please, Stro. Please, I'm beggin' ya. Don't kill me..."

In that instant, McFarland's knee dropped to Laskey's chest and the razor-sharp blade sank home just below Laskey's right ear. With a twist of his wrist, McFarland took the blade around Laskey's throat, under his chin, and up to the other ear. Laskey's eyes remained open in ultimate horror, but his head lolled to one side.

McFarland stayed as he was for several seconds, holding the knife hilt-deep in Laskey's throat, and then his eyes cleared and he glanced around, as if he had suddenly awakened from a dream. Jerking the knife from Laskey's throat, he wiped the blade clean on the dead man's shirt, sheathed it, and turned toward the others.

"Jasper, you and Holland finish loadin' them hides and tyin' 'em down. The rest of you get ready to move out."

Curt Jasper was a young man, maybe twenty-two, and he had yet to attain the hard, embittered look of the others. Even though McFarland had spoken to him, he continued to stare at the flies crawling over the yawning wound just below Laskey's chin.

McFarland's eyes hardened again as he watched the young man. "You hear me, Jasper?"

"Why'd you have to do it, Stro?" Jasper asked in a breathless voice. "He didn't do nothin' to deserve that. Sure, a little roughin' up, maybe, but not—"

McFarland was upon him in three strides, and his knuckles cracked across the young man's jaw. Jasper staggered two steps backward and his fingers gingerly stroked his chin.

"Don't never talk back to me, boy," McFarland said in a low, menacing growl. "Don't never talk back to me! Do as you were told and do it now!"

"Sure, Stro, sure," Jasper said, stooping to pick up a hide. But his eyes never left Laskey's throat.

By the time Tim Boggs' horse cantered onto the home property, the sun was slanting toward the horizon and he stared straight ahead with hatred burning in his heart. His brothers, Daniel and Martin, had completely blocked his mind, and when he passed by the first pocket of cattle, he didn't even bother to glance in their direction. But another man had been studying them with keen interest, and now he moved his horse out of the shadows of a cut bank and swung in behind young Boggs. His tall frame appeared to have been stacked perilously atop the saddle, and when his long bony fingers moved to clear the coat from his long-barreled Colt, they moved as if stilled in time.

"Pardon me, young man," he said in a low, commanding voice.

Startled, Tim pulled up on his reins and spun his mount around. His hand was moving toward his gun, but he stopped the movement with the next rumbling words.

"Don't do that. I have no desire to kill you."

Tim steadied his horse and continued to watch the motionless rider, some twenty yards away.

"Who are you?"

"The Reverend Thomas Pope."

"What do you want?"

"To do the Lord's work in peace. May I come forward and talk with you?"

Tim watched the skeletal rider suspiciously. "Yeah, sure. I guess so. Just keep your hand away from that gun, all right?"

"My pleasure. If you would be so kind as to do the same?"

Both men moved their hands away and Pope urged his horse forward. "Would you happen to know who owns these cattle?" he asked cordially.

"Of course. My father does. Why?"

Pope pulled his horse in beside Tim's, and a frigid, funereal smile crossed his thin, bloodless lips. "Nothing important," he replied. "I was just noticing the brand. Double G. What does that stand for, if I might ask?"

"Boggs. Our family name is Boggs, with two Gs."

"I see. Where are you headed now?"

"Home."

"May I ride with you? I think I have some business to discuss with a man who works on your place. Is there a Jake Barnes in your father's employ?"

Tim hesitated before responding. Even though Jake was as rough as they came, Tim still liked him and respected him for

110

the way he treated him like a man, and because he didn't bow to his father's every demand.

"Why do you want to know?" Tim asked suspiciously.

"He and I were friends in Mexico a while back. We had a business arrangement together at the time, and I wish only to settle an old debt I owe him."

Tim's mind was weary from lack of sleep, and he sensed nothing ominous in the minister's purpose. "Sure, Jake works for us. Ride along with me, we're only about an hour from the ranch."

"God bless you, son, I'll just do that."

It was dark when Tim and Pope reined in before the house. The building was dark, which was a complete surprise to Timothy.

"Wonder where they are?" he asked himself as he stepped down and tied his horse to the rail. "Pa's almost always here this time of night."

"I have no idea," Pope replied, surveying the place and noting where the other buildings were. "Perhaps an emergency came up."

"Maybe so. Come on in and I'll make some coffee," Tim offered, stepping onto the porch. "There's whiskey, if you're a drinking man."

"That I am, son" Pope said, swinging a long leg over his horse's rump and looping his reins around the rail. "But only in moderation."

"Same here, so let's forget the coffee, then. I'm needing a drink myself right now."

After Tim lit the lamps, he offered Pope a seat at the kitchen table while he went to the drainboard and poured two liberal shots into less than clean glasses.

"These glasses aren't exactly the cleanest in the territory," he said, squinting at the fingerprints on one while he moved toward the table, "but I guess whiskey is supposed to sterilize things pretty—"

His mouth froze open and he stopped stock-still and stared at the barrel of the Buntline, pointing at him just above the surface of the kitchen table.

"This is a pretty good sterilizer too, son," Pope said in a kindly voice, "so just stay calm, sit down, let's drink our whiskey, and you won't get hurt. It's not you I'm after."

"You're not . . . you're not a preacher at all, are you?" Tim demanded, showing no fear of the gun. "I trusted you, damn you!"

"Now let's not get upset, son, it wouldn't be a healthy thing to do. Like I said, sit down and have your drink and I'll have mine."

Tim slowly sank onto a chair and shoved the whiskey glass across.

Pope's face was nearly devoid of expression as he nodded, lifted the glass, and took it halfway down in one gulp. "Not bad whiskey," he allowed, "and I'm thankin' you for it. To answer your question, no, I'm not a reverend, but I have made my peace with the Lord and I abide by His word. Things haven't always been that way."

"What do you want with Jake?" Tim asked.

Pope smiled easily. "Jake Barnes," he said musingly. "The meanest man I ever did meet. But still, he pulls his pants on one leg at a time, like the rest of us. What do I want with him? To kill him, son, just to kill him."

"Why?"

"Because he stole something of mine. Like about a quarter of that herd out there that your pappy calls his own. Like I said before, me and Jake were partners at one time."

Tim took a sip of whiskey, grimaced, and shook his head. "I know Jake's got a pretty cloudy past, but I can't believe he's a thief."

"Believe it, son, believe it. He's the only one that could've done it."

"Done what?"

"Took my cows. Or at least my half."

"What do you mean by that?"

Pope downed the rest of his drink and waved the long barrel toward the kitchen. "Why don't you save yourself a lot of walkin' and just bring the bottle in here?" Pope accurately read the hesitation in Tim's eyes. "And leave your gun here on the table. That way nobody gets hurt."

With a casual shrug, Tim laid his Colt on the table, retrieved the whiskey bottle, and shoved it toward Tom Pope as he sat down again.

"Thank you, son. Thank you indeed," Pope said, pulling the cork from the bottle with his teeth and pouring generously. He inclined the bottle toward Tim's glass, but Tim declined with a shake of his head.

112

"Suit yourself. Whiskey'll rot your guts out anyway, but since I haven't got anything left to rot, I think I'll just have another little drink." Pope took up his glass again while watching Tim closely. "You asked me a question, and a man deserves an answer."

"I'd appreciate one."

Pope continued to gaze at Tim, but a certain wistfulness came into his eyes. "Me and Jake were partners in a cattle deal, highgrading stock from a Mexican spread called the Granada Grande, about seventy miles south of the border. We'd both led a pretty rough-and-tumble life and we wanted to settle down, get some decency. When we had about two hundred head, Jake went north to arrange a deal while I stayed south to cover our tracks and keep the suspicions down. Looks like old Jake hooked up with your pa, which was pretty smart, because the Double G of the Granada Grande is almost exactly the same as the Double G your pa uses on his cattle.

"Anyway, Jake never came back with my half of the take. I told the folks at the Granada Grande that I knew who had stolen two hundred head of their beef, they put a reasonable price on his head, and here I am. Jake was a good old boy, but I don't like being left holding an empty gunnysack, if you know what I mean."

"When was this?"

"About two years ago. I've been on his trail ever since."

Tim frowned and tried to think back. "I wasn't with my father at that time. I was still in school."

"In school, huh? Weren't you a little old?"

"Yeah, but my ma insisted."

"Good for her." Pope's eyes narrowed. "Do you know anything about cattle?"

"Yeah, I suppose so," Tim replied with another shrug. "As much as the next person, I guess."

"About Mexican cows?"

"I didn't know there was any difference."

Now Pope smiled warmly. "There's a world of difference, son. Anybody that knows about Mex-cut cattle could spot—"

There was a clatter of hooves in the yard, and Pope's mouth froze while his eyes darted toward the open doorway. "Listen! Think that's your pa and Jake?"

Tim studied the sounds. "Yeah, I suppose it is."

With amazing agility for one so tall and lank, Pope sprang

away from the table and ducked inside the kitchen doorway. "Go meet your pa, son, just like you always would. Stand just inside the front door, and remember, this Buntline is hell for making holes at short range. Tell Jake to come on in here, you want to talk to him."

Undecided, Tim paused with his hands on the table.

"Do it, son!" Pope said in a harsh whisper. "You don't have much chance of outrunning a bullet."

Tim stood and moved to the front door, just as boots clattered on the front porch. "Howdy, Pa. Jake."

Boggs' voice boomed in the stillness. "Where the hell you been, boy!?"

"Ridin', Pa. Just ridin' by myself."

"Ridin' by yourself, hell! We got work to do around here. First I send Daniel and Martin a-lookin' for you, then me and Jake and the rest of the hands gotta go lookin' for them!" Boggs snatched a chair, sank down, and grabbed the whiskey bottle. "What the hell's goin' on around here, anyway?"

Tim's heartbeat quickened. "Did you find Dan and Marty?"

"Hell no!"

Jake Barnes stood just inside the doorway, studying Tim's gun and the two used glasses on the tabletop. His hand edged closer to his Colt while his eyes searched the room, until they came to rest on Tim. Tim rolled his eyes toward the kitchen door, and Barnes' hand flashed toward his holster, but he was too late.

Pope stepped into the room and leveled the Buntline at Barnes' chest. "Hold it right there, old pardner, or you're a dead man."

Barnes froze momentarily with his eyes locked on Pope, before his arm went limp and he smiled at the man behind the long-barreled revolver.

"Hello, Tom. What brings you to these parts?"

Boggs held the whiskey bottle suspended over a glass, and stared at Pope in slackjawed surprise. "Now who the hell are you?"

"One question at a time, fellers," Pope said, circling the table to cover all three men. "My name is Thomas Pope, mister, and I've come to kill your hired hand there."

"Kill me, Tom?" Barnes asked. "You're a little old to take up bounty huntin' again, ain't you?"

"Not when the price is right, Jake. And the price offered

by the Granada Grande is right, not to mention a little unfinished business between you and me."

"What the hell's—"

"Shut up, Boggs. This is between Jake and myself."

For the first time that Tim could remember, his father fell silent without argument.

"Unfinished business, Tom? I'm afraid you'll have to explain that."

"Glad to, even though you couldn't help but know. You walked out with my half of the take from that herd. I didn't take kindly to that."

There was a look of genuine surprise on Barnes' face. "I did what, Tom?"

"When you brought the herd north, you were supposed to send my half of the profits back, which seems to have slipped your mind now, just like it did then."

"You're wrong, Tom. Put the gun away and let's talk about this like friends would."

"Like hell I will, Jake. If we were friends, it wouldn't have taken me nearly two years to find you, now would it?"

Barnes shrugged helplessly, a gesture that seemed out of place, coming from his brawny shoulders. "Didn't know you were lookin' for me."

"Didn't know? Did you think I'd just let you skip with my half and not come looking for you?"

"I didn't skip with your half. It was sent back to you, just like I said it would be."

Now it was Pope's turn to smile in a weak, thin-lipped manner. "Sure it was. By carrier pigeon, I suppose?"

"No, by his two sons," Barnes said with a nod toward Boggs. "After we made the deal. Hoss there paid for half of the herd, which was to be sent back to you, and I kept my half of the stock and threw it in with his cattle as an investment."

"He's right, feller," Boggs snapped. "It happened just like Jake said it did."

"Isn't that sweet?" Pope said with a chuckle. "One man lies and the other swears to it. The Lord don't look kindly on liars, Jake, and neither do I."

"So you're a God man now, huh, Tom?"

"That I am. And when I finish my business with Jake Barnes, I'm gonna give my life up to the service of the Almighty."

"What I'm tellin' you is the truth, Tom. I did send that money back with Hoss's two sons."

"Then what happened to it?"

"Beats hell out of me. If we could find Daniel and Martin, we'd ask them."

A cunning look came into Pope's gray eyes, and he shook his head. "What good would that do? Even if you sent that money with them, which I doubt, it's gone now and I'm left with nothing. Except the price on your head." Pope wagged the barrel of the Buntline toward the door. "Let's go, Jake. We've got a long ride ahead of us."

"Sure, Tom, have it your way," Barnes said with another shrug. "See you, Hoss, Tim." He stepped to the doorway while Pope moved around the table, then, spinning to his left, he ducked out of sight, and drawing his Colt and firing in the same instant, his bullet smashed through the windowpane and tore into Pope's chest.

A surprised look filled the tall man's eyes while his Buntline tilted forward and dangled from a stiff finger by the trigger guard. Splintered glass sprayed around the room while Pope hung there, seemingly suspended by invisible wires, until he slowly folded up like a marionette and crumpled to the floor. Both Tim and Boggs were too stunned to move, but Barnes darted back inside with his gun cocked and held before him. Then he slowly lowered the hammer, holstered the gun, and moved forward to kneel beside Pope and gently roll him onto his back.

"Tom? Can you hear me, Tom?"

Blood bubbled from the hole in the old man's chest, but his eyes fluttered open and he tried to focus on the face above him. "Guess . . . guess you were right . . . Jake. Too . . . too old for this bus . . . business anymore."

"Tom, listen to me. I did send that money. I want you to know that."

The eyes closed once before slowly opening halfway again, and a pained smile crossed Pope's lips. "I believe you did, Jake. I've got no hard . . . no hard feelings toward you. I just wish . . ."

The eyes closed to narrow slits, Pope's head tilted sideways, and he was dead.

Barnes' head slowly turned upward toward Boggs, who had not yet moved. "Damn your two boys, Hoss. They took Tom's money. Now they'll have to face me, as will you if you side with 'em."

"Now hold on a minute, Jake. There must be an explanation of some kind."

"You call it an explanation. I'll call it a lie."

Timmy's eyes were locked on his father's face as well. "Did you know those were stolen cattle, Pa?" he asked softly.

"Well, I . . . well, Timmy . . . I . . ."

Barnes' face was hard and he stood slowly with his hand drooping toward his Colt. "Don't lie to the boy, Hoss. I thought he knew."

"Well, the subject never really came up."

"He knew, Tim," Barnes said without taking his eyes off Boggs. "Leastwise, he didn't ask any questions. An experienced cattleman like your pa couldn't of helped but know. We were goin' to unload the whole Mexican herd this fall on the Eastern market, where nobody would be the wiser."

Tim shook his head in disbelief. "I can't believe it, my own father a cattle thief! And to think I felt a little shame about marrying an Indian girl!"

The words came out before Tim could stop them, and Boggs bolted to his feet. "You *what*?"

"That's right, Pa," Tim said evenly. "I'm going to marry Kita Wak, Red Hawk's daughter."

"You little whelp!" Boggs raged, lunging toward Timmy. "No son of mine is going to marry no Indian! Not while I'm alive!"

Boggs' fist reared back to strike, but stopped at the deadly sound of Barnes' voice. "Touch that boy again, Hoss, and you won't be alive to worry about it."

Both men looked at Barnes, and it was obvious he had meant what he said. His fingers hovered over the grips of his Colt. "You want to beat on somebody that deserves beatin', Hoss, find the other two. I'll gladly help you with that."

"What the hell's goin' on around here?" Boggs asked in dismay, lowering his fist and reaching for the whiskey bottle. He tilted it to his mouth, drank deeply, then wiped his lips in disgust.

Boots clattered on the porch, and a hired hand named Williams burst through the door. He glanced once at Pope and then his eyes sought out Boggs.

"Hoss, there's a man outside who says he wants to talk to

you. Says his name's McFarland. He's got four riders with him and looks to be a buff hunter to me."

"What the hell's he want?" Boggs growled.

"Didn't say," Williams replied.

"What in the jumped-up Jesus is goin' on around here?" Boggs asked again as he stamped toward the door.

McFarland sat his mount before the porch, and watched the big man stride from the building to stand on the top step with his hands on his hips.

"I'm Sam Boggs. What's your business with me?" he demanded.

McFarland smiled. "Evenin', Mr. Boggs. Right pleased to make your acquaintance."

"Cut the bullshit. State your business."

"Glad to." There was almost a twinkle of delight in McFarland's eyes. "I reckon you been lookin' for your boys?"

"I have. What about it?"

"Thought you might be. I know where you can find 'em."

"Get on with it, man! Where?"

"At the crossin' where the creek feeds into the Wahilla Reservation near the northeast corner of your property." McFarland smiled again, picked something from his nose with a dirty finger, wiped his hand on his shirt, then said flatly, "They're dead."

"What? You can't be talkin' true, mister," Boggs said, glowering into the darkness while taking a threatening step downward.

"I am for a fact. And I know who done it."

Boggs stopped on the bottom step with a jolt. "Who?"

"Seen it with my own eyes," McFarland said while a gleeful giggle tickled his throat. "Sure did, seen it with my own eyes."

"Who, dammit, man! Who killed my sons?"

"The Arapaho. Must've been ten of 'em. Took your boys by ambush. They didn't fire a shot, didn't have a chance."

Even in the dark, McFarland could see the burning hatred in Boggs' eyes. The Scotsman touched the brim of his hat with the tips of two fingers while turning his horse away. "'Night, Mr. Boggs. Happy huntin'."

Boggs stared after the retreating riders until they were swallowed by the darkness, then turned and walked back into the house on numbed legs. Barnes and Tim had been standing behind him, and they too went inside, followed by the hired hand.

Boggs sank into a chair and stared blindly at the tabletop while the rage built in him. "Williams?" he finally said, without looking up.

"Yeah, Hoss?"

"Go back to the bunkhouse. Tell the boys we got a war on our hands. I want every man armed to the teeth, with plenty of extra ammunition. Tomorrow mornin' I want all of you to fan out to the other homesteads hereabouts. Tell every rancher you can find what happened to Daniel and Martin, and tell 'em to be here by daybreak, day after tomorrow. Tell 'em we're gonna wipe those goddamned Arapaho out, once and for all. Now git!"

"Sure will, Hoss," Williams replied, sprinting toward the door.

The room was silent for nearly a minute before Tim said softly, "You know Dan and Martin killed Gray Wolf, don't you, Pa? He was Red Hawk's son."

"Damn your Injun-lovin' hide, boy! You don't know that for true!"

"I do, Hoss," Barnes said quietly. "Dan told me about it. He thought it was kinda funny, as a matter of fact."

Boggs spoke slowly, grimly. "I don't give a damn who they killed. I only care about who killed *them*. And, day after tomorrow, I'm gonna get even."

Tim stared at his father momentarily before spinning on his heel and running out the door.

"Where you goin', boy?" Boggs roared.

The only answer was the drumming of hooves on packed earth.

eleven

It would have been difficult to find a less enthusiastic man in all of Wyoming Territory than Larry Watkins as he angled his horse toward the Wahilla Reservation with the first tinge of pink touching the eastern horizon. The color of the dawn sky made him think of blood, and he wished he were anywhere other than on his way to meet with Red Hawk to tell him of the chief's daughter's injury. He was entertaining serious doubts regarding the merits of his occupation, and suffering the discomfort of a hangover which, in his opinion, was one of stellar magnitude, and made each step his horse took a painful ordeal.

And when he crossed the reservation line, the sight of two warpainted braves approaching on galloping ponies did little to cheer him. They turned in front of Watkins' mount and stopped.

"Good morning," he said pleasantly, trying to ignore the fact that his hat had suddenly become too tight for his head. The two Arapaho stared at him silently, ominously, and Watkins felt a tingle run through his scalp.

"I am here to speak with Chief Red Hawk," he managed, striving for an authoritative tone and failing.

Neither warrior spoke, but only continued to watch him impassively, and Watkins found himself wondering if they ever blinked their eyes. Then he wondered why in hell he would be thinking about a thing like that at a time like this.

Searching his mind for another approach, Watkins said quickly, like a drowning man clutching at a straw, "I come in peace."

The warrior to the left merely nodded and turned his pony in indication that Watkins should follow, which Larry did, while the other Indian fell in behind him.

Watkins had noticed the rifles lying across their laps and while the tingle quit his scalp to shiver down his spine, a sudden hatred for Matt Kincaid filled his brain. "This is not for me," he mumbled. "Being an Indian agent is bad enough, but being cannon fodder is out of the question. Or was," he added as an afterthought.

The lead brave turned to stare back at Watkins, and Larry smiled weakly. "Just warming up," he said with a limp shrug.

The warrior turned back and urged his mount to a gallop, the very thing that Larry had tried to avoid on his ride out from the agency, but he had no choice other than to kick the flanks of his horse. The gelding responded, and Larry held onto the saddle horn while hard leather slapped against his butt. "That's all right, horse," Watkins said in a low moan, "I don't like you, either."

Wisps of smoke from several campfires drifted aimlessly on the thin morning air, and the smell of boiling meat wafted on the breeze as they rode into Red Hawk's camp. At least fifty braves were seated around a larger, central fire, and all of them wore green-and-white paint smeared across their faces. Remembering his mission, Larry closed his eyes and wished he were delivering anything, even a case of syphilis, instead of the message he had to relay. The warrior to the rear grunted and motioned with his rifle barrel that Watkins should step down, which he did while the braves slipped from their ponies' backs. With a warrior flanking him on either side, Larry was escorted to the side of the fire away from the smoke, where Red Hawk was seated. Some words were spoken in rapidfire Arapaho before the chief looked up at the uneasy agent.

"You have something to say to me?"

"Yes, yes, I have." He could feel the weight of fifty pairs of unfriendly eyes on his face, and he felt a sudden desire to have to go to the toilet, but he contained the impulse and tried to concentrate on what he would say. "I am the Indian agent...uh, 'er, I represent the United States Government, Bureau of Indian Affairs."

"I know who you are, Mr. Watkins," Red Hawk said in a tone indicating neither welcome nor hostility. "You have come to Wahilla land at an unfortunate time. We are preparing to avenge the death of my son at the hands of white people."

Larry swallowed hard. "That's why I'm here, sir. To stop you."

"To stop us?" Red Hawk asked with an easy smile. "You, alone, are going to stop us?"

"Well, I...I didn't mean it exactly like that. I'm here to try and talk you out of it."

Red Hawk shook his head almost sadly. "There is no more time for talk. My warriors will wait no longer. This is the morning of the fourth day."

"I know that, Chief," Larry said quickly. "And that's why I was asked to come here."

"By whom?"

"By Lieutenant Kincaid."

"He has found the killers?"

"No, no, he hasn't."

Red Hawk looked into the distance. "Then we have nothing to talk about."

"Yes we do, sir. Something very important." Larry knew exactly what a condemned man felt like when asked to say his final words. He hesitated several seconds before clearing his throat and saying, "Your daughter is wounded and she might die."

Red Hawk's eyes snapped to the agent's face. "Kita Wak?"

"If that is her name."

"How do you know this?"

"Because she is at Outpost Number Nine right now, with a stab wound in her stomach."

"Who did this?"

"According to my understanding, sir, she did it to herself. That's what Lieutenant Kincaid said. He also asked me to tell you that she is asking for you and her mother." Larry could almost feel the blazing heat in Red Hawk's eyes and he swallowed hard again to try and clear what felt like a ball of cotton from his throat. "If you have the time, Red Hawk," he added weakly.

"There is no reason for Kita Wak to stab herself, Mr. Watkins."

"Apparently she didn't see it that way, sir. But don't ask me, I only know what the lieutenant told me."

"These things you say are true?"

"By God, they'd better be!"

After staring at the horizon again for long moments, Red Hawk rose to his feet in a single motion and, turning toward a tipi, called several words in strong Arapaho.

The flap moved to one side and a middle-aged woman, obviously beautiful in youth but now thickening with age, stepped out. Concern was written on her face as Red Hawk continued to speak in his native tongue. The woman nodded and ducked back inside, and Red Hawk turned to his warriors and spoke a lengthy phrase before turning to Watkins again.

"We will go to see her."

"That's nice, Chief," Larry said, extending his hand. "Have a good trip and—"

"You will go with us."

"I will?"

"Yes you will. You will be our . . . what is the word?"

"Hostage?" Larry asked, hoping he might be wrong.

"That's it, hostage. If Kita Wak dies, or is harmed in any way other than that of which you speak, you will die."

Instinctively, Larry tried to back away, but his path was blocked by the braves who had closed in behind him. "Now look, Chief. I'm not involved in this at all. In fact, I didn't even want to come here, but—"

"You will go," Red Hawk said with finality. "There is no more time for talk."

"Goddamn you, Kincaid," Watkins said as he was led to his horse.

Colonel Melvin Cooper stalked before Captain Conway's desk like a tiger on a leash, and the cigar in his mouth appeared to be large enough to have been a third arm. He was a small man, not quite tiny, but small enough for his tailored uniform to provide him with an uncanny resemblance to a toy soldier. One hand was pressed to the small of his back while the other reached up to grasp the smoldering log protruding from his mouth. It might not have been fair to accuse Cooper of having a "little man" complex, but at five foot six, he carried a chip on his shoulder large enough for anyone under the rank of colonel to clearly visualize. The pencil-thin mustache above his lip appeared to have been painted on with black ink, and his thin hair was slicked back with enough pomade to grease a wagon wheel. He paused from his pacing long enough to snatch the brandy decanter from Conway's desk, take a sip, and then resume his marching.

"It's not good, Captain. Not good at all," he said around the puffs of smoke escaping his thin lips. He turned to cut another swath past Conway's desk and looked at him with indulgent eyes. "Not that I don't understand your problems here, but I don't like it one bit."

Knowing that Colonel Cooper was a man thoroughly in sympathy with Phil Sheridan's way of thinking regarding the Indians, Conway flicked an ash from his cigar and smiled while leaning back in his chair.

"What don't you like, Colonel?"

"Anything. Everything. Nothing. I was sent here by the inspector general to determine why your command received such low grades in your battlefield-readiness report, and what I find is an army outpost barely equipped to fight an insurrection at the local orphanage, let alone a full-scale Indian war."

"There are copies of all my requisition forms and correspondence regarding that matter in this folder." Conway took it up and waved it once before dropping it on the desktop. "And you're more than welcome to look at them again if you so choose."

Cooper waved his cigar in impatient disgust. "I've seen the damned things, all two hundred of them, or however many there are. I have no desire to look at them again."

"Very well, sir. But they do indicate that we've asked, time and again, for the supplies and replacements we need, to no avail. If we are to maintain this command in the state of readiness desired by the inspector general, this will have to become more than a one-way flow of communication. We need new rifles, preferably repeating Spencers, extra ammunition for weapons qualification, boots, saddles—not to mention men to wear them and sit in them—mounts, clothing, rations, to receive our pay on time, and on and on it goes. You can inspect me all you want, Colonel, but you'll never see any more than what regimental headquarters sees fit to equip my men with."

Cooper nodded and puffed on his cigar. "You have to understand, Captain, these are tough times financially. We all have to tighten our belts until Congress approves some additional military funding."

"Easy Company has gone to the last notch on that belt-tightening you mention, Colonel. We have tightened beyond the point of combat efficiency, and if it weren't for the quality of my men—officers, noncoms, and privates alike—this outpost would stand for nothing more than a mockery of what an army installation is supposed to represent."

"Those are hard words, Captain," Cooper said, trying to drop his high voice to a menacing level. "I am a fair man, but I'll not brook insubordination."

Conway would have laughed, had it not been for his military training. "Insubordination? Since when, sir, is the truth regarded as insubordination?"

A tiny pout formed on the Colonel's lips. "It's not *what* you said, Captain, it's the way you said it."

"Forgive me, sir. But I'm sick of this entire supply-and-pay problem, and as far as I'm concerned, the chain of command is as worthless as tits on a stud mule, if you'll pardon my saying so."

"Captain," Cooper said with an indulgent smile, "there is no such thing as a stud mule."

"Exactly my point. If there isn't any such thing as a stud mule, what in hell's name is it doing with tits?"

Cooper nodded, as though his military mind had grasped the comparison. "Of course."

Conway continued, "We are being required to do a job here that few units in this man's army could accomplish, even *with* the proper supply channels. It's damned well high time Easy Company was given first nod on a few of these requisitions and troop levies that come down, and to hell with the damned garrison troops back in Washington."

As though suddenly weary of it all, the colonel sank into a chair and crossed his stubby legs. "Your command did stand a good inspection, from a presentation point of view," he allowed almost reluctantly.

"These inspections, in and of themselves, are ridiculous, Colonel, as I'm sure a man of your obvious intelligence is well aware. It's like inspecting a robin's nest for eggs in mid-November. What the hell do you expect to find?" Conway was warming to his subject, and he knew he was treading on thin ice, but he wanted to have his say at any cost. "I've got a unit in the field right now, my first platoon, with the finest officer I've ever known in command, First Lieutenant Matt Kincaid. But the replacements we received to fill out that platoon would better have been sent to cooks' and bakers' school instead of a mounted infantry unit! What we need are competent men, well trained and armed with the best weapons available, to complement an officer of Kincaid's stature. But what do we get? The rejects from every outfit that hasn't fired a single shot in anger since the Civil War, if even then."

"Yours is not the only command in the United States Army, Captain. Please keep that in mind."

Conway leaned back in his chair and took a deep drag on his cigar, then let the smoke trickle out, before saying, "Have you ever faced a tribe of Indians, painted for war, ready for battle and suicidal without doubt, like the Cheyenne, perhaps?"

Cooper shifted uncomfortably in his chair. "No, unfortunately I haven't. My considerable logistical skills have taken me into other arenas of combat."

"Like inspecting this outpost, Colonel?" Conway asked.

Cooper sighed heavily. "Yes, like inspecting this outpost and others just like it. It's a thankless job, Captain, but somebody has to do it."

"I understand that, sir. But just once, just one time, you should hear the war scream of an Arapaho, Sioux, Cheyenne, whatever, bent on killing and heedless of death. It's a blood-curdling thing, Colonel, especially when you know your men are ill-equipped, poorly trained, underpaid, and usually misfits recruited from among the most unruly of civilian riffraff. Their survival, and your own as well, rests entirely in your hands and the decisions you make. And then, later, when your unit doesn't pass an IG combat-readiness inspection, you have to wonder why. Who gives a shit? My men, and others like them, prove themselves in the field, Colonel, not standing in front of a bunk. Sure, inspections are necessary, but needless inspections certainly are not."

The conversation had taken a turn that Colonel Cooper had not wished for, and he cleared his throat unnecessarily before saying, "Speaking of Indians, Captain, would you mind telling me what a naked Indian girl is doing in the bachelor officers' quarters?"

"You must mean Kita Wak."

"I mean whoever that naked Indian girl is who is lying in the bachelor officers' quarters."

"That's Kita Wak. She is the daughter of Red Hawk, one of the proudest chiefs of the entire Arapaho nation."

Cooper smiled derisively. "So much for her credentials, Captain. You still haven't explained what the hell she's doing there."

Conway studied the senior officer closely. "She just might be preventing a war, sir, at the most. At least, we are trying to save her life."

"Come now, Captain. What ever happened to herbs and spice and everything nice that the Indians are supposed to be so damned proud of? We have to help the poor red men, of course, but we don't need to baby them. Why can't her people take care of her? And what, heaven forbid, would happen if we had a need for those quarters for officers of senior rank passing through this area?"

Conway rose angrily and poured a drink from the brandy decanter. "They can sleep on the fucking *ground* for all I care. And they will too, before that Indian girl is moved."

Even the eagles on his shoulder boards seemed to cringe while Cooper stared up at the towering captain, and his voice was barely above a whisper as he tried to regain the position that was his by rank. "This is not a rest home for wandering Indians, Captain. It is supposed to be a military installation."

Anger flashed in Conway's eyes and he turned sharply toward the colonel. "Nor is it a funeral parlor, Colonel. That girl didn't wander in here. She was brought by the son of a homesteader. The *white* son of a *white* homesteader."

"What in the world would a white boy be doing—"

"He loves her, Colonel. And he got her pregnant."

"Good God, man!" Cooper exploded, jumping to his feet, the top of his head coming level with Conway's broad shoulders. "We can't have that!"

"We're not being asked to have it, sir," Conway said with a wry smile. "The girl is."

The captain's droll remark sailed right over Cooper's head. "Think of the consequences, man!"

"I have, and that's why she's being medically treated to the best of our limited ability. I'd have gotten the regimental surgeon out here if I thought he would come, but I'm sure he, like the rest of them, would just be glad to know that she's about to become *a good Indian*. So a couple of the wives, mine and Sergeant Cohen's, with help from Sergeant Rothausen, my mess sergeant, are doing the best they can to keep her a *live* Indian."

"And what if she dies here, Captain? What if this Chief Red . . . Red Bird or whatever . . ."

"Red Hawk."

"Red Hawk. What if he finds out? What happens then?"

"We'll have to play it one card at a time. If Red Hawk doesn't know about his daughter already, he will soon enough. Kincaid will see to that."

"Kincaid? Lieutenant Kincaid? Why in hell's name would he do a thing like that?"

The smile forming on Conway's lips was not one of cordiality. "Because he respects Red Hawk as a man first, an Arapaho second. The man has a right to know his daughter's life is in danger."

Cooper shook his head in dismay. "I don't understand, Captain. I just don't understand."

"I know you don't, and you never will as long as your only concern is how much dust a white glove can collect. You administrative people, no matter what your rank, haven't got the slightest idea of what we're dealing with out here, Colonel. We see the Arapaho as people, human beings, not animals to be slaughtered like—"

An urgent pounding rattled the captain's door. "Yes?" Conway asked.

"Sergeant Cohen, sir. Excuse the interruption, but I think we've got a problem on our hands."

"A problem? What kind of problem?"

"A big problem, sir. Red Hawk is waiting outside the front gate. He's got fifty warriors with him and they're all painted up for the path."

"Thank you, Sergeant," Conway said calmly. "I'll be right out."

"Painted up for the path, Captain?" Cooper asked with widening eyes. "What did he mean by that?"

"Warpaint, Colonel. Red Hawk is going on the warpath.

I'd say your inspection of this facility is officially over, sir. Now you just might have the opportunity to look down the barrel of a gun. With your permission, sir?"

Conway pulled on his hat as he stepped into the sunlight, then crossed the parade with ground-eating strides. Behind him, walking quickly with an occasional hopping skip, Colonel Cooper scurried along, his dress saber nearly dragging the ground.

Red Hawk, his wife, and Larry Watkins sat their horses side by side in front of the gate. The warriors were arrayed in a single rank some fifty yards away. Immediately behind Watkins, a warrior waited with his rifle loosely aimed at the agent's back.

Conway couldn't help noticing how magnificent and fierce Red Hawk looked, mounted on a splendid black and white war pony. Green and white paint zigzagged down his face like lightning. Twin eagle feathers hung limply from his braided hair in the absence of wind, and Conway mentally compared him with the image of the same bird perched upon Cooper's tiny shoulders.

Just before they got to the gate, the Colonel caught up with Conway and panted up toward his ear, "Warpaint is illegal, by terms of the treaty."

Conway's eyes held on Red Hawk's face and he continued to walk. "A lot of things are illegal by terms of that goddamned treaty, Colonel. Like not providing the supplies promised to the Arapaho."

"You'll have to arrest him, Captain."

"Like hell I will."

"I order you to."

"The hell with your orders, sir. I am in command here, and unless you wish to relieve me of that command, you'll abide by my decisions."

Conway stopped abruptly and the little colonel bumped into him before backing two steps away.

"Why are we stopping, Captain?"

"To get one thing straight. Are you relieving me of my command, Colonel? If so, you go out and arrest Red Hawk."

Cooper's eyes went immediately to the Arapaho chieftain, and as quickly back to Conway's face.

"No, Captain."

"No, what, sir?"

"No, I'm not relieving you of command."

"Good. Then keep your mouth shut and listen. You might learn something," Conway said, turning again toward the gate.

It was impossible to tell whether Larry Watkins' body sagged from relief or exhaustion, but whatever it was, he appeared ready to topple from his saddle. He smiled weakly when Conway stopped before the horses, and raised a limp hand.

"Hello, Captain. I'm Larry Watkins. I *used* to be the agent out at the Wahilla Reservation."

"Nice to meet you, Mr. Watkins," Conway said, ignoring the hand Watkins now offered, while his eyes remained on Red Hawk's face. "I am Captain Conway, commander of Outpost Number Nine."

The Arapaho nodded. "I am Red Hawk, son of Red Eagle. I am chief of the Wahilla Arapaho."

"I'm pleased to meet you, Red Hawk. I have heard many good things about you from Lieutenant Kincaid. You and your people are welcome here."

"Thank you, Captain. We do not come here to make war with you. This man"—he inclined his head slightly toward Watkins—"has told me that my daughter, Kita Wak, is here. Is this true?"

"Yes, it is true."

"And that she has been injured?"

"She has."

"Is she dead?"

"No but she is very ill. I cannot promise that she will live but we are doing the best we can for her."

Red Hawk nodded again, but his face remained impassive. "Thank you, Captain. Beside me is my wife, Nona Wak. She would like to see her daughter."

"Of course," Conway said, stepping aside and brushing the colonel back with a sweeping motion of his arm. "Please enter. I will take you to her myself."

"The agent will wait here with Running Fox until I return."

If Larry could have slumped any deeper into his saddle, he would have done so, but as it was, he merely stared at the captain with pleading eyes.

Conway glanced once at Larry, then back to the Arapaho. "Whatever you wish, Red Hawk. Please follow me."

The bright sunlight brought out the deepest hues of Conway's polished black boots and dark blue uniform with light blue piping, which contrasted with the dull brown of the parade he was now crossing with the two Indians walking their ponies behind him. He stopped in front of the bachelor officers' quarters and turned toward Red Hawk.

"Kita Wak is inside here, first room to the right. She slips in and out of consciousness, so I don't know if you'll be able to talk to her or not."

Red Hawk and his wife slipped from their ponies' backs, and with the chief in the lead, they followed Conway into the building.

For a man so fat and generally given to temper tantrums, Dutch Rothausen's fingers worked deftly as he tied the last knot of the clean bandages in place. Flora dabbed at the Indian girl's forehead with a cool, damp cloth, while Maggie folded new wrappings off to one side. All three of them looked up when Conway and the two Arapaho stepped into the room.

"How is she, Dutch?" the captain asked his mess sergeant. "Any change?"

"Not much, Captain. She's opened her eyes a couple of times and stared straight ahead, but she never says nothin'. One good thing, though, the fever broke about an hour ago."

Conway turned to the Indians behind him. "These are Kita Wak's parents, Red Hawk and Nona Wak. Red Hawk, I'd like you and your wife to meet my wife, Flora, Maggie Cohen, and Sergeant Rothausen."

All parties nodded cordially, with the exception of Nona Wak, who moved cautiously to her daughter's side. The girl was beautiful as she lay there with her bronze skin surrounded by a fresh, white pillowcase while her brushed, shining hair flowed on either side of her head like twin black rivers. Her eyes were closed, and her long, slightly upturned eyelashes nearly touched her high cheekbones.

Nona Wak touched the girl's face gently before turning back the single blanket and top sheet to study the bandages. Her lips worked in a barely audible singsong chant until her hands went to Kita Wak's lower stomach. The movement of her hands and the chant stopped instantly while she listened to the girl's womb with her fingertips. There was a grave look in her deep brown eyes as she turned to face Red Hawk and speak to him in Arapaho.

A pang of anguish crossed the chief's face in that single,

unguarded moment, and his eyes went to his daughter's face. Then any hint of emotion was gone and he looked across at Conway. "Who brought her here?"

Fearing for Tim's safety, Conway decided not to tell any more than he had to. "A young man. A white man. I'm not at liberty to tell you his name right now, but he has promised to tell you all he knows about this. All I know is that he says Kita Wak stabbed herself, that he loves her, and that she loves him. Anything else he has to say, you'll have to hear from him."

A hardness tightened the chief's face. "Why can't you tell me his name?"

"Because he is a good man and deserves the right to tell you of his involvement with Kita Wak at the time and place of his choosing."

"I understand. We will go now."

Flora moved forward and placed her hand on Nona Wak's arm. "Nona Wak, you are welcome to stay here as our guest until your daughter has recovered. She can't be moved just yet, and I know it would help her regain her strength if she knew her mother was by her side."

There was no hint of understanding on Nona Wak's face as she looked into Flora's compassionate eyes.

"Does your wife speak English, Red Hawk?" Conway asked quietly.

"She does."

"Fine, thank you. Go ahead, Flora."

Flora smiled pleasantly and squeezed the Indian woman's arm ever so gently. "We wish your daughter no harm, only health and happiness. We feel the same toward you. A cot will be put up in this room for you, so you won't have to leave her except when you wish. Your meals will be brought to the room for you, and if you need anything else, all you have to do is ask."

There was still no outward sign of emotion, but a hint of warmth came into Nona Wak's eyes.

"Please," Flora said. "Won't you stay? Do it for me as well as your daughter. I would like to get to know you and to understand your ways."

Red Hawk spoke swiftly in Arapaho, and Nona Wak's head nodded slightly.

"She will stay. I must go now," Red Hawk said, turning toward the doorway and striding toward his pony.

Conway followed the Indian outside and watched in silence as he swung up on the horse's back. Red Hawk pulled up on the hackamore and then looked down at the officer.

"Thank you, Captain, for all your kindness. You have saved my daughter's life, and I will not forget that."

"Where are you going now, Red Hawk?"

The chief's lips tightened. "To do what I must."

"And that is?"

"To avenge the death of my son Gray Wolf."

"Lieutenant Kincaid will find the killers and bring them to justice. He's already promised you that."

"No. His three days passed with the rising of this morning's sun. There is no more time. My people will wait no longer."

"Then your people are wrong, Red Hawk. You came here in peace and my soldiers will not try to stop you. But it is foolish to allow more blood to be shed between our two peoples."

"Blood has already been shed, Captain. That of my son. I will do what I must."

Their eyes locked in silent understanding for several seconds before Red Hawk pulled up on the hackamore again and the horse backed away. "The agent is yours. I have no more use for him."

The pony whirled on its hind legs and galloped toward the main gate, and Conway saw the warrior who had been holding his gun trained on Watkins' back turn his mount and follow Red Hawk.

Larry turned weakly in the saddle and watched the war party race across the plains, before sinking slowly to one side and toppling from his saddle.

Colonel Cooper's head jerked from Conway to the fallen man and then to the receding warriors. Then, making a decision, he ran across the parade as fast as his stubby legs would carry him, while his right hand tried to control the bouncing saber by his side.

"They're getting away, Captain! They're getting away!" he yelled, stumbling and falling flat on his stomach before leaping up again. "Mount the company and go after them!"

Conway said as he passed the colonel, walking in the direction of Watkins, "You go after them if you want, Colonel. My troops are staying here. Excuse me, there's an injured man over there."

Dumbfounded, Cooper could only stare at the captain's back, seemingly mindless of the thick layer of dust covering the front of his otherwise impeccable uniform.

twelve

They were not tidy packages, the two lifeless forms spread on the ground and covered with dull gray army blankets. As rigor mortis had had plenty of time to set in, they lay there with arms and legs stiffened in odd and awkward positions, so that the blankets covering them bulged in grotesque shapes. Saddles, bridles, and other riding gear were stacked nearby, and the stench of rotting buffalo carcasses was carried strongly on the morning breeze. In the distance lay two more corpses, disfigured by bloating and stiff in death, waiting only to become carrion for the creatures of the prairie. The two horses had been dragged away from the streambed by a detail from First Platoon, and now, as the troopers were forming ranks again for the day's patrol, Windy Mandalian glanced upward at the hard blue sky.

A dozen or more black objects circled in patient orbits on motionless wings while lowering slowly toward the feast spread across the plains, and waiting for the living, moving figures below to depart.

"Never could figure out how in hell they do that, Matt," Windy muttered absently.

"Figure out who does what?" Matt replied without looking up from the cinch strap in his hands.

"Those damned buzzards. Gotta be the laziest sons of bitches on God's green earth. Never move their wings, never do a damned thing but coast around up there in the sky all day and wait for some poor bastard to break his neck. They gotta get up there some way, but I'll bet you a dollar the lazy bastards don't fly. Must be a big high rock around here somewhere that they just jump off of."

Matt turned with a grin. "How do they get up on the rock?"

"Ain't got that figured yet," Windy said, giving up on the buzzards. "But however they do it, you can bet the lazy assholes don't walk."

"I didn't know buzzards upset you so much, Windy."

"Well, Matt, I ain't gettin' no ulcers over it, they just kinda piss me off. Got it too damned easy, that's all. I wonder who eats the buzzards when they cash in. Or maybe they just don't die."

Kincaid lowered the stirrup and adjusted the foot iron. "Don't see a lot of dead ones lying around. What the hell are you so speculative about this morning?"

"Nothin'," Windy replied, biting off a chunk of tobacco for his first chew of the day. "Like I said, buzzards just kinda piss me off. Where we goin' now?"

"Much as I hate to do it, I guess we'll have to ride over to the Boggs place and tell the old man about his sons so he can give them a decent burial. I'd do it here, but he might want them closer to home. After that, we'd better find Black Wing damned quick and put some questions in his direction."

"Think Boggs will know it was Arapaho that killed his boys?"

"I hope not. Not yet, anyway."

"If he does, we got war."

"I know that, Windy. That's why we've got to find Black Wing damned quick."

Windy chewed in silent contemplation. "I've been wonderin' about McFarland. He was skinnin' buff damned close to here, as your nose might tell you. Then, yesterday afternoon, we find him cuttin' a trail toward Boggs' place, 'stead of toward town. That strike you as strange?"

"Yes, it did then and it does now. What are you getting at? That maybe he found Daniel and Martin, maybe saw the whole thing, and went to tell Boggs to rile him up?"

A stream of brown juice squirted from Windy's lips before he spoke again. "That's what I'm thinkin'. If he's behind all this, as we both think he is, then who would stand more to gain than him by tellin' Boggs what he wants him to hear? Boggs ain't known for havin' the coolest head in these parts."

"That's an understatement if I ever heard one," Matt said, placing a foot in his stirrup and swinging into the saddle. "Even though I hope you're wrong, your logic sounds accurate as hell. I'm sure we'll find out when we talk to Boggs. Let's go."

The farther the platoon went onto Boggs' land, the more longhorns they saw grazing in the distance. After they had ridden for nearly three hours, Private Callahan moved his horse up from the rear of the column and reined in beside Sergeant Olsen.

"Private Callahan requests permission to speak with the lieutenant, Sergeant."

While Olsen didn't necessarily like the private, he had seen a spark of good soldiering in him on patrol. "Why do you want to see the lieutenant, Callahan?"

Callahan motioned toward a pocket of longhorns no more than fifty yards away. "About them cattle over there, Sarge."

"What about 'em?" Olsen replied, glancing at the stock and shrugging. "They've got horns, four legs, and a tail. Why would that be of interest to the lieutenant?"

Callahan smiled. "The only thing about 'em that wouldn't be of interest is the tail, Sarge. Let me tell it to the lieutenant an' he can do the thinkin' 'twixt his own ears."

"Why not tell me?"

"Why tell it twice?"

"This better be good, Callahan," Olsen said with a glower at the private. "Lieutenant Kincaid!"

Matt turned in the saddle and looked back. "Yes, Sergeant?"

"Private Callahan requests permission to speak with you, sir."

"All right. Send him up here."

"Like I said, Callahan, this had better be damned good. Permission granted."

Callahan grinned easily. "Trust me, Sarge, it will be," he said, urging his horse forward to the head of the column.

Callahan saluted as he came up beside Kincaid.

"What's on your mind, Private?"

"You know I'm a Texas boy, don't you, sir?"

"Yes, I'd heard that."

"Well, I been 'round Texas longhorns since I squeezed past my mama's knees, an' I know a fair bit about 'em."

"That's fine. Now what's your point?"

Callahan pointed toward the pocket of cattle once again. "I'd like to take a little closer peek at them beef over yonder, if you don't mind, sir."

Matt glanced toward the longhorns and then back at Callahan. "Why?"

"Got a hunch, sir. Give me five minutes and I'll tell you somethin' 'bout them cattle that nobody here knows but me."

"What about them?"

"Have I got the five minutes, sir?"

"We're kind of in a hurry here, Private."

"Five minutes, sir. That's all I ask, five minutes."

"Very well, Private," Matt said, raising his hand above his shoulder and stopping the column. "You've got your five minutes."

"Thank you, sir," Callahan said, moving his horse cautiously toward the longhorns to avoid spooking them. He circled slowly around the pocket of cattle, studying them, comparing them, and before his time was up, he cantered back to the lieutenant's side.

"Just like I thought, sir," Callahan said with a bright smile. "Them ain't the real thing."

"Had me fooled," Windy said with a chuckle. "I'd of swore those were cattle."

Matt watched Callahan closely. "What do you mean, they're not the real thing?"

"Windy's right, Lieutenant. They *are* cattle, jus' not the right kind."

"I'm listening."

Callahan pointed toward the nearest pair. "See them two right there, sir?"

Matt nodded. "What about them?"

"See how one's got shorter horns than the other, an' the one on the left is shorter'n the one on the right?"

"I see. Is that unusual?"

"'Pends on what side of the border you're on, sir. The one

on the right is from Texas, sure 'nuff, but the one on the left was stole."

Now Matt looked at the pair with more interest. "Stolen? From where, and how can you tell that by just looking at them?"

"Easy, if you're a Texas boy. An' stole' from where? That's easy too. Mexico."

Kincaid looked over at Windy. "You making any sense out of this, Windy?"

"Yup. The little one over yonder speaks Spanish. That tall feller speaks English. Ask 'em."

"There's more to it than that, Windy," Callahan said with a pleased look on his face. "I been watchin' these beef for better'n an hour now, and I'd say at least a fourth of 'em is Mex-cut."

"What does 'Mex-cut' mean, Private?"

"I'll get to that in a minute, sir, but let me 'splain the difference first. That big one on the right's spread would go maybe six feet from horn tip to horn tip. The other one, maybe four feet at the most. Now in Texas, when a cow drops her calf, usually in early spring, March to May, the calves is castrated no later than the end of May, which makes 'em steers like the two over yonder. It's the early castration what makes the Texas longhorn have such a spread. But with Mex-cut cattle, it's a whole 'nother matter. The calves is allowed to run with their mama till they're weanin' age, about a year later. They ain't castrated until *after* they been weaned and their horns has already commenced to grow. That's why the Texican cows have got a much wider horn span than Mex cows. And that's how I know that at least a fourth of this herd is from Mexico, an' stole for sure."

Matt studied the cattle nearest to them and nodded in agreement. "I'll be damned, Private, I think you're right. I can tell the difference myself, now that you've pointed it out."

"Wouldn't have to point it out to a Texas brand inspector, Lieutenant. He'd spot 'em in a second."

"Is that how you know they're stolen?"

"Partly. Live beef ain't legally allowed across the border 'cause of disease and such, besides the fact that Texas cattlemen don't want no competition from down south. But there's one more thing that points them Mex-cuts up to be hot. Even though both them steers have Double G brands, one of 'em has a little bit tighter curl to the top of the G than the other one. 'Course, you wouldn't be able to tell about that, either, unless you was lookin' for it. A buyer from the East wouldn't know that, sir, and, if the price was right, maybe he wouldn't give a damn anyway. No doubt about it, one out of every four of them steers got their legs wet in the Rio Grande, and likely got some moonlight in their eyes as well."

Matt studied Callahan with new respect. "Are you absolutely certain of all that you've told me, Private? Certain enough to stand up in court and repeat what you've said?"

"I ain't too long on dealin' with the law, Lieutenant, but I'd do it if you *ordered* me to."

Matt smiled at the emphasis on the word 'ordered.' "You will be ordered, when and if the need arises for your testimony. Fall back in ranks now, Private, and thank you very much for coming forward with this information."

The two soldiers saluted smartly. "You're welcome, sir. I wouldn't put myself to the trouble for anybody but you, sir," Callahan said sincerely, before moving his horse along the line.

"So we've finally got somethin' on Boggs, huh, Matt?" Windy said, continuing to stare at the herd.

"Looks like we have, Windy," Matt replied. "But now it doesn't seem as pleasing as it would have before."

"Why's that?"

"Well, two of his sons are dead and the third one is in love with the Indian girl he got in trouble. Seems like a bad run of luck for anybody, even a bastard like Boggs. But I intend to confront him with this stolen-cattle issue. If Callahan is correct, as he seems to be, then maybe we can use that knowledge to take a little of the bark out of Boggs' bite as regards his feud with Red Hawk. On the other hand, if it doesn't, that just gives us another problem to deal with. Let's move 'em out."

It was nearly noon and they were halfway to the Boggs ranch when they saw a rider moving slowly toward them, but off to one side. He was hunched over in his saddle and the horse appeared to be picking its own way across the prairie with no concern for direction.

"That feller looks like he's hurt, Matt. Shall I ride over and check him out?" Windy Mandalian asked, lifting the reins from his horse's neck.

"Yes, do that, Windy," Matt said, halting the platoon once more. "We'll wait here for you. Somehow he looks familiar to me."

140

"I was thinkin' the same thing," Windy replied as he turned his horse to intercept the apparently unconscious rider.

Kincaid watched the scout approach cautiously, lift the revolver from the man's holster, and then raise his head up to study his face. Windy gently freed the reins from the rider's tight grip and led the horse toward the waiting Kincaid.

"Who is he, Windy?" Matt called as the scout neared.

"Don't rightly know, Matt, but he's one of McFarland's men. He's hurt purty bad, but still alive. Got a bullet through his back and out the right side."

Kincaid jumped from his horse and moved forward quickly to help lower the man to the ground. "Bring that horse around here to give him some shade, will you Windy?"

"Was just gonna do that, Matt."

"Sergeant Olsen!" Matt called over his shoulder.

"Yessir?"

"Bring the medical kit and a canteen of water on the double."

"Yessir."

While waiting for the medicine and water, Matt tore the man's shirt away and examined the blood-blackened hole in his side. When he looked up, he shook his head; there would be no need for the medical kit.

"Here you are, sir," Olsen said, handing the canteen down and bending to open the satchel.

Kincaid took the canteen while saying, "Thanks, Sergeant, but there's no need to open that. There's nothing we can do for him except try to make him comfortable."

Matt splashed some water on his hand and dampened the man's chapped lips before moistening a piece of shirt and sponging off the rider's forehead.

"What's your name, son?" Matt asked, after listening to the faint heartbeat in the young man's chest.

The man's tongue touched his lips in a quest for more water, and his eyelids fluttered open.

"Water. More water," he moaned in a weak, crackling voice.

"I can't let you drink, but you can suck on this," Matt said, pressing the damp cloth to the man's lips. "You've got a hole in your stomach, and water would do you more harm than good."

The young man tried to nod while sucking greedily at the cloth.

"What's your name and who did this to you?"

141

"My name's Jasper. Curt . . . Jasper."

"Who shot you, Jasper?"

"Stro."

Kincaid looked up at Windy. "Who'd he say?"

"Sounded like 'Stro' to me."

"Tell me again," Matt said, leaning closer. "Who shot you?"

"McFarland. Strother McFarland."

Matt's eyes hardened. "Why did he shoot you, Jasper?"

"Because . . . because I wanted to get away. I don't like what he's doin' no more. He . . . killed Laskey just like he did them cattle and that range hand, 'cept he had to use his knife 'stead of an arrow." Jasper's eyes closed momentarily before opening weakly again. "Can't I have more water, please?"

"Sure, Jasper, sure," Matt replied, soaking the cloth again and returning it to the young man's mouth. "Did you say McFarland shot Dowler and those cattle?"

"Yup, he did. And . . . and he killed Laskey for no reason a-tall. 'Cept he gave him a Sioux arrow 'steada Arapaho. That ain't no reason to kill a man, is it, Lieutenant?" Jasper asked, turning to look up at Kincaid's face.

"No, Jasper, it isn't. When did McFarland do this to you?"

"Last . . . last night. We went to the Boggs place so Stro could tell him 'bout the killin' of his boys. Stro said he saw Arapaho doin' it, but he was lyin'. He was skinnin' buff with us when it happened."

"But he told Boggs he saw the Arapaho do it? Why?"

" 'Cause . . . 'cause he said if we could get them to fightin', we'd have the buff all to ourselves. But I didn't like what he did to Frank. Laskey was my friend and I didn't like it. After we . . . we left Boggs' place, I tried to get away. It was dark and I thought I could make it, but Stro, damn him, he's got eyes in the back . . . back of his head." Jasper grimaced in pain and Kincaid knew it had to be torturous for the man to try and talk.

"Just take it easy, Jasper. Just take it easy."

Jasper looked up again, and his eyes found Kincaid's face. "I wanted to find you, to tell you the truth 'bout what Stro was doin'. It just ain't right what . . . what Stro's doin'. I . . . ."

Matt patted the young man's shoulder and gazed into the distance. "No, it's not right, Jasper. A lot of innocent people might die because of him." He looked down at Jasper again. "There's not much I can do for you except . . . ."

The young man's eyes stared sightlessly at the sky, and the

sucking sound came no more from the hole in his stomach. Matt gently pushed the man's eyelids closed with the tip of a finger before standing slowly. "Correction, Jasper," he said softly. "There's *nothing* I can do for you."

"Shall I get a burial detail to workin', Lieutenant?" Olsen asked.

"Yes, do that, Sarge."

Kincaid looked across at Windy. "That's three men to McFarland's credit that we know of, Windy, not to mention another three that died because of what he's done."

"Six men and ten cows, plus thirty-five buffalo in four days? That McFarland feller seems to have a hell of a thirst for killin'."

"Yeah, and how many more to come, if we can't stop it before the battle begins?"

"How're we gonna do that, Matt? Red Hawk only gave us three days, we're on the fourth one now, and Boggs already knows about his kids. There's too much wood on the fire, and it looks to me like the stew's about to boil over."

"It is. We've got to catch McFarland and put him between Red Hawk and Boggs. Maybe that way both sides will listen to reason, if they know the one guilty man is going to hang."

"Then we're not going to Boggs' place?"

"No need to, now. Whatever he's going to do, he's already set in motion, I'm sure of that. The same goes for Red Hawk. As soon as that detail finishes burying Jasper, we'll cut cross-country and try to intercept McFarland."

Windy spat out his wad of tobacco and rinsed his mouth with a drink from the canteen. "There's one more feller you haven't mentioned, Matt."

"Who's that?"

"Black Wing. If he killed them two brothers, he just might have a little too much starch in his feathers to settle down easy. Sure, he done it for revenge, but he might feel that two dead men in exchange for his little brother ain't quite enough."

"I know, Windy, but we'll have to take this a piece at a time. Let's get McFarland first, and then worry about Black Wing afterward. If Daniel and Martin *did* kill Gray Wolf, and Black Wing *did* kill them, then I'd say that score's settled."

Windy grinned and squinted toward the sun. "That's a whole passel of ifs, ain't it, Matt?"

"Yeah. It's an iffy damned world."

• • •

The dancing flames of their small fire caused yellow fingers of light to lick and probe the surrounding darkness while the twelve young warriors roasted strips of antelope meat over glowing coals. A bow and a quiver full of variously marked arrows, some red and yellow and others green and white, lay beside Black Wing's right foot, seemingly unnoticed. But when he finished his last bite, he laid his roasting stick aside and took up the quiver.

"Where did you say you found this, Bear Catches Fish?" he asked a brave directly across from him. "Inside a hollow log?"

Bear Catches Fish looked up from the blackened strip of meat in his hands. "Yes, Black Wing. I followed the buffalo hunters as you told me to do, and the small, bearded one hid it there."

"And the bow as well?"

"Yes, the bow as well. It was near their last camp, the one from which they took the thirty-five hides. It was well concealed, covered over with fallen limbs and sticks, and if I hadn't seen him put it there, I would never have found it myself."

"You have done well, Bear Catches Fish. I'm sorry you missed the ambush of the two brothers, but you will not miss the next one."

"Next one?" Crooked Nose asked. "I thought we had avenged the death of Gray Wolf."

The heat in Black Wing's eyes had nothing to do with the fire as he glanced sharply at Crooked Nose. "Those two were strictly in payment for my brother's death. This time we will get the man who caused his death, and he will join those who actually killed him."

It was Crow-in-the-Rain's turn to speak. "Do those arrows tell us who caused Gray Wolf's death?"

"Yes they do. When the Blue Sleeve lieutenant talked with my father, he told him of cattle being killed with Arapaho arrows and the death of a white man by a Sioux war arrow." Black Wing turned the quiver in his hands while he examined the shafts without touching them. "We have no Sioux war arrows, nor does anyone else near the Wahilla Reservation. But now we know who does... or did."

Crooked Nose hesitated before speaking again. "Haven't we done enough, Black Wing? We have already gone against the wishes of our chief."

"And now you wish to go against mine, Crooked Nose?" Black Wing asked, standing slowly and pulling his shoulders back. "My father is not here for you to worry about, but I am. You have three choices, Crooked Nose. Leave us now and go back to my father's camp, stay with us and say nothing to me unless I speak to you, or fight me hand to hand, to the death. Which will it be?"

Crooked Nose tried to match Black Wing's stare, but failed and diverted his eyes and tried to concentrate on his food in silence.

"Which will it be?" Black Wing demanded, his tone growing ever more stern. "Tell me now!"

Crooked Nose glanced up, then back down. "I will stay here," he said just above a whisper. "And say nothing."

"Then you are welcome under those terms," Black Wing replied, sinking again to his crosslegged position on the ground and taking up the bow. "I wonder which of our brothers he killed to get this? And why he wants to start another war between us and the white men?"

"He is a hunter, my friend," Crow-in-the-Rain said. "There are not many buffalo left, and if we are fighting the white men, and they are fighting us, he will have complete freedom to take the remaining few."

"You are wise, Crow-in-the-Rain. But he is not. He is foolish, as most greedy men are. And he will die for it." Black Wing looked at Bear Catches Fish. "Where was the bearded one when you last saw him?"

"I followed them until the sun was at its peak in the sky yesterday, but I had to leave when the Blue Sleeves came. About an hour later, the Blue Sleeves went back toward Big Trees, and the bearded one went in the direction of the flaming-haired white man's house. When they left there, the hunters headed in the direction of the trading post with three packhorses loaded with hides."

Black Wing smiled. "Then that is where they will go. At what time of night was this?"

"The moon was well above the horizon."

"Good, Bear Catches Fish. They could not possibly make it to the trading post in less than two days. We will be waiting for them on the afternoon of their second day, when they think they are safe. But we must ride all night to get there, to where the trail leads through the bluffs. We will go now, and tomorrow Gray Wolf will have his final revenge."

145

Lean and hard, the young warriors moved like mountain cats as they quit their campfire and trotted to their ponies. And when they mounted and rode away, there was no sound except the dull drumbeat of hooves striking grass.

Strother McFarland interrupted his humming long enough to wipe the perspiration from his brow and glance toward the midafternoon sun. His shirt was damp with sweat, but he grinned when he turned to look back at the three riders behind him, each leading a packhorse laden with hides.

"We'll split it four ways instead of six," he said to himself, while trying to remember where he had left off with his tune. "I know I hit that boy real good last night, even if I couldn't find him. But the vultures'll find him, just like that damned Laskey. Neither of 'em was worth more'n buzzard-bait anyway."

He started humming again, and then thought of something. "Jenkins!" he shouted over his shoulder without turning. "Get your worthless ass up here!"

While he waited for Jenkins, McFarland wondered why the others were holding back from him. He hoped it was for the reason he suspected: they were afraid of him. He considered fear to be a much better working tool than praise, and he knew that none of his men would cross him as long as the sight of Laskey's severed throat was still vivid in their minds. He also knew they would never quit him, because their trails would inevitably cross again one day, as was the way with prairie drifters, and when they did, each man knew in his heart that Strother McFarland would kill him without so much as blinking an eye. The men behind the Scotsman were trapped, and the small, bearded man loved it.

"Yeah, Stro? You called me?" Jenkins asked, as he pulled up beside McFarland with the trailing packhorse on lead.

"Weren't callin' yer goddamned mother!" snapped McFarland. "When we get these hides sold, I want you to do somethin' for me."

Jenkins eyed McFarland nervously. "Sure, Stro. You name it and you got it."

"That's a right healthy attitude, Floyd. 'Member the last time we was to town? And that little blond-haired gal down to the whorehouse?"

Jenkins shivered because he did remember, even though he

would rather have forgotten. Her name was Cindy, and while she was rather thin, she was also pretty in a pallid sort of way. But what he remembered most was what McFarland did to her. After taking what he had paid for, McFarland had forced the girl from the room at knifepoint, down the backstairs, and toward the stable, where a young stud donkey was being boarded. Wearing only a nightgown, which the Scotsman had quickly stripped away, the girl had been tied in a prone position on the floor with her legs spread apart. Jenkins had been trying to sleep in the hayloft at the time, and the sound of the animal's braying awakened him in time to see McFarland press his hand against Cindy's crotch and then rub it across the donkey's nose. He could still see the curl of the animal's lips as it sniffed the pungent odor of the woman's sex organs while its huge, dangling penis became hard and erect. And he would never forget McFarland's maniacal laughter as he watched the dumb animal try to mount the terrified young woman, whose screams were muffled by the gag tied around her mouth. Jenkins had shrunk back out of sight as the frenzied donkey sank to its hind knees while probing frantically with the terrible red object, which finally sank home. Jenkins had feared for his life at the time; the mere fact that he was alive was ample evidence that McFarland had not been aware of his presence.

"Yeah, Stro, I remember her," Jenkins said without enthusiasm. "I remember. What about her?"

McFarland chuckled, and his eyes were bright with anticipation. "I had a hell of a good time with that little ol' gal, and I'd like to see her again. But I don't think she'll be wantin' to see me. Guess I gave her more'n she could handle that night, if you know what I mean."

McFarland looked over at Jenkins, and there was a testing hardness in his voice, which became anger after Jenkins' prolonged silence. "You *do* know what I mean?" he demanded.

"Sure, Stro, I know what you mean," Jenkins said quickly, with a forced, nervous chuckle. "You're hell on wheels with your pants down."

"I am, for a fact," McFarland replied, satisfied with the words he'd heard. "Anyway, what I want you to do is buy her a couple o' drinks and then take her to her room. I'll be waitin' there with a little surprise for her."

"Stro, look, I—"

"You what!"

"I don't like to—"

"Do what, Jenkins?" McFarland snarled.

Jenkins fidgeted with the reins in his hand. "Well, Stro, it's not that I—"

McFarland eased the knife from his belt, and its shining blade glinted in the sunlight while he ran a thumb along the steel. "Laskey was a right good friend of yours, weren't he, Jenkins?"

Jenkins tried not to look at the knifeblade, but his eyes would not obey. "He was all right, Stro."

"'Member that new grin I gave him?"

"Sure, I remember. Be purty hard to forget."

"Want one to match?"

"No, Stro, I sure don't."

"Then do as I tell you, with no sass." McFarland glanced toward the sun, and then at the pass between the buttes, which was only perhaps three hundred yards away. "We should be in town by eight, maybe nine o'clock. First thing I want you to do is get that gal for me. I want to see her squirm with just a little bit more peter'n she can handle. You gonna do that for me, ain't ya, Jenkins?" he finished with a challenging stare.

"Sure, Stro, anything you say," Jenkins replied, while his hand massaged his throat and his eyes tore away from the blade. "Just put that damned knife away and I'll do anything you say."

McFarland laughed wildly while sheathing the knife. "Knew I could count on you, Jenkins. We're a hell of a team, you an' me."

"Yeah," Jenkins replied, allowing his horse to fall back with the others again. "A hell of a team."

McFarland was perhaps twenty yards ahead when they entered the canyonlike passage through the buttes and he pulled in his horse and stepped down. The other riders stopped, maintaining the distance between them as their leader unbuttoned his pants and urinated, while massaging his groin.

Even these hard men of the plains felt a sense of revulsion as the little Scot shook his penis one more time than was necessary before beginning to stuff it in his pants again.

During this interlude, no one had noticed the twelve Arapaho ponies, six to the front and six to the rear, suddenly emerge from the shelter of the buttes and block passage in either direction. And there was no point in attempting to draw weapons, because each stone-faced warrior held a rifle in his hands, and there was no doubting their intention to use them.

Black Wing was in the center of the six braves to the front, and he nudged his horse forward with the bow and quiver full of arrows held in one hand.

Forgetting his open fly, McFarland stared, slackjawed, at the Indians, with one hand still inside his pants. The contrast of green and white warpaint on Black Wing's face was intensified by the blazing sun, and his countenance was a mask of hatred.

"Howdy," McFarland said cautiously. "Somethin' I can do for you?"

Black Wing stared down impassively from atop his mount while he held up the objects in his hand. "You lost these," he said without emotion.

McFarland's eyes were riveted to the bow and quiver, but he tore them away to stare at the Arapaho's face, and there was the first hint of fear in his eyes.

"Them ain't mine."

"Yes they are. And by them you will die," Black Wing said, riding past McFarland and toward the others. He stopped in front of Jenkins while his eyes went to each of the riders. "Did you help in this deception against the Wahilla Arapaho?"

"Nossir," Jenkins said quickly, with an affirming glance at the men on either side of him. "All we wanted to do was take a few hides. Ever'thin' else was his idea."

Black Wing watched them in silence for a long moment. "Do you wish to live?"

"Yessir, we sure do," Jenkins replied.

"Do I have your promise never to be seen on or near the Wahilla Reservation again, and that what buffalo remain will be left to the Arapaho people?"

"You got it, mister."

Black Wing looked toward Crow-in-the-Rain, in the center of the rearward six, and nodded. The warrior raised his rifle and fired three quick shots, one each into the necks of the packhorses, and the animals dropped under their heavy loads.

Jenkins and the other two settled their skittish horses down and awaited their fate while Black Wing continued his expressionless stare. "Throw your weapons to the ground."

Colts and Winchesters dropped silently to the grass, while McFarland watched from a distance with widening eyes.

Black Wing nodded. "You three can go," he said softly. "The bearded one will stay with us. If I ever see any of you again, or hear of what is about to happen today, you will suffer the same fate as your friend. Is that understood?"

The three men nodded sharply while Jenkins said, "You got our promise on everything, mister, and believe me, you'll never see any of us again."

Black Wing watched them, and his dark eyes were all the emphasis his threat needed to give it an unfailing quality of truth. "You can go."

"Jenkins! Holland! Fanning!" McFarland screamed as he watched the three riders turn their mounts. "You can't just leave me here!"

"The hell we can't, McFarland," Jenkins called over his shoulder. "You dug your own grave, now sleep well in it."

"You bastards! You dirty bastards!"

"Fuck you, Stro, and your donkey as well," Jenkins said, and the three were gone on horses bolting to a run.

One of the warriors started to dismount to pick up the weapons on the ground, but he stopped with the raising of Black Wing's hand. "Leave them. We came here for only one thing, and that is all we will take."

thirteen _____

"I'm not goin' back, Lieutenant, not for you or nobody else. There ain't enough men in the whole United States Army to make me go back and face what Stro's gotta go through." As if being in the midst of an entire platoon of mounted infantry still was not enough to insure his safety, Jenkins glanced nervously over his shoulder in the direction from which he and the other two skinners had just come. "Them Injuns is painted up for war, and McFarland is gonna be the first to fall. Ol' Bill Jenkins, that's me, ain't got no intention of being the second."

Kincaid watched the three men before him and noted the unanimous expressions of fear on their faces. "Did any of these Indians have a name?"

"Didn't need one," Jenkins said, shaking his head. "Their leader, the one who talked to me, had a look in his eyes that I'll never forget, and I wasn't about to ask no questions."

"How long ago was this, Jenkins?" Windy asked.

"'Bout two, maybe two and a half hours ago."

"Where?"

"At the place where the trail leads into the buttes."

"How many Indians were there?"

"Dozen, at least."

"Sound like Black Wing's band to you, Windy?" Matt asked, turning to look at the scout.

"Could be, Matt. Numbers sound about right."

"That's what I was thinking." Kincaid turned back to the buffalo hunters. "From what I understand, none of you were directly involved in McFarland's overall plan. Is that correct?"

"Sure 'nuff is. Stro's the one what done all the shitty stuff. The three of us was just hired to skin buff for a percentage. Ain't got a damned thing left to show for our work, either," Jenkins finished glumly.

"I think you've gotten everything you deserve, Jenkins," Matt said flatly. "You can go now."

Jenkins glanced over his shoulder once more. "You goin' after them featherheads?"

"We are."

"You didn't see us, remember? We didn't say one damned word to you. Black Wing, or whatever his name is, kinda made a point of tellin' me to remember that."

Kincaid looked at the three men silently, in revulsion, for several seconds. "Like I said," he told them finally, "you can go now."

"And mighty glad to be gone," Jenkins said, turning his horse out and sinking the spurs home.

Kincaid watched the three mounts race across the plains before turning to Windy. "Kind of makes you wonder what it's all about, doesn't it, Windy?"

"Yes it does, Matt. Protecting that kind of scum is the hardest part of this deal. Think we'd better go check out McFarland?"

"Yes," Matt replied while squinting at the lowering sun. "We haven't got a hell of a lot of daylight left, but we'll go as far as we can this evening and then head for the Wahilla Reservation in the morning. We're kind of chasing ghosts here, it seems, and every time we show up someplace, we're a day late and a dollar short."

"Yup. We're definitely a day late as far as your agreement with Red Hawk is concerned. But as far as McFarland goes, time won't be too important to him now."

152

"I suppose you're right, but still, we have to take a look."

"Might be a good sight for those recruits back there to see. They won't be forgettin' it, that's for sure."

Sinking behind low-hanging clouds in the west, the sun was a flaming, blood-red ball on the horizon. The prairie was silent except for the whistle of an increasing wind. Dust eddies swirled off the buttes, and a swarm of flies rose from the dead packhorses as the platoon pulled up beside them. There was an eerie feeling about the quiet in the hushed softness of the spreading sunset.

Kincaid looked at the horses, and then at the weapons laying scattered on the ground. "You think they took McFarland with them, Windy?" he asked, turning in his saddle and searching in all directions for some sign of the little Scotsman.

"Nope. He ain't goin' noplace."

"Then I wonder..."

"Look up there, Matt," Windy said, pointing toward the high ground.

All eyes turned upward in the direction indicated by the scout. There, hanging upside down and stripped to the waist, were the earthly remains of Strother McFarland. He had been tied, spread-eagled, to an outcropping of rock. A single arrow protruded from his lower belly, and from that arrow hung a bow and quiver.

They moved their horses closer to the dead man, and when they did, they could see the blood-matted beard around his face and the blood caked in his hair. But it was the eyes that created the most bone-chilling effect. They stared sightlessly at nothing, and had dried like prunes in the heat of the afternoon sun. They had not blinked, and even if the Scotsman had lived, they would never blink again. The eyelids had been cut away.

"Goddamn!" one of the recruits muttered from back in the ranks. "Wasn't just killin' the poor bastard enough?"

"Not for the Arapaho," Windy replied softly. "He had been a liar in life, and that is their way of making sure his spirit doesn't lie in death."

"What do you mean by that, Windy?" another young soldier asked.

"Look a little closer, and you'll see that his tongue's been cut out too. That's so that his spirit will never talk again. And as for the eyelids? The Arapaho have a saying that goes something like this: 'If the truth is to be seen in the light of day, the eyes must always be open.' They figure McFarland's spirit will see nothin' but the truth from now on. From my point of view, he ain't never gonna see nothin' a-tall again."

"They shot him low with that arrow for a purpose as well," Kincaid offered. "It was his own arrow, and they wanted him to die slowly and painfully, just as they figure the original owner of the bow must have died. They're pretty damned thorough, when it comes to revenge. Remember that, if you ever kill an Arapaho in anything other than honorable combat. And it's not a bad thing to keep in mind if you give one of them your word and don't try to live up to it. Might as well cut him down, Sergeant Olsen, and then have a detail bury him. He doesn't deserve it, but it's regulations."

Timothy Boggs stepped down from his weary mount and knocked on the door of Sergeant Cohen's quarters. He was exhausted and hungry, but he tried to smile when Maggie opened the door.

"Good evening, ma'am," Tim said, taking off his hat and holding it before him. "May I see Kita Wak?"

He had not allowed himself to think the worst, and now he watched hopefully while waiting for her reply.

There was an almost divine tenderness about Maggie's roundish face as she looked deeply into the young man's eyes. "I'm sorry, son, but—"

Tim's face tightened. "She's all right, isn't she? She's not—"

Maggie smiled softly. "No she's not, Tim. What I started to say was, she's not here in my home. She's over at the bachelor officers' quarters. Come, I'll take you to her." Maggie stepped from the doorway and paused to lay a hand gently on Tim's arm. "She's improving, and I think she'll live, and the baby as well. But her mother is with her now. You'll have to face her."

"Thanks for the warning, Mrs. Cohen," Tim said, his voice filling with resolve. "As long as Kita's all right, then nothing else matters. I'll have to face her mother sometime, and I guess now's as good a time as any."

"You're a good young man, Tim. You look tired and half starved to death. After you've seen her, come back here to eat and rest."

"Thank you, ma'am, but no. I've got to find Lieutenant

Kincaid after I see Kita. But I'll need a fresh horse."

"I'll talk to my husband. I'm sure he can arrange that. Let's go to Kita now."

The room was dark and hushed by twilight shadows as Tim stepped inside, with Maggie standing just behind him. Nona Wak looked over from where she stood beside her daughter. Her expression betrayed no emotion.

Maggie made the introductions, saying, "Nona Wak, I'd like you to meet Timmy Boggs. He is the one who brought your daughter here and saved her life. Tim? Meet Nona Wak, Kita's mother."

"Pleased . . . pleased to meet you, ma'am," Tim said, crushing his hat nervously in his hands.

Nona Wak watched him impassively until finally she nodded her head in greeting.

"How is Kita?"

Again, her regal head nodded slowly.

"May I talk to her?"

Nona Wak's eyes went to the girl's beautiful face as she lay there in what appeared to be a comfortable sleep. A third time the woman's head nodded, and Tim moved forward to lay a hand on Kita's arm. "Kita? Can you hear me? It's Tim."

Her eyelids fluttered open and a radiant smile broke across her copper-hued face. "Hello, my Timmy. I am very sorry for what I've done."

"Don't be sorry, honey. Don't waste your strength on being sorry. Just get well and take good care of our son."

"Do you still want me?"

Moisture glistened in Tim's eyes and he blinked to keep back the tears. "I want you, Kita. More than ever, I want you."

"And I want you and I want your son now. I've told my mother of my love for you. She knows about our baby."

"And I will tell her of my love for you, Kita," Tim said, holding Kita's hand now and turning toward her mother. "I love your daughter and I want to marry her, Nona Wak. I want to raise our child in peace and happiness, and to teach him all the things a man must know. I am asking your permission now, as I will ask your husband's when I see him. I truly love your daughter, and I want only to care for her and make her happy."

Nona Wak watched them silently until she spoke in a husky, strained voice. "It will be a difficult thing. There will be much hardship for both of you."

"Maybe, but we can live with that. We love each other

155

enough to overcome any difficulties that might arise. It would be less difficult if you could give us your help and understanding."

"I can give these things," Nona Wak said softly. "But Kita Wak is the daughter of an Arapaho chief, and you are the son of a man who hates the Arapaho. Your love for each other will have to be strong. Very strong."

"I'll talk to them both," Tim said with determination. "I'll make them understand."

Nona Wak shook her head sadly. "No, you will not make them understand. There is too much hatred. My son Gray Wolf is dead at the hands of white men, and my other son, Black Wing, would probably kill you both if he knew of your love for each other. Red Hawk is understanding and kind, but he is also very proud. He would have had his daughter marry Crow-in-the-Rain, a proven warrior. And Crow-in-the-Rain would kill you for having taken something he thought was his."

Anger flashed in Kita's eyes. In English, she said to her mother, "I am not a horse, to be stolen or traded. I do not believe in the old ways of our people. I will marry the man I love, and that man happens to be Timmy. I would kill myself before allowing another man to touch me."

"Yes, I am sure you would," Nona Wak replied. "And if the war between our peoples cannot be stopped, you may have to." Nona Wak looked at Tim. "You have my blessing, but unlike my daughter, I still believe in the old ways of our people. I obey my husband. It is him that you must persuade. But that will not be easy. Tomorrow morning the Wahilla warriors will avenge the death of Gray Wolf."

Tim pulled away and turned toward Maggie. "Can you get that horse for me, Mrs. Cohen? I've got to go and find Lieutenant Kincaid, and I haven't got a minute to lose. Two of my brothers were killed, and my father thinks it was done by Arapaho. Tomorrow morning he and the other ranchers in the area are going to avenge their deaths. Many will be killed for nothing, if both my father and Red Hawk can't be stopped."

"Of course, Timmy," Maggie said, clutching her skirts and running toward the door. "I'll get it myself."

"Thank you for your understanding, Nona Wak," Tim said, looking at the Indian woman. "I do love your daughter, and nothing will stop me from marrying her."

"Be careful, my Timmy," Kita called as Tim stepped through the doorway. "Come back to me."

Tim paused. There was a boyish grin on his face. "I have the two best reasons in the world to live, Kita. You and our baby. I'll be back."

And then he was gone, running toward his horse to remove its saddle and throw it on the army mount.

Sam Boggs looked at the men surrounding him before turning to stare at the two crosses topping twin mounds of freshly dug earth behind the house. "Today we buried two of my sons. They were killed by Arapaho. By this time tomorrow there'll be twenty times as many featherheads scattered across the prairie."

Mumbled grunts of agreement came from the thirty mounted ranchers, their sons and hired hands, and they gripped their rifles more tightly.

"Kincaid ain't gonna like this, Hoss," Jake Barnes offered as the lone dissenting voice. "Especially when he finds out what your boys did to that Indian kid."

"Who's gonna tell him?" Boggs growled.

"Tim," Barnes replied simply.

"You backin' away from a fight, Jake?"

"You know better'n that, Hoss. Forgettin' that fact would be your biggest mistake."

Boggs glared at Barnes' expressionless face while the light of dawn crept across the yard. "Jake, you and me have been friends for a long time, and I aim to see that it stays that way. Now I'm going after the bastards what killed my boys, and to hell with the army, Kincaid, and anybody else who don't like it. Are you in, or are you out?"

"I'm in," Barnes said, shrugging. "Just want you to think about what you're doin', that's all. I'll be right beside you when the shootin' starts."

"Good. Any of you other fellers want to back out? If so, do it now."

The tight-lipped settlers shook their heads, and Boggs nodded his approval. "Fine, then let's get on with it. We've done enough talkin' and now it's time to fight."

Boggs lashed his spurs across his horse's flanks and galloped onto the plains, with the thirty riders fanned out in a line behind him.

There was a kind of sadness in Red Hawk's eyes as he looked at the fifty warriors mounted and prepared for battle. *So it will happen again*, he thought. *All those dreams and all the talk of peace are gone, and the Wahilla will die before the guns of the Blue Sleeves. They are too many for us to fight, and more will come and my people will be killed, like those at Sand Creek. But*, he reminded himself, *we cannot cringe like dogs struck by their master. I must avenge the death of my son or they will never listen to my advice again and they will not respect my judgment.*

"Is there no word yet of Black Wing?" Red Hawk asked the brave nearest him.

"No, Red Hawk, there is not."

"He has been gone two days and we can wait no longer. The Blue Sleeve lieutenant has not returned, even though he has had more time than we agreed upon." Red Hawk looked at the warriors again and raised his voice so that all could hear.

"Hear me, my brave ones. Again we wear the warpaint of the Arapaho people, and today we will avenge the death of Gray Wolf. It will be the first time in battle for some of you, and I want you to listen well. We will take no women or children, we will take no horses or weapons. We have learned that the white settlers have gathered and are preparing to attack us, and they are the ones we will fight. They are men, as are we, and we will kill them in fair combat. There will be no scalps taken, and we will bring our dead and wounded home with us. Is that understood?"

The warriors raised their weapons skyward and there was excitement and anticipation in the air, that of men suddenly being freed who have long been held in bondage. Red Hawk noted this, and again his heart was saddened. *They do not know the fate that awaits us after we do what we must*, he thought. *They are proud warriors and anxious for battle, and I alone must suffer the consequences of these actions. They do not understand the white man's hatred for us, and that treaty I signed with the army generals is nothing more than paper to them.*

Red Hawk looked down at an old man who had proven himself well in earlier battles with the white men. "Tell Black Wing where we have gone, old one, when he returns."

The old man raised his hand and nodded while Red Hawk turned his horse away and rode onto the plains with the fifty warriors spread out in a long line behind him. The sun was well above the horizon now, and their shadows stretched out before them like long, black, serpentlike creatures slithering across the grass.

"I think it's gonna get worse before it gets better, Matt," Windy said, swinging onto his saddle. "I've got a feelin' about this day that I ain't likin' a whole lot."

"Me too, Windy," Matt replied, moving his horse to the head of the column. "This has been a long patrol and it doesn't seem like we've accomplished a whole hell of a lot."

"Yeah, guess so. After ridin' all over hell's half-acre, about the only thing we know for sure is that McFarland started the whole damned mess. That and the fact that Boggs' cattle are more fond of beans than potatoes."

"Well, we'll head for the Wahilla Reservation and hope that the death of McFarland will be enough to cool Red Hawk down, and if we knew for sure that Boggs' boys killed Gray Wolf, and that Black Wing killed *them*, and if . . ." Matt shook his head, as if to clear the confusion from his mind.

Windy cut off a chew of tobacco and grinned as he thumbed the cut from his knifeblade into his mouth. "Like you said, Matt, it's a damned iffy world."

"Sure as hell is. The only one thing I know for sure is that we've got everybody on both sides thoroughly pissed off at us."

"That seems to be a problem we see quite a bit of."

"Yeah, and if this thing turns into a real war, we're going to have Regiment on our ass as well."

"Fuck Regiment," Windy said, spitting and squinting toward the rolling plains. "Ain't one of 'em could find his way home from the shithouse. Now who the hell's that?"

Kincaid glanced over at the bay horse streaking toward them at a dead run from a quartering angle. "Beats hell out of me, Windy, but whoever he is, he's in a hell of a hurry," Matt replied, raising his hand and halting the column. "Doesn't that look like Tim Boggs?"

"Sure does, and he's ridin' an army horse."

Tim pulled the horse to a sliding, plunging stop, and he was nearly out of breath as he looked at Kincaid. "Thank God I found you," he panted.

"Hold on a minute and get your breath, Tim. Why have you been looking for me?"

After taking several deep breaths, Tim pushed the hat back

from his eyes and relaxed slightly in the saddle. "My pa and the other ranchers around here are on their way to the Wahilla Reservation. Pa knows the Arapaho killed my brothers, and he's out for blood. Red Hawk is leaving the reservation this morning to avenge Gray Wolf's death. There's going to be one hell of a battle if we can't get between them."

"We found the man who started the whole thing, Tim. His name's McFarland, and Black Wing killed him yesterday."

"McFarland? He's the one who told my pa about Daniel and Martin."

"I know. And what he said was mostly the truth. But we don't know for sure who killed Gray Wolf, and that's—"

"I know who killed him," Tim said without hesitation. "It was Dan and Marty."

"How do you know that for sure?"

"They told Jake about it. He'll back up what I say."

"Then there's no need for a battle, the way I see it," Windy offered. "All the guilty ones are dead."

"You and I and Tim know that, Windy. But Boggs and Red Hawk don't. What time was your pa leaving his place this morning, Timmy?"

"At daylight, maybe an hour ago."

Now Matt turned to the scout. "Windy, if Boggs is heading toward the reservation and Red Hawk is on his way here, where would be the best place to try and intercept them?"

Windy scratched his neck and chewed silently while he thought.

"You said at dawn, Tim?" he asked finally.

"Yes, sir. At dawn."

"And Red Hawk's leavin' 'bout the same time. That'd put 'em runnin' into each other about noon, probably someplace close to those washouts along Winter Creek. Be a good place to start lookin', anyway."

"How long will it take us to get there, Windy?" Matt asked, lifting his reins.

"If we get the lead out of our asses, we might make it around noon ourselves."

"Consider the lead removed," Matt replied, urging his horse to a run.

It was shortly after twelve o'clock when they heard the first scattered shots, but they could see nothing because of the rolling swell before them. And when they reined in atop the high ground, they looked down and saw twelve Indian ponies streaking across the prairie at top speed with their riders bent low and firing backward while thirty more horses raced behind them at a dead run. Puffs of smoke preceded the sound of weapons fire as the pursuing riders fired inaccurately from their running mounts.

"That's Pa and the others!" Tim yelled.

"Yeah, and I'd wager that ragged group in front is Black Wing and his boys," Windy said. "Musta got jumped."

Matt pointed at the swale toward which Black Wing's pony was heading. Fifty warriors were waiting there, knowing the white men would come to them.

"The perfect ambush," Kincaid said. "Your pa and his friends will be dead in less than a minute. Let's go!"

The army mounts pounded down the hill, forming a battle line as they moved, and Kincaid shouted, "Have the men fire a few rounds over their heads, Sergeant! We've got to get their attention, and they haven't seen us yet!"

"Yessir! Fire a volley, but keep 'em high!"

The Springfields exploded with a deafening roar, and Kincaid saw Boggs look up in surprise while reining in his mount, with the others following suit. The Indian ponies raced away and disappeared over the rise, and Matt yelled at Windy, "Take two squads and get Red Hawk! I'll take care of Boggs! Bring him to the top of the rise."

"Gotcha, Matt!" Windy replied, breaking to the left and signaling for the two squads to follow him. The platoon broke into two groups and Matt slowed his mount to halt before a glowering Sam Boggs.

"Now what the hell do you think you're doin', Kincaid?" Boggs snarled. "We damn near *had* those bastards!"

"No you didn't, Boggs. They damned near had you. You were riding straight into a classic Arapaho trap."

"Like hell I was!"

"Matt's right, Pa," Tim said. "There must be fifty of 'em waiting right over that hill."

"You shut up, boy! I'll take care of you later."

"No you won't, Pa," Tim said evenly, unaffected by his father's heated gaze. "There won't be any 'later' as far as you and me are concerned."

"Why were you in pursuit of Black Wing and his band, Mr. Boggs?" Kincaid asked, knowing he had to break the impasse between father and son.

Boggs tore his hate-filled eyes from Tim's face and looked at the lieutenant. "'Cause I jumped 'em on my ground."

"There is nothing in your homestead agreement with the government that gives you the right to shoot anyone crossing your property."

"Maybe not, but I got a personal right to protect what's mine. I've got one range hand dead 'cause of them feather-heads—"

"Correction, Boggs," Matt interjected. "You've got one range hand dead at the hands of another white man. His name was Strother McFarland, and you talked with him the other night. He was killed yesterday afternoon by Black Wing."

Boggs looked confused, but he persisted, "That don't bring back my two sons, Kincaid. They was killed by them Injuns over there, and by God they'll pay for it!"

"And I suppose that'll bring Daniel and Martin back to life, right, Boggs? Just like the death of your two sons brought Gray Wolf back to life?"

Boggs' eyes shifted nervously. "I don't know nothin' 'bout no Gray Wolf... or whatever you said," he replied sullenly.

"Yes you do, Pa. I told the lieutenant what Daniel told Jake." Tim's eyes shifted to the foreman. "Would you tell Matt the same thing if it were necessary, Jake?"

"I would," Barnes said without hesitation. "I've done a lot of wrong things in my life, but I never have killed a sixteen-year-old boy."

"Jake, damn you! I trusted you, and now—"

"Forget it, Hoss." Barnes looked at Kincaid. "Whatever you want to know about anything that's happened around here is up to you. I'll answer your questions honestly."

"Thank you, Jake. We're going to need some honest answers."

"Matt!"

Kincaid turned and looked toward the rise, where Windy, Red Hawk, and Black Wing waited. He waved and shouted back, "We're on our way!" Then he turned back to Boggs. "Boggs, I want you and Tim to come with me," he said, reining his horse toward the rise and moving out as though expecting to be followed without question.

Boggs hesitated and Tim started to follow Kincaid, then stopped and turned toward his father. "Come on, Pa. You're in enough trouble now, don't make it worse, please?"

Boggs' shoulders seemed to droop, and he slouched in the saddle like a beaten man as he moved his horse forward to follow Kincaid up the incline.

The Indian chief and his son faced the white settler and his son, and there was but five feet of prairie grass between them, with Kincaid sitting his horse on one side of Sam and Tim Boggs, and Windy sitting his on the other.

"Hello, Red Hawk," Matt offered. "I'm sorry I didn't return within the three days you gave me."

Red Hawk nodded, but his eyes were locked on Boggs' face. "I am sorry too, Lieutenant. Now we have no choice but war."

Boggs straightened in the saddle and pulled his massive shoulders back. "If it's war you want, dammit, then it's war you'll get!"

"There is no further need for war, Red Hawk," Matt cut in. "Your son has avenged Gray Wolf's death."

Red Hawk's gaze shifted to Black Wing, and even the carefully impassive expression on his face couldn't hide the surprised blink of his eyes.

"Isn't that true, Black Wing?" Matt continued. "You are responsible for the deaths of Martin and Daniel Boggs?"

"Are the words of the lieutenant spoken in truth, Black Wing?" Red Hawk asked.

"Yes, my father, they are true. They were the men who killed my brother."

"How do you know that?"

"Because I heard them talking and laughing about it just before they entered the stream at Big Trees where they were killed."

Kincaid watched the young Indian warrior. "And how about McFarland? You killed him as well, did you not?"

Black Wing's eyes showed no fear of the truth. "Yes, I am the one. Bear Catches Fish saw the bearded one hide the bow and quiver, which he used to try and bring guilt to the Wahilla Arapaho. He admitted this to me before his death. The others heard him as well."

"What does all this mean, Lieutenant? Are the guilty ones all dead?"

"Yes they are. Now your two peoples can live side by side in peace."

"Like hell," Boggs growled.

"He is right, Lieutenant," Red Hawk said almost sadly. "We have nothing in common except our hatred for each other."

"You are both wrong. In addition to your hatred, you have two other things in common."

"What's that, Kincaid?" Boggs asked sullenly.

"You are both under arrest, for one."

"Under arrest? You got cause to arrest that Injun—and you damned well better—but you got nothin' to take me in for."

"Wrong again, Boggs. You're under arrest for possession of stolen cattle."

Now Boggs' beady eyes darted to his son's face and his lips curled to form a scathing word, but Matt stopped him before he could say anything.

"Tim told me nothing about it, Boggs. One of the men in my command was a Texas cowhand before joining the army. He spotted your Mex-cuts instantly. And he is certain that a Texas brand inspector will have even less difficulty." Matt looked again at the Arapaho chief. "And you, Red Hawk, are under arrest for a violation of the treaty. Wearing warpaint is in direct violation of that document."

Boggs looked away, and the weariness swept over him again, while Red Hawk continued to watch Kincaid. "I understand and accept that, Lieutenant. But you mentioned two things that we have in common. What is the second?"

"You are both about to become grandfathers." Kincaid's gaze wandered from one man's shocked face to the other. "And your mutual grandchild will be half Indian and half white. The blood of which you are both so proud will be intermixed and red, just like everybody else's."

"Timmy, is this true?" Boggs asked raspingly, as though his throat had suddenly gone dry.

"Yes, Pa, it is. I love Kita Wak and I will marry her. I am very proud to be the father of her child." Tim could feel the Arapaho chief's eyes on his face, and he turned to confront him. "Red Hawk, I love Kita and she loves me. We will be married the minute she is well enough, and I ask you both for your permission and blessing, just as I ask it of you, Black Wing."

There was absolute silence on the rolling crest while the

four white men waited for Red Hawk's reply. Finally, there was a barely perceptible nod of the chief's head before he turned his horse and rode toward the warriors waiting in the swale below. Black Wing hesitated, then wheeled his mount and left the rise with no outward indication of acceptance to the man who would be his brother-in-law.

fourteen

The two officers were resplendent in their dress uniforms, even though there was a hint of discomfort in the way they occasionally ran a finger around inside the stiff collar surrounding their necks.

"Never could stand these damned things," Conway said as he poured from the brandy bottle, handed a glass to Kincaid, and took a seat behind his desk.

"Me neither, Captain," Matt chuckled while raising the glass in salute and taking a drink. "But the agony is for a worthy cause, I guess."

"Suppose so. Damned funny the way things turned out, isn't it?"

"Yeah, but it's for the best. As soon as Kita is well enough to ride, Boggs is going to loan some of his hands to Tim so they can take that herd back to Mexico. And I guess he's giving them enough money to set themselves up in a small spread down there someplace. The way I understand it, mixed marriages aren't as uncommon down there as they are here, and it'll give them a chance to start out with a clean slate."

166

Conway sipped his drink and watched Kincaid over the rim of his glass. "What about the Barnes fellow?"

"He was most cooperative, and Tim speaks very highly of him. He offered to take the herd back and turn himself in, but I don't see where anything could really be gained by that. He made a mistake and will earn nothing from it, and the Mexicans will profit by the weight gain their herd achieved on this good grazing land, not to mention the natural increase in their herd, so nobody should really have a bitch coming."

"I think your suggestion about what to do with Red Hawk and Black Wing was the best way to go," Conway said, reaching for a cigar before changing his mind and closing the lid on the small box. "Damn, guess I won't have time for one of those."

"No, I don't think you will. About Red Hawk and Black Wing? There is no point in punishing Red Hawk; he was only doing what his rank and tribal customs required him to do, and he was reluctant even at that. We need him as the leader of the Wahilla, and he has to save face to remain their chief, not to mention the fact that he is the best man to keep the peace. And as for Black Wing, he only killed those who were guilty and deserved their fate. In truth, if it hadn't been for him and what he did, there would have been no way to prevent a war between the two sides. If he has any punishment coming, it will come from his father. Red Hawk doesn't think too highly of his son's taking tribal matters into his own hands."

"No, I suppose not," Conway said with a heavy sigh. "Guess it's about time to go, huh, Matt?"

"Yes it is," Kincaid replied, downing his drink in a single gulp and standing. He watched the captain's weary effort to rise from his chair, and a grin spread across his lips.

"Ever done anything like this before, sir?"

"Hell no, and I never want to do it again. If I'd wanted to be a preacher, I would have joined the clergy instead of the mounted infantry."

"These are rather strange circumstances, I'll agree to that, Captain," Matt replied with a chuckle. "You marrying a white boy and an Indian girl—shotgun wedding, no less—with her lying down and him standing up and their fathers standing right behind you and hating each other with more passion than a cat and a dog would under the same circumstances. There is some humor in it, sir, if you look at it properly."

167

Both officers stepped from the building and adjusted their hats to their heads. "If there is any humor in this situation, Lieutenant, I fail to see it," Conway said with a nervous glance at the bachelor officers' quarters, while tucking the Bible uncomfortably beneath his arm.

Matt laughed openly now. "Well, look at it this way, sir. Stranger things *have* happened to Easy Company. And besides, if they hung around here, you just might have had to deliver the baby."

"God, no!" Conway said with a shudder. "Don't even think about it. Thank Christ that's Maggie Cohen's department. We've got more than we can handle here, and I'm beginning to think we should have finished that bottle off before we even tried this."

"A drunken army officer is one thing, sir, but a drunken preacher? Never. May I?" Matt asked, holding the door aside for the commanding officer.

Captain Conway gave Kincaid a pained look and trudged inside as though a gallows awaited his arrival.

SPECIAL PREVIEW

Here are the opening scenes
from

EASY COMPANY AND THE BIG MEDICINE

the next novel in Jove's exciting
new High Plains adventure series

EASY COMPANY

coming in July!

one _____

It was the summer of 1855 along the banks of the upper Missouri. It was a hot but dry day, not unpleasant, and the songs of birds were in the air. But Second Lieutenant Warner Conway, sitting astride his army mount, was oblivious to such niceties. Rather, he was appalled by what he saw.

Spread out before him was a scene such as he'd heard about but never seen. Native Americans, Indians, dead or dying without a blow from the white man having been struck. Devastated by fever, they lay about, plagued by chills, dreadful aches, and finally rashes that phased into ugly lesions. Mercifully, death soon brought release.

"They have no natural defenses," said Captain Wilbur, "not against any of our diseases—measles, cholera, scarlet fever, and this, the worst, smallpox."

Lieutenant Conway dismounted and stood beside his bay gelding. He was a young man, tall, rangy, and heavy-boned. He would probably put on weight over the years, but his frame would carry it easily. He glanced at his captain, who'd remained mounted.

Captain Wilbur was a short man, heavily torsoed but short.

Mr. Conway's eyes, though he stood on the ground, were almost level with those of the mounted captain. It was one reason why Mr. Conway had dismounted; astride his horse, he towered over the captain, and he knew that made Captain Wilbur uncomfortable and testy.

"Isn't there anything they can do?" asked Mr. Conway.

"There's nothing *anyone* can do once they get it," said Wilbur. "I hear they can give some kind of shots now that might prevent it, but . . ."

Conway eyed the shallow craters on Captain Wilbur's face. He'd wondered about them.

"Yes, Mr. Conway, I've had the damn disease. That's what caused these things you're looking at."

"Sir! I wasn't looking at—"

"Yes you were, Conway, but I don't mind. In Europe, back in the last century, everyone was supposed to have had it at one time or another. But you haven't, have you?"

"No, sir!"

"Then you just stay where you are. Matter of fact, if the wind starts blowing our way, you take off. You hear me? That's an order."

"Yes, *sir!*"

"That's how it gets passed. Contact, or someone breathes it into the air and someone else breathes it in. It doesn't live long in the air, but then it wouldn't take long to get from that camp to here, given a brisk wind."

Conway started paying very close attention to the prevailing air currents.

"*I* can't get it anymore, y'see," the captain went on, "because I already had it. At least that's what those bastards in the Sanitary Corps say. They better be right."

They'd ridden out of Fort Leavenworth—Captain Wilbur, Lieutenant Conway, and a platoon of mounted infantry—and followed the Missouri north and northwest. Along the way they'd encountered a few sites where tipi poles still stood and human bones lay scattered about, obviously the ruins of Indian camps.

"They had the right idea," the captain had said. "Didn't help, but it was the right idea."

"I don't understand, sir," Warner Conway had said.

The captain hadn't explained then, but he did now. "As I said, there's nothing to be done except isolate the sick ones

172

and stay the hell away. There may have been some healthy ones left in this village, but they're long gone, leaving these to die. A week, a month, a year from now, this village will look like those others we passed. Tipis collapsed and rotting, bones picked clean. But the ones that got away, they may be sick anyway—it takes a while to show up—and may be passing it on to someone else right now." He shook his head. "You know, Lieutenant, some say that before we'd seen or shot a single goddamn Indian, any of these Plains Indians anyway, we'd already killed about half of them."

Conway frowned, and the captain continued, "Sure. The white man, the Spaniards, they brought all these diseases with them, starting with Columbus. Smallpox, measles, about any you can think of. And the story goes that about fifty years ago, some war party into New Mexico—Pawnee, I think—brought smallpox back up to the lower Platte. Spread from there down to Texas, cutting a swath. Then, about fifteen, twenty years ago, there was another big smallpox epidemic, north of here but right along this Missouri. Brought by steamboat passengers, best guess. Slowly spread farther on up the Missouri. Cut some tribes in half. Damn near wiped out the Mandan and Assiniboine. The Mandan were a farming tribe, didn't have anywhere to run or any way to get there. Crow, Blackfoot, they all nearly got cut in half. And that was well before we started shooting them. I'll tell you, if it wasn't for those diseases, we'd have our hands full, clearing out these red bastards."

Conway, recently out of West Point, wasn't sure that "clearing out these red bastards" was official United States Government policy, or the right idea, but... "What about the Indian medicine I hear talk about, sir?"

"Not worth a hoot in hell, Lieutenant. A lot of mumbo-jumbo that doesn't add up to much. Keeps them busy, keeps them fooled, keeps them happy sometimes, but that's about it. 'Course, having a happy, satisfied mind will sometimes cure what ails you, you know that. You get way down in the dumps and your body starts feeling bad. But they've got this idea that everything's caused by evil spirits that have entered the body, and the way to get better is to wash the evil spirits out. That's why they have all those sweat boxes. And sometimes sweating *is* good, too, like if you got a runny nose or something. But listen to this. They had another big epidemic a while back, again thanks to us—cholera."

173

Conway frowned, thinking he recalled something. . . .

"You know what the symptoms of cholera are," the captain asked, "what shows you're sick with it? Vomiting, diarrhea, liquid pouring out of the body. You damn near dry up and blow away. The way to treat it is to pour liquids in, not take them out. But what does the Indian do? Sticks a man with cholera in a sweat box. Thinks it's *good* if he's vomiting—that means the evil spirits are being expelled." The captain shook his head.

"So all these people will just die," said Lieutenant Conway, "and go off to the Happy Hunting Ground."

Captain Wilbur snorted. "Only if the Jesuits have gotten hold of them. Or the Methodists. The Methodists have been out here working their butts off, trying to convert these heathen. The Happy Hunting Ground is just the Indian version of Christian heaven. Most Indians have some idea or other about what happens after death, but it rarely has anything to do with heaven or hell." Captain Wilbur laughed. "Heaven and hell are for *us*, Mr. Conway. There aren't going to be any Indians there. No niggers, either."

Conway frowned. Captain Wilbur eyed him suspiciously.

"You're not one of those abolitionists, are you, Conway?"

"No, sir," Conway replied judiciously, "but there seem to be an awful lot of them without me."

"Abolitionists? Or niggers?" Wilbur grinned. "They're already having arguments right there at the fort. There's a bunch that says that slaves ought not be allowed into Kansas. Hell, I don't see why not. Half the states have them, why not all? But I'll tell you, Conway, this is '55, we've got an election next year, an' the next four or five years will tell the story. If things continue on the way they are, I figure that in another ten years you'll see this whole damn country divided up into two separate countries, and nobody's going to be able to stop it."

"Are you thinking of a war, sir?"

"A war? Not a chance. Americans killing Americans over slaves? Over niggers? Not a chance. No, if it happens, it'll be peaceful. Tell you what, though. As long as we've got nigger slaves, we might as well have Indian slaves too."

"But this is their land, sir."

Wilbur smiled coldly. "It *was* their land. No more."

Conway's eyes suddenly widened and he stiffened. They were looking down from near the crest of a bluff, and suddenly rising up before them, not twenty yards away, was a tall figure shrouded in black—a dark, spectral presence.

He stood still, staring at them, a tall Indian. His head was hooded and his eyes were in deep shadow, yet they were clearly visible, seeming almost to glow.

Conway went cold.

The Indian's mouth opened and closed twice, without uttering a sound.

"Like a fish," muttered Captain Wilbur. "He's trying to breathe."

The Indian continued to stare, unblinking.

"Stoic bastards," declared the captain, "and nothing scares them. They...they aren't human, it seems. But you'd better get the hell out of here, Lieutenant, especially if he gets any closer."

Lieutenant Conway thought of Flora, his new bride, a delicate flower plucked from Maryland's fertile fields. A fine thing it would be to carry plague back to her warm bed.

"Funny thing is," said Wilbur, "can't say these Indians haven't had their revenge."

"How's that, sir?" asked Conway, keeping his eye on the Indian.

"Best anyone can figure, about the time we were shipping them smallpox and measles and God knows what else, they were sending us the so-called 'French disease' by return ship."

"The French disease? Do you mean syphilis, sir? Isn't that...well, *French*?"

"It is *now*. And Italian, and English, and everywhere else, including right back here in America. But the best anyone can figure, it didn't show up until after Columbus and his boys started messing around with those Indians, down in Mexico or south of there somewhere. The word is that the Indians down *there* had it because, being short of women or something, or like any old farm boy, they kept sticking it to their goats or sheep or whatever. Anyway, that's what *they* got it from. And that's what the Indians gave *us*, in return. Pretty fair exchange, I'd say."

Conway shuddered and remarked carelessly, "I suppose you've had *that* too, sir."

Captain Wilbur glared at him. "I should say *not*, Lieutenant, and you'd best be careful who you accuse of such foul behavior."

Conway stared at the gaunt, ghostly figure at the edge of the bluff, searching for the eyes that no longer glowed. "Sorry, sir. I meant nothing by it."

The Indian turned and vanished as quickly as he'd appeared.

The hell he had "meant nothing by it," recalled Captain Warner Conway, commanding officer of Easy Company, a mounted infantry company stationed at Outpost Number Nine, on the High Plains of Wyoming in the year 1877.

It was summer again. Captain Conway stood by the window of the orderly room, staring out over the parade. As predicted, he had filled out that rangy frame, and now he was not only tall but large. A large, decisive, formidable officer who clearly remembered Captain Wilbur, the officer who had tried to convince him that the Indian could not be reshaped to fit the white man's civilization.

Well, maybe he couldn't, but Captain Wilbur hadn't been much of a help. And if anyone had ever deserved the "French disease," it had been that pint-sized warrior.

The split in the country had come, as Wilbur had predicted, but war had come also, as Wilbur had not foreseen. Wilbur had chosen to fight and die with the Confederacy; Conway had chosen to go with Honest Abe, and had never regretted his choice. And being on the winning side had nothing to do with it. Being on the *right* side was what mattered.

Warner Conway always recalled the story of Lincoln correcting the man who, during the War, had prayed that God was on their side. Lincoln had told him that rather he should pray, or hope, that they were on God's side. And that was the way Warner Conway had felt about the War. Win or lose, he'd been on the side he felt he should be on.

But he also respected the beliefs of those who opposed him, the beliefs of men he respected. But Captain Wilbur had not been among them.

He suddenly wondered why he was having these thoughts.

The person standing outside the orderly room, the black-shrouded figure that blocked Captain Conway's clear view of the parade, was what had prompted the grim recollection. It had reminded him of the dying, shrouded Indian who had stood

176

on the bluff overlooking the village and the headwaters of the Missouri, and who had fixed Conway with his burning, accusing eyes.

This figure turned about abruptly and, seeing Conway through the window, smiled. But his eyes also had a glow, an unworldly gleam, like those of the Indian long ago. Warner Conway walked outside.

"Father McElroy," said Warner Conway.

"McElroy, yes," answered the man, beaming, "but I am not Catholic, Captain."

Warner Conway was not in the best of moods, hadn't been for several months, if not years. And his memory had just reminded him unnecessarily that twenty-two years before he'd been a second lieutenant, that he'd emerged from the Civil War a first lieutenant, and that not too long after that, he'd made captain. But here he was, still a captain. Time, and promotion, had seemed to stand still. "Then what the hell are you?" demanded Warner Conway.

"Merely a minister of God, a simple man of—"

"That's right, a humble shepherd." Conway took a deep breath of hot, dry air. "What was it—Methodist?"

"Presbyterian." McElroy sighed. "Still Presbyterian."

Conway nodded. "That's right. The Methodists came through last week. And some Jesuits, but they were headed much farther west, Oregon country, if I'm not mistaken."

"There is room for all to do God's work."

Conway nodded again. He couldn't remember the last time he'd been to a church. Then he brightened. "The Whitmans, they were Presbyterians, weren't they?" He watched a shadow fall across McElroy's face. "Yes, I'm sure they were. Hope you plan to do things a little differently than they did." McElroy frowned, and Conway went on, "The Whitman massacre? You've never heard that mentioned?"

"We have, Captain Conway," said McElroy heavily, "many, many times. Marcus and Narcissa Whitman were most dedicated, most zealous, most determined to *force* the heathen down the road to divine grace. Unfortunately, they were also dogmatic and unbending. They had nothing in common with the Indian and there was no rapport, rather the opposite. And it seems a cruel paradox that the one time they were truly trying to help those Cayuse Indians—the measles epidemic?—the Cayuse thought they were trying to poison them with their

177

medicine. It's truly ironic that that was what led to the massacre."

"Mmm," agreed Captain Conway, "ironic indeed. The Whitmans, as I understand it, were not just rigid but unpleasant. Do you count many of their kind in your group?"

"I, Captain, am probably the most disagreeable," said McElroy, beaming at him.

"Aha . . . Well, then, when do you plan to leave for the reservation?"

"We are already there. Or rather, members of our mission have already moved among the Indians and are preparing the neophytes for my disagreeable arrival."

Did he ever stop beaming? "The Cheyenne are not the pushovers that the Sioux were," Conway pointed out.

"The Sioux took very readily to the concept of one God," said McElroy, a trace of irritation in his voice. "One single Spirit, the concept of grace, of heaven and hell—"

"The Happy Hunting Ground," Conway interjected.

McElroy grimaced slightly. "Saint Peter guarding the Gate with his bow and arrow."

"An interesting notion. But you misunderstood me. What I meant was that I think you will find the Cheyenne much less amenable to conversion."

"In our hands, perhaps," allowed Reverend McElroy, "but not in God's hands. Whosoever He shall wish to convert, He shall convert."

"The Cheyenne are kind of old-fashioned."

"So was Mary Magdalene, from the oldest of fashions, harlotry."

Captain Conway's jaws clamped shut. He'd never won a religious debate and was now old enough to know better than to try. He turned to reenter the orderly room, muttering, "Go with God, Father."

"Thank you, Captain," said McElroy.

In the orderly room, Corporal Four Eyes Bradshaw, the bespectacled company clerk, was eyeing the telegraph equipment suspiciously; it had just made a brief, mysterious noise.

"I think there are men out working on the lines, Corporal," said Captain Conway.

First Sergeant Ben Cohen looked up from his daily strength reports. "That's probably Merkin, from Olsen's platoon. Private Merkin thinks he knows something about telegraphs, about 'lectricity."

"Evidently he does," Conway commented.

The captain stepped to the door of the company adjutant's office. The adjutant, Second Lieutenant Matt Kincaid, stood quickly behind his desk, folding his pocket knife and putting it hastily in his trouser pocket, then snapping a salute while brushing a small pile of wood shavings off his desk with his other hand. This series of motions was not lost on Captain Conway as he returned the salute of his second-in-command; he knew that Kincaid was wont to carve up his pine desk whenever time lay heavy on his hands, a habit doubtless left over from his school days. Indeed, the desk appeared to Conway to have become smaller recently, the wooden victim of long sieges of boredom. Conway figured it was a relatively harmless habit, so he never commented on it.

"Apparently those missionaries have already begun converting Mr. Lo," he said. "Has anyone talked to the agent?"

"Mallory?" Kincaid said. "I did. I rode over the other day and tried to discourage the whole thing."

Conway genuinely liked Kincaid, in whom he saw something of himself as he had been some ten years ago. They were almost the same height, though Kincaid was somewhat slighter of build, a lanky, rawboned man with a sort of rugged handsomeness about him that, in a more civilized and cosmopolitan setting, would turn the heads of many a comely young woman.

Kincaid continued, "I told Mallory the Cheyenne weren't going to swallow all that God and heaven and hell dung."

"Dung?" wondered Captain Conway, smiling thinly.

"According to the Cheyenne it is. I argued with him for hours. Lot of good it did. As you well know, the Bureau of Indian Affairs thinks the War Department speaks with a forked tongue. But besides that, you might have noticed that one or two of these Presby missionaries are *fe*male, and one in particular has got Mallory reciting the Bible backwards and forwards."

Captain Conway nodded understandingly. "But that's still not going to help McElroy and his friends get through to Mr. Lo."

"Yeah," Matt said, grinning, "but I suspect Mallory's interests lie—or *lay*—elsewhere at the moment."

Unfortunately, Mallory's interests were not working out. The object of the agent's affections, Miss Amy Selby, was proving unusually devoted to her mission and resolutely chaste. Her fawnlike eyes might moisten and gleam at the thought of an unbaptized Cheyenne babe, but let Bob Mallory gently finger her fall of cornsilk hair and whisper suggestions—rather tame ones, too—into that delicate pink bud of an ear, and those soft, wet eyes would freeze over. As a result, Mallory was passing many a troubled night.

"There is but *one* God," thundered a voice through the windows of his agency. Mallory glanced out crossly. What troublemaker was this? The BIA could feed them, clothe them, house them, and properly educate their children, but tamper with their religion? *That* was asking for trouble. But hell, what could he expect from missionaries?

"*You* claim that this is not so," the voice went on, blasting Mallory's uneasy peace of mind, and he went outside to bear witness (to a slaughter, he privately hoped).

The speaker was black-robed, as usual, but pink-complected, with a great bonnet of curly orange hair. "You *do* say there is a principal god who lives above, but then there is also a benevolent god who lives beneath the ground, who has similar powers, and besides *them*, there are the four great spirits that dwell at the four points of the compass. Surely the great Cheyenne have little need for so many spirits, so many *demons*. They only serve to confuse."

The speaker, one Reverend Pilcher, eyed his congregation, as unfriendly a group as he'd ever seen.

"No," he continued resolutely, "there is but one God, Our Father, who lives above us, in *heaven*, or, as your friends the Sioux have come to believe, the Happy Hunting Ground."

Eyes hardened in the congregation as they recognized the reference to what they regarded as the dim-witted Sioux. Friends, perhaps, but simple and gullible.

"And there are no powers from the four winds, but there *is* a power, an *evil* power, that lives deep beneath the ground in a place called hell. He too is powerful, but his power is bad, he works to destroy, to make you suffer. And when you die, if you are not loved by God in heaven, and taken to His bosom, Satan, in hell, will gather you and take you below to never-ending pain.

"But listen! Your god Heammawihio—*hē' ămmă* does mean 'above,' and *wī' hio* does mean 'chief,' but *wī' hio* also means 'spider,' and it *also* means 'white man' "—he raised his hands, turning his pink palms out, and puffed out his pink cheeks, as if to emphasize his whiteness—"and it also means mentality of a higher-order.

"You know the white man is of superior intelligence. We know things of which you know not. We have instruments of magical power and force. And we tell you that these things are all ours as a gift from the *one God* . . . and they can be *yours* when you accept that one God, when you *believe* . . ."

The Reverend Pilcher paused, sweating. It was damned hot. Why couldn't they have gone on a mission to a more northern tribe of heathen?

He saw the Indian agent grinning at him. He saw him raise his fist and call out, "Give 'em hell, preacher."

Pilcher once again eyed his congregation, largely breech-clouted, though some wore ill-fitting cotton shirts and trousers. A truly stone-faced group.

He noticed one Cheyenne standing apart from the rest. This man, or at least as much of his skin as was showing, appeared to be painted red. And his leggings and shirt looked as if they might have been fashioned from old lodge-skins. He held in the crook of his left arm something that looked like a combination of bow—strung with two strings—and lance, the complete thing about five feet in length. Near one end was tied the stuffed skin of a red-faced Louisiana tanager, and the rest of the lance was adorned with various mysterious symbols. The Cheyenne now transferred the bow-lance from his left to his right, passing it, however, behind his own back. He glared fiercely at Pilcher for a moment and then, with the same behind-the-back movement, returned the lance to the crook of the left arm. The lance head never touched the ground, never even came close.

Finally, this strange Cheyenne opened his mouth and said, "Let us stay and listen." Whereupon the whole damn bunch got to their feet and walked off.

Pilcher's mouth dropped open, and Mallory grinned at him.

"What in the he—" sputtered the Reverend Pilcher. "That is, what in the world was *that*? Who was that . . . *red* man?"

"That was a *Hohnŭhk'e.*"

"A what?"

"It's a word that sort of means doing just the opposite of what is said. We call them, in English, Contraries. And that's what the Cheyenne call 'em too, when they're talkin' English. It means that when one of them wants to say yes, or agree, he

181

says no. Ask a Contrary to go away and he comes nearer. There are about two or three in a tribe. Anyway, these Contraries are special and are taken seriously. And you better not step in a Contrary's tracks, or let them step in yours, or else you'll go footsore and then lame. Let me tell you, it's bad business messin' with a Contrary."

Pilcher found his voice. "And that was a *weapon* he was carrying?"

"Nope. Oh, they carry it into battle all right, but it's only used to *touch* the enemy, to count coup. You know what that means?"

"It's French for 'blow,' isn't it?"

"Well, yeah, but what it means to the Indian is just touching the enemy. Don't even have to kill him, just touch, with something you're holding in your hand."

Pilcher was already confused, and Mallory explained, "Look. Say there's a fight. One brave rushes the enemy with . . . hell, he could be holding a goddamn *twig*. But he just touches the enemy with that twig and yells, 'I'm first.' Then another Indian touches the same enemy and yells, 'I'm second.' And so forth. Only three count as honors. But in a big battle it's hard keepin' track. An Indian sees someone lying there, could be dead already, but he touches him, or probably fetches him a full-fledged whack with his battle-ax, and yells, 'I'm second' or whatever. Probably accounts for the fact that after some of these battles the dead look like they've been chopped up a wee bit more than necessary. Likely just some braves trotting along, one after another, whacking away, and counting coups. Get it?"

Pilcher had, but wished he hadn't. These Cheyenne obviously had rites and symbols sufficiently complex as to make Christianity seem like child's play. Conversion was clearly going to be a long, tough haul.

"But what does the Bureau of Indian Affairs intend to do about those . . . barbarisms?" Pilcher asked, outraged.

"Nothing, I hope," said Mallory, "if they got any sense. We'll feed 'em, clothe 'em, give 'em shelter, school their kids, but I hope no one in the bureau's planning to mess with their religion. *You* can, but—"

"There was no trouble with the Sioux."

"These ain't Sioux, preacher. The Cheyenne and Sioux are

friends, all right, but the way you and me are friends. I ain't about to become a Presbyterian and you ain't about to become a Lutheran."

Pilcher stared at him for a while. "You're *Lutheran*? Why? Have you really ever thought about it?"

"Oh, for cryin' out loud." Mallory shook his head, grinning. Then he got serious. "Hey, look, preacher, you know where Miss Selby's hiding herself? I ain't seen her all day."

"I believe she went off to try to baptize a newborn babe."

Mallory nodded grimly. "*That'll* put her in a good mood," he said.

Crying Eagle, Yellow Bead, and White Bull met in the shadow of a sod hut. The hut had been built for the Cheyenne by the BIA, but the Cheyenne preferred to live in their tipis. All their robes, blankets, and skins were cut with the circular, conical tipi in mind. The tribal council sat in a circle, braves danced in circles, the sun, moon, and stars swept across the heavens in great arcs. The flat planes and squared corners of the Americans' huts were foreign and unsuitable to these young Cheyenne (and many Cheyenne youths), as was the full range of American life and customs.

"Have you watched the elders," asked Crying Eagle, "when the Black Robes speak? They sit with their mouths open and they nod. When the Black Robes say the earth god is evil, they nod. When the Black Robes say there are no other gods but the Black Robe god, they nod."

"They are only trying to please," suggested Yellow Bead. "The agent has let the Black Robes come among us. If the Black Robes leave unhappy, the agent will be mad and we will eat less, have less to wear."

"That would be bad," said Crying Eagle. "Then we would have to kill him and take what is ours."

"But the elders say we should keep the peace," said White Bull. "And the elders are wise."

"Wise? Look at us. We have no guns, no horses, no freedom. That is wise? A *child* could have led us to this reservation and stripped us of our manhood."

"Ah, Crying Hawk, you are too suspicious, and too warlike. This life is not bad. It is easy. The women do not have to work so hard—"

"Because the agent tries to get *us* to do women's work. He tries to turn us into women. But the way the Americans do this evil thing is guileful like the snake, like—"

"Speak clearly, Crying Hawk," said White Bull.

"It *is* clear. The agent and the Black Robes tell us we can only have one wife. Well, what single woman can do all the things that must be done for a warrior—clean his clothes, raise his children, cook his food? And when one wife is running blood, as they do with each moon, where can the healthy warrior turn if he has no other wives? He must go to another woman—to a relative or to another man's wife—and that will bring shame."

"Yes, that is so. We must have two wives, at least."

Yellow Bead and White Bull nodded, and Crying Eagle despaired; two wives were all it would take to make them happy. "But do you not understand," Crying Eagle pressed them, "how the American is planning to destroy us? Do you not remember stories of how they brought the great sickness and many of our people died? Half were left to rot and dry up and be blown across the plains. Now they say they are trying to save us. The Black Robes are going to save us. Ha! Are we, my brothers, to believe them? *Can* we believe them?"

White Bull and Yellow Bead frowned. "It is many a moon since we wore the blue paint," said White Bull, "but I have kept some."

"I too," said Yellow Bead, showing some eagerness.

"Good," said Crying Eagle. "Good. We are ready. The elders' medicine is weak. To have brought us from the triumph at the Greasy Grass to this poor place is to lose much medicine. If they do not show more wisdom, if their medicine proves weak..."

"How goes it, Reverend Pilcher?" asked another missionary.

"Not well. They are fearful and superstitious in very strange ways." He wondered if he could get the concept of Contrariness across to this brother. "And they remember the days when white man brought pestilence among them, and they are wary."

"We shall overcome their resistance, though."

"Amen. But I do wish it weren't quite so hot."